Rode He On Barbary?

A collection of short stories

Richard Parsons

Published by
MELROSE BOOKS

An Imprint of Melrose Press Limited
St Thomas Place, Ely
Cambridgeshire
CB7 4GG, UK
www.melrosebooks.co.uk

FIRST EDITION

Copyright © Richard Parsons 2014

The Author asserts his moral right to
be identified as the author of this work

Cover designed by Jonathan Duval

ISBN 978-1-909757-13-4

All rights reserved. No part of this publication may be reproduced, stored in a retrieval system, or transmitted, in any form or by any means electronic, mechanical, photocopying, recording or otherwise, without the prior permission of the publishers.

This book is sold subject to the condition that it shall not, by way of trade or otherwise, be lent, re-sold, hired out or otherwise circulated without the publisher's prior consent in any form of binding or cover other than that in which it is published and without a similar condition including this condition being imposed on the subsequent purchaser.

Printed and bound in Great Britain by:
Martins the Printers, Spittal, Berwick upon Tweed

Contents

1	Terry's Trump Card	1
2	The Phillimore Andante	7
3	The Legacy	10
4	The Enemy	17
5	The Threat	22
6	At the Graveside	28
7	In The Piazza delle Erbe	32
8	The Nightcap	37
9	William's Word	43
10	The Announcement	49
11	The Making of a Duchess	52
12	A Sticky Meal	61
13	In The Archipelago	66
14	Dedication	74
15	Counselling	79
16	Reunion	84
17	Safe	89
18	The Valley of the Shadows	95
19	Carnival	103
20	The Night Carnivore	111
21	The Beggar	116

22	Brinsley	120
23	The Woman on the Moor	125
24	Rode He on Barbary?	130
25	The Madonna of Saint John's Wood	135
26	Remembrance of Things Past	143
27	In the South	148
28	Mrs Patel's Cat	152
29	Symposium	157
30	The Head of Personnel	162
31	East of the Khyber	167
32	On the Fields	172
33	Something Understood	178
34	The Treasure	183
35	Just Friends	188
36	Death in Moscow	193
37	The Night Auditor	200
38	The Vladimirka Road	207
39	Dumping	211
40	The Table by the Window	218
41	National Heroine	224
42	Senior Citizens	233
43	The Beast Inside	240
44	Alma Mater	246
45	On the Beach	251
46	A Dish to Die For	257

About the Author   269

Terry's Trump Card

"A perfect bloody shambles," muttered Andrew Thomas MP, filling his large mouth with hot buttered toast. At this time, the Tea Room of the House of Commons was usually crowded. Outside, the riverside terrace was starting to be covered with thin London sleet. A good moment to be indoors. The House was an excellent Club. You could do most things inside it, if you knew the ropes. Andrew might speak petulantly, but he was fundamentally a cheerful soul. A happy sybarite by nature, with the gift of the gab, he made the ideal Parliamentary Private Secretary for a harassed Minister.

"I was sorry to miss the show," said his friend Jonathan Perkins MP, pouring himself a second cup of the hot, strong tea. "I'm sure your Minister's speech had comic potential. But I had to receive a dreary deputation from my constituency. They're upset about the proposed new wind farm to be built on the Moors."

"Comic potential," growled Andrew. "I suppose you could call it that. But I work for the wretched man. It's not funny to me when he falls flat on his face. You can afford to be objective. But just wait, your time will come."

RODE HE ON BARBARY?

Both men had entered the House three years earlier. Seething with ambition, they were professional politicians without any real outside interests. After university, Andrew had gone to work for the Party while Jonathan had risen through Local Government. They had started equal, but Andrew had forged ahead by being appointed as Parliamentary Private Secretary to Terry Franklin, Minister of State for Special Projects. It was the first step up the ladder, or rather the greasy pole. Jonathan had so far remained, to his chagrin, a back-bencher. One of the whips had opined that he laughed too much for British politics.

"I don't understand why your man had to introduce the Bill," said Jonathan. "Surely that should have been a job for your Secretary of State."

"So we thought," agreed Andrew. "But Prendergast's aged Mum is on her last legs down in Truro, and he insisted on attending the deathbed. So the unfortunate Terry Franklin had to step in at the last moment."

"A bit hard on him."

"And us too," snapped his friend. "You know Terry's slow, ponderous manner. He always has to have everything explained to him in immense detail. And now there simply wasn't the time. It's a hugely complex Bill and it fell to poor Terry to propose it to the House."

"Surely the Private Office must have had a speech ready for Prendergast?"

"Of course. But that wasn't enough. Franklin had to be prepared for interventions and questions. These would need off-the-cuff replies. Terry couldn't get away with just reading the speech. He actually had to understand it. We mobilised an emergency briefing session. Bang went the lunch-hour."

"I see you're making up for that now," commented Jonathan drily as Andrew savaged an impressive slice of plum cake.

"Terry cancelled a delicious lunch at the French Embassy and put a wet towel round his head. I was brought in to give moral support. Private Office rushed to prepare a series of cards, typed very big, giving a series of points to make and replies to objections."

"You mean they treated him like the complete idiot he is."

"You could put it like that. We went the whole hog. When Terry rose to speak from the Front Bench, there was quite a good House. The Opposition scented blood from the start. The Officials' Box was packed with the brains of the Ministry. The Permanent Under-Secretary was seated next to the Principal Private Secretary, both looking as if they were attending an execution. I was in the Chamber myself of course, poised to carry notes between the officials and the Minister. That's all one has to do as a PPS."

"You must have enjoyed that," said the cynical Jonathan.

"Not at all. When you work inside a hard-pressed Ministry, you do develop a certain loyalty. Terry was nervous as hell. I could see him sweating. One couldn't help feeling sorry for the man. It's a terrible thing in public life to suffer from the consequences of over-promotion."

"Not one of my problems," commented Jonathan drily.

"It all began to go wrong pretty quickly. Terry started droning away, but the Opposition were waiting to pounce. They wouldn't have treated Prendergast like that. That shit Fownes-Parker raised a perfectly lethal Point of Order and the Speaker did precious little to protect Terry. Then he lost his place and his notes fell to the floor. The Opposition burst into rude guffaws and even some of our own people were sniggering. I kept bringing over helpful cards from the Officials' Box but, by now, Terry was incapable of taking in a new briefing. He ended by just repeating platitudes and not dealing properly with any of the detailed points. It was a total disaster. The house was reduced to derisive laughter."

"I'm sorry," said Jonathan.

"I hope you mean that. Terry is quite a decent old thing and he's always been kind to me. He will be completely devastated. A public failure in the House can hardly be lived down. I must go up to his room now and let him weep on my shoulder."

"Hasn't he got a wife for that? That good-looking woman with the long black hair."

"Drusilla? She has her own life. Keeps rather to herself, it would seem. She's into garden design."

As Andrew walked along to the Minister's room, he planned his strategy. There was no blinking the fact that the man had quite badly blotted his copy book. No doubt he would be tempted to give up the struggle, to abandon his wrecked political career. He must be encouraged to take the longer view, to remember that memories were short and time a great healer.

The Parliamentary Private Secretary found his Master, with the usual blank look on his face, reading his evening paper.

"Ah, there you are, Andrew," said the Minister with a welcoming smile. "How did you think it went?"

The PPS blinked. He had not been prepared for such a stark question. Surely the Minister could see for himself that he had disgraced the Ministry and made himself into figure of fun.

"Well, you got through it," he replied cautiously. To his surprise, Terry's impassive features melted into a smile.

"Thank God for that," he said happily. "Do join me in a celebration drink. I always like a post-mortem. I got a bit confused, you know. I expect you noticed that. All those sub-paragraphs and the different chapter headings."

"Didn't the little notes help?"

"Not much. There were too many of them, like the pigeons in Trafalgar Square. I felt a bit odd at one point. Should have had a proper lunch."

"You ended rather abruptly," said Andrew.

"I was told to."

"Told to?"

"You brought it yourself. That note from the Permanent Under-Secretary."

Andrew remembered Sir Hector's message now. It had been contained, rather unusually, in a sealed-down envelope.

"You can read it if you like," said the Minister amiably. It was short.

"Minister of State," read Andrew, "sit down at once."

"So I did," explained Terry calmly.

"That was rather cheeky of him," commented Andrew.

"It seemed a good idea to me," said the Minister. "Would you like a boiled sweet?"

Andrew gulped. He had not been prepared for this display of sang-froid.

"I found it all a bit of an ordeal," continued Terry. "As you may have spotted. But the House seemed to be enjoying it and I found that encouraging. Somebody told me the Whips had taken note. I suppose that could be quite helpful to my career. If Prendergast decides to pack it in, they could be needing a new Secretary of State. I've got to push off now, as you know. That wretched dinner with the construction engineers in deepest Essex."

"Is Drusilla going with you, Terry?"

"No. I'm sending her to represent me at the Estonian national day. Would you be an angel, Andrew, and escort her? Take my invitation and make my apologies."

"It will be a pleasure."

Later that evening Andrew had a chance to discuss Terry's performance as he lay in bed in Terry's flat in Kennington with Terry's wife Drusilla.

"Are you sure he doesn't suspect?" asked Andrew as he gently massaged Drusilla's shapely rear.

"Not a thing," she replied happily. "Don't stop. I adore that."

"Then he must live in a dream."

"Of course he does. It's the only thing that makes him just tolerable."

"I don't think he realised today what a ghastly mess he had made in the House."

"He wouldn't," cooed Drusilla happily. "He's so terribly stupid."

"Intense stupidity," echoed Andrew. "Too dim to know when they're all laughing. It's a tremendous advantage for a politician, isn't it? You might call it Terry's trump card."

The Phillimore Andante

"Have you got anything to say in your defence, Mr Phillimore?" asked Mr Justice Haslemere. "Before I pass sentence?"

"Indeed I have, my Lord," said Roland Phillimore, a tall, gangly Old Marlburian who looked as if he could have done with a good haircut. "I did not mean to kill that wretched violinist, horrible though his intonation was. It was only manslaughter, as even the Prosecution have conceded. If my wife and I hadn't been having dinner for her birthday at that Hungarian restaurant; if I hadn't drunk too much Imperial Tokayi; if there hadn't been a sharp knife handy, I wouldn't have stuck it into the damned fiddler and caused all that blood. But the truth is, I was driven beyond human endurance. That miserable little man had just begun to play my Andante. My famous Andante. I simply can't bear hearing that piece.

"'Why?' you may well ask. I'll tell you why, my Lord. Then you will understand and let me off lightly. I am a major composer of classical music. I have written eleven operas, twelve symphonies – more than Beethoven – three piano concertos, a wealth of chamber music, innumerable songs. I have taught at the Royal Academy and in Vienna, Budapest and Bismarck, North Dakota. I am greatly respected in the higher reaches of the musical world.

"For this, I have given up everything else. And I mean everything. I never had time to teach my children how to ride a bicycle. I have never ironed a shirt. I never learned how to make an omelette or even to boil an egg, which I am told is quite easy. In fact, I am useless around the house, as my wife frequently remarks. I have lived my life in a frenzy of creative activity. Like Mozart, you might say, except that I did not die young.

"And what is the result of this huge, life-long expenditure of energy? Do they play my Symphonies at the Proms? They do not. Are my song-cycles, my delicate settings of Emily Bronte and Walt Whitman, performed at the Wigmore Hall? They are not. Has my great opera, my five-hour Genghis Khan, been snapped up by the Royal Opera House? The full score came back by return of post. They say I am old-fashioned, unduly tonal, a thing of the past. Just because I am not a handsome boy you could photograph in tight jeans, or some young dolly bird with big boobs and a come-to-bed pout."

Mr Justice Haslemere stirred uneasily. The Court Usher gave him a discreet dig in the ribs, fearing he was going to sleep again and might even snore.

"And what, out of all my massive oeuvre, do they still play?" quavered Phillimore, his thin voice rising with the intensity of passion. "Just one little thing, a mere trifle. The slow movement from my violin sonata in G, beefed up for exiguous string orchestra. It lasts for four and a half minutes and has a pretty little tune which came to me in the bath. The famous Phillimore Andante. Very convenient for the sloppy and light minded. I detest the Phillimore Andante. As poor old Boccherini might have felt about his Minuet, or Paderewski with his bloody Minuet in G. The damned piece reminds me how much effort I put in, how little I got out. Every time I hear that cursed sound, I see red. It is a perpetual symbol of my own devastated career.

"So now you will understand, my lord. I was driven beyond endurance. I was not my usual urbane self. I feel certain you will show mercy."

"I find your explanation quite unconvincing," responded Mr Justice Haslemere with a slight start. "Indeed it verges on the time-wasting and merely frivolous. You have committed a very serious crime, Phillimore, and I am obliged to impose the maximum sentence."

There was a wail from the Public Gallery as the prisoner's aged mother was led from the Court. Mr Justice Haslemere did not notice. There would be time, he thought, for a large gin and tonic in the upstairs bar at the Garrick before lunch. These creative geniuses were all a bit nutty. Thank God he had expended his own mental energies in the more profitable field of criminal law.

The Legacy

Selling books, I suppose, is like selling anything else. You have to get the details right, to marry the product with the customers. I've always enjoyed reading, though I didn't go on to University. Too busy looking after Mother, who had all those years of illness before she died when I was nineteen. Now, three years later, I often felt lonely in my one-room flat near the Old Pier. At least in Mr Wheeler's bookshop you got plenty of human company. I enjoyed talking to the browsers and making unsought suggestions about what they might like to buy. Mr Wheeler sometimes said I was a gem, though he never offered an increase in salary. On Sunday evenings, unlike everyone else, I used to look forward to Monday mornings. The bookshop was better than walking alone along the front towards the Dolphin Pool.

I remember well that winter afternoon when Mr Deverel came into the shop. Mr Wheeler was upstairs in his flat, enjoying a siesta, I supposed. He often did that nowadays since taking to a spot of whisky with his lunch. I didn't mind being in charge of everything myself. It was good to know that the old boy trusted me. Mother had treated me as a retarded child, right up to the end, bless her. I could bear that in Mother, but not in Mr Wheeler, whose stained old suit should have been binned long ago.

You could see at once that Mr Deverel was a cut above the usual run of our customers. He was well dressed in a smart sports coat with grey flannels and a nice red shirt and tie. He wasn't young, but there was a touch of distinction about his grey hair, and he had kind, amused eyes.

He wanted a book on Venice and I managed to advise. "Have you read all these books?" he asked approvingly.

"I do my best, sir," I said. We got into conversation and he seemed to be in no hurry to leave. I wondered if he fancied me. That is not unusual among the old queens who seem to be so numerous in this part of the Sussex coast. I am on the short side and look as if I might be cuddly and complaisant.

Lots of people think I'm gay. I can sense that without being told. I don't know that I am, that's part of my trouble. If I surrendered to that side of me, I could go out to the gay clubs and at least find myself a bit of company. But I imagined that I'd got a bit of a crush on Fiona, the girl I happened to sit next to at the Theatre Royal. We'd gone out together two or three times, but nothing much had come of it so far. I wanted to settle down with her and become more like other people. I was confused, that's the trouble. Perhaps I always would be.

"Do you run this place all on your own?" asked Mr Deverel after we had exchanged names.

I explained about Mr Wheeler and how he liked to take a nap in the afternoon. Mr Deverel smiled and went off with the Venice book

He was back two days later. Again in the afternoon. I somehow thought he would be. He wanted more books on Italy. He was planning to go there in the summer. He was obviously not a silly sun-seeker, but someone who planned his holidays with care and knowledge.

"We shan't be sticking to Venice," he explained. "This time we shall be doing a bit of the Veneto, too. Padua, Treviso, Vicenza, Asolo. So much to see."

I wondered who he meant by 'we'. He came back several times, always in the early afternoon when he could be sure of catching me on my own. Obviously he was offering me friendship. I was happy to accept that. God knows I needed friends. But I didn't like the idea of being cruised by a rapacious old queen. I had had quite enough of that from Canon Droitwich. I was rather reassured when he suggested that I should come for a drink after work one day 'to meet the family'. Now I could visualise a nice white-haired Mrs Deverel and some civilised grown children of about my own age.

It wasn't like that though. It turned out that he lived in a beautiful Regency flat on the sea-front with a younger man called Toby. The children proved to be a pair of rather capricious Siamese cats. Toby was younger than Angus Deverel and only slightly older than me. I quite liked the look of him. He was dark and slim and had worked in the catering trade. Angus was socially grander, a retired civil servant who had once been a mandarin in Whitehall. He came from a moneyed background, too. In some ways I felt closer to Toby. Well, I wasn't going to do anything to split them up. That wasn't my way.

I soon got to know them well. They kept inviting me

to dinner. Toby was a splendid cook and they took me a lot to restaurants too, sometimes we went on excursions, to Chichester, or Arundel, or places like that. I appreciated their friendship and I enjoyed the fun. I was seeing even less of Fiona now, but she didn't seem to mind. I don't think she had ever really cared much about me. But Angus Deverel did. I felt sure of that. He kept looking at me in a cool, appraising way, as if I were some valuable antique at Sotheby's he was thinking of bidding for. I could imagine what he had in mind, and I didn't like it at all. An old man like him would never attract me. Besides, it wouldn't be fair to Toby.

Toby was a dark horse. He didn't talk much. Perhaps he was frightened of displaying some huge gap in his knowledge. He wasn't cultured and expensively educated like Angus. Sometimes I thought he was actually avoiding me. But then, every now and again, he would give me a lovely smile. It was like the sun shining out after a storm. Toby was a simple person, in the best sense; a refreshing contrast from his devious old partner.

We got to the stage when they would invite me to come over for the whole weekend and sleep in their comfortable guestroom. Sometimes they would have friends to dinner, always Angus's, never Toby's. Gay mostly, but not invariably. Interesting people whom I might otherwise have met in the bookshop, but never socially. Actors, literary agents, high-level journalists. It was a damn sight better than cooking myself a lonely supper and watching the soaps.

One night I got stuck on the sofa with Isabel, a woman casting director, not much younger than Angus. He was showing off his Oriental treasures in the library and Toby, poor Toby, was doing the washing-up. I could see she wanted to talk.

"I gather you have become rather important to Angus and Toby," she began conspiratorially.

"Did they tell you that?" I replied. "They have certainly been very hospitable."

"Angus is keen on you," she continued. "He's always had a soft spot for the young."

That might have sounded bitchy, but it didn't come out that way. I knew she had been a genuine friend to Angus for many years. Somehow I felt I could talk to her.

"Angus has his relationship with Toby," I pointed out. "I would never do anything to damage that."

"That won't last," said Isabel.

"What on earth do you mean?"

"Angus is very ill. I suppose he hasn't told you."

"Ill?" I was shocked. He looked fragile, but I had put that down to age.

"He doesn't want it to be generally known. But you're special. He has prostate cancer. It's a long business. They gave him chemotherapy, but it didn't do the trick. And now he's too old for the radical operation. Don't tell him I told you. Just be kind to him."

I had this conversation in mind when, the following weekend, Angus knocked on the door of my bedroom as I was trying to get off to sleep. I felt obliged to let him in.

"I thought we could have a little natter," he said hopefully, sitting down beside my pillow. "You don't mind, do you?"

"No, of course not."

"Toby is asleep already. It's a good moment to talk."

He put out a gnarled old hand and started stroking my hair. He must have sensed that I didn't care for that, because he didn't go any further. I began to understand his motives better now, in the light of Isabel's disclosure. Poor frightened old Angus, facing the valley of the shadow of death, lusted after some new young flesh to help him, however briefly, to forget. But did it have to be mine?

"I wanted to explain to you," continued Angus. "I'm very fond of you, you know. You must have realised that. You're a sweet, intelligent boy; and very attractive, too."

"Thank you, Angus dear," I murmured. "I'm grateful for your affection. But there's one thing we have to get straight. I'm not interested in older men. Not in that way, at least."

"I know that," he replied. "I sensed it from that first afternoon. I don't want you for myself. I'm not going to last long. I overheard Isabel letting that cat out of the bag. Our Italian holiday will probably be the last. Toby will be left here. He won't be short of money, but he'll be badly in need of companionship."

"I'm terribly sorry, Angus …"

"Thank you. Enough of that. It's Toby we have to think about now."

"Surely you have a lot of friends."

"They won't bother much with Toby. Not in the long run. They will be kind to him, but he's not in their world and never could be. He only comes alive for them because of me."

There was truth in that, I knew. That was why, at dinner parties, Toby seemed satisfied to spend much time in the kitchen, preparing his mysterious brews.

"Toby requires someone of his own age, or even younger," continued Angus. "He's fond of you, too. I think you would find him a good partner."

"So that's why you picked me up in the first place."

"I suppose so. You're not hurt, are you?"

"No, of course not." I was not so sure about that. I did feel a bit deflated. Did he mean that Toby and I were both vulnerable people? Two matchsticks who needed each other's support if they were to stand upright?

"I wanted to leave you for him," said the older man.

"As a kind of legacy?" I asked, a faint note of bitterness in my voice.

"You could call it that. Do you know Rosenkavalier? At the end, when the FeldMarschall gives up young Octavian to Sophie." Trust Angus to add a cultural touch. I giggled to think of him as a FeldMarschall. I felt that, even in the dark, he was giving me one of his well-bred smiles. He kissed me on the forehead and wished me good night.

"Think about it," he added softly, moving to the door. He shut it behind him with a gentle click.

I did not sleep well that night.

The Enemy

The warm wind whistled, as I peered out into the threatening darkness. In this part of the world, at this time, you had to be careful if you wanted to go on living. Around us were the Troodos Mountains in western Cyprus, and these were the 1950s. As British soldiers, we were representatives of the colonial oppressors to the EOKA terrorists, dedicated to using violence to get us out and hand the island over to Greece. Our company was potentially a sitting target. No wonder I wanted to make sure young sentries were straining their ears for every crack of a twig, every hoot of an owl. You couldn't fire at the locals first. They had the initiative. Frankly, it was damn frightening, though we all tried hard not to show it.

It had all been different in France nearly fifteen years before. Then it was the other way round. The Germans had taken over the Chateau and were occupying the village. We were hiding out there in the wooded darkness, waiting for an opportunity to blow them up and so put out of action an important railway junction. I had been seconded from the army and parachuted into Occupied France to work with the French Resistance. After the war, the French understandably tended to exaggerate the value of their Resistance to the Allied war effort. Many had been all for a quiet life. But there had been some brave men and women who risked torture and death to try to undermine the huge power of the German army. I suppose I was the right sort of young officer to send them. With my French mother, I was almost bilingual, although brought up in England. I had a talent for other languages too.

The key to knocking out the German detachment, they said, was to destroy the Chateau where their Commanding Officer was billeted. We know nothing about him, but that wasn't the point. In war you kill your enemies and he had to be eliminated. With the aid of a friendly local worker, we had managed to install an explosive device in the wine cellar of the Chateau. It would be detonated as soon as I gave the signal. We were waiting till after midnight to make sure that the German General was shut away in his room. There was a lot of waiting in the war.

It was a bright moonlit night. We never cared for those nights, threatening as they did the welcoming darkness in which we preferred to carry out our exploits. I remember the clouds scudding across the face of the moon, the chime of the church clock at midnight. Otherwise, the Chateau and the whole village were very quiet. I gave the signal to go ahead. We waited in a moment of agonising apprehension. Then a huge explosion followed, sending the Chateau up in a garish, unnatural light. Nobody could have survived that. We ran quickly down to the river, where a boat was waiting to rescue us. At the river mouth, a larger ship would take me back to England. I felt exhilarated, rather pleased with myself.

"A job well done," said my debriefing officer when I got back to the big house in Kensington. "Eliminating General von Hildesheim has been a major coup. Reports say he was killed outright with his Chief of Staff and ADC. He was considered to be one of the brightest of the younger German generals and might have had a big future. Now we were wondering whether you might like a little trip to Norway."

After the War, I continued my army career. By sheer chance, a holiday in the late '40s brought me back to the same region of France where I had worked with the Resistance. When my background became known locally, I was hospitably received by some in the village, though others stayed away. It was not considered tactful to dig too closely into the events of the Occupation which had divided families and provoked lifelong resentments among the French themselves. The inn-keeper's wife, whom I remembered from wartime days, soon became a useful ally.

"I have often wondered about the German General," I said to her one evening as I downed a pint of her powerful cider. "Von Hildesheim, the one we killed. Was he a bit of a brute?"

I was hoping, I suppose, that she would say yes. I had imagined him as terrorising his region, threatening to take and shoot hostages. Perhaps, in some obscure way, I felt a sense of guilt, even though I had only been doing my duty. Was that the subconscious reason why I had chosen that part of France for my holiday? It would have been so easy to go south, to remote Savoy, or unravaged Provence. My lingering doubts would be so easily dispelled if I could be assured that I had eliminated a monster.

But Madame Deffand wasn't having any of that.

"He wasn't a bad man at all," she said firmly. "I saw quite a lot of him, you know. He used to come into the private bar here for a drink from time to time. It was his way of trying to be friendly to us in the village. The Germans often liked to do that. It made life easier for them. It was only when the villagers turned against them that they began to show their teeth."

"Didn't the Resistance object? Your having the General in here as a customer?"

"They encouraged it. My husband was with them secretly, you see. They trusted us completely. They wanted us to get information about German plans. And we did sometimes."

"What was von Hildesheim like? As a human being."

"Very polite, well brought-up. He was a regular officer, you see, in the German cavalry, not one of those Nazis. Just doing his duty for his country, I suppose. He was very fond of classical music. Played the piano himself, up at the Chateau. We used to hear him often in the evenings. Mozart, Schubert, Chopin. He was longing for the war to end. To get back to his family at home. They sent a much worse man to replace him. He was the one who shot the hostages."

A General who played Chopin! Not at all the brute I had hoped to hear about.

A few years later, I found myself posted to Germany, to the British Army of the Rhine. Some haunting apprehension made me want to make enquiries about the von Hildesheims. I found that they had an estate near Hanover, badly battered but still intact. I made an excuse to visit their Manor House, pretending that we were interested in buying local farm produce. At that difficult time the Germans were keen to find ways of building up their fortunes again. The door was opened by a white-haired lady in middle age who introduced herself as the Baroness von Hildesheim.

We got talking and I told her about my wife and children. She spoke about her late husband who had died during the war. It was indeed the same General I had killed in France.

"Do tell me about him, Baroness," I said in as casual a tone as I could manage. I was feeling bad, but of course I didn't want her to spot that.

"He was very keen on your country," she replied. "As a young man, before joining the Army, he had spent a year at Wadham College in Oxford reading English. He loved music and painting too. He hated Hitler and his horrible Nazis. If he had lived, I am sure he would have been involved in that plot against the Führer. They were already taking soundings. My husband was the ablest of the potential conspirators. If he had lived, the plot might well have succeeded, and perhaps have been brought off earlier. That could have shortened the War by one year."

I drove off down the long avenue of lime trees, full of strange thoughts.

And now, out there in the dark, Cypriot night, there are EOKA resistance fighters – terrorists, as we now call them – who are out to kill me, as the local British military commander. They don't know, or care, that I am personally favourable to the concept of Cyprus deciding her own destiny, and long for the Greeks and Turks to live in peace. I must be marked for death, quite impersonally, because I happen to be the enemy.

It's a funny old world, isn't it?

The Threat

By the middle of the twenty-first century, the world was in turmoil. In many countries, famine and disease had been spread by a series of disastrous wars. There had been the war of the two Chinas, the war between the Koreas, the Moslem-Christian war across the Mediterranean, the war between Israel and her combined Arab neighbours, and the nuclear war between India and Pakistan. The next item on this fearsome agenda was expected to be the looming struggle between the United States and China, a veritable Armageddon in the making. This terrible cycle of human folly had, of course, been set off earlier in the century by President Bush's doctrine of the pre-emptive strike. He had persuaded the credulous that wars need no longer be fought solely in self-defence; but that any country could invade any other if they thought they were in danger of attack.

In spite of all this, the United Nations still existed, uttering despairing cries for calm reflection and peaceful negotiation. Some thought it was more important than ever that the warring nations should at last take co-operation and debate seriously. Many speeches on this theme had been made by the well-meaning Secretary-General, Sampson

Adekunle of Nigeria. But so far Governments, inspired only by national interest, had refused to take him seriously.

"We must try something else," groaned Adekunle, looking sadly out of his office window across the East River in New York. "The time has come for desperate measures."

"I have been thinking about that," said the Deputy Secretary General, the elegant François Trichet of France.

France and Britain had lost their seats on the Security Council. Indeed, they were not even in the General Assembly under their own names. The European Union was now represented at the United Nations, at day-to-day diplomatic level, by Ambassador Palamos of Greece, a brother-in-law of the Greek Prime Minister, whose appointment was known to be due to that relationship. Palamos, who was elderly, showed a disturbing tendency to sleep through important negotiations and then wake, with a start, to make some totally irrelevant proposal. He could not be got out until it was some other member's turn. The real voice in New York of the European Union, now representing the whole of Europe, was the Deputy Secretary-General. It had been generally accepted that this key office should be held by a European. Within the EU, it had also been agreed that this European should be a national of Britain, France and Germany, much to the chagrin of Italy, Spain, Poland and all the other European states. Now, with the Neanderthal giants, America and China, about to lock horns, Trichet came as near as any other being to representing the vestigial sanity of the human race.

"Feel free to give me your ideas, François," said the Secretary-General hopefully.

"In moments of difficulty," replied the urbane

Frenchman, "I ask myself what Voltaire would have recommended. Admittedly, he died three hundred years ago. But, in his cynical way, he understood the unchangeable human spirit. It's petty jealousy, its childish ambition and yet, just occasionally, its capacity to display faint streaks of redeeming nobility."

Sampson Adekunle quite liked his Deputy, but he did find his ultra-civilised, round-about, method of operation decidedly irritating. In moments of crisis, it was best to come straight to the point, as they were inclined to do in his own Yoruba homeland. And all moments, these days, seemed to be ones of crisis.

"What do you advise?" he almost snapped.

"We shall soon be approaching the World Hunger Summit," replied Trichet. "This year it is to be in New Zealand. A nice quiet spot in the wilderness of the South Island, far removed from the usual noisy demonstrators. They have deliciously succulent roast lamb. All the world leaders will be there. Including you, Sampson. After dinner on the first evening, I think you should summon a very special, very private meeting. Just the Presidents of the United States, China and Europe and the leaders of India, Canada, South Africa, Brazil and Japan. And me, of course. Unfortunately, it's too far away for the Pope." In the old days the ancient nation states of Europe would have pressed to sit at the top table. But these times were long since past and now France, Britain and Germany had to speak officially, at Head of government level, through the voice of a retired hairdresser from Luxembourg.

"And what are we to propose at the meeting?" asked the Secretary-General.

"I'll tell you," replied Trichet, lowering his voice. "But it is essential that we should not be overheard. This is a desperate last throw for the world. An alternative to allowing the wretched leaders to be pushed into wars by the bellicose sentiments of their own people."

"Humans need to have someone to hate," pointed out Adekunle. "We have found that out in Nigeria."

"Exactly. So we will give them someone they can hate safely. Without destroying the world."

A month later they sat together in an upper room of the large, lonely, wooden hotel overlooking the wild beauty of Milford Sound in New Zealand. Out there was only the Antarctic. Each leader felt put out by the instruction that they should come alone, without their usual supporting cohorts. There was no need for interpretation since nowadays all leaders spoke English. The President of the United States felt specially bereft without his female Security Adviser who usually told him what to think. The President of Europe secretly wished he was back at home in the cosy atmosphere of his old barber's salon in the nicest section of Luxembourg. The Prime Minister of India was suffering from athlete's foot, and the President of China from after-dinner flatulence. The female Prime Minister of Japan suddenly remembered that she had forgotten the birthday of her second favourite grandson. They might be the most powerful people in the world, but they were not young and the excellent dinner, a speciality of World Hunger Summits, had been a shade too heavy.

After a preliminary welcome, the Secretary-General handed over to his articulate Deputy. Trichet, unabashed, unfolded his bold plan. A lesser man might have felt nervous in the presence of such great potentates, but a capacity for feeling timid was not in the Frenchman's repertoire.

There was a silence after he had finished his exposition. The leaders looked stunned.

"Could we really pull it off?" asked the American President, Homer Fairchild. "In my experience, you can't fool all the people all the time. I know that because I've tried."

"It would be essential for us all to work together," said Mrs Ishiguru of Japan. "Corroboration from such different parts of the world might just do the trick."

"The sheer cheek of it is awe-inspiring," pointed out Tom Biltmore of Canada. "I like that. No-one could even imagine it, much less suspect us. Let's give the people what they need. An enemy to fight."

Adekunle beamed at Trichet. It was a bold move, but better than letting the world end through man's folly and childish refusal to compromise.

Shortly afterwards the American Government announced, to an astonished world, that there had been disturbing activity in Nevada which appeared to come from an extra-terrestrial agency. A probe from outer space was suspected. This news was received worldwide with considerable suspicion. Until China came up with a similar story. There had been a moonlight landing near the Tibetan frontier. After that, terrifying news came thick and fast. A crater had opened up in Germany, in the Black Forest, indicating that a saucer-like vehicle had crash landed there. A total power black-out in South Africa suggested that the lines had been cut by something other than human hands. In the Amazonian basin of Brazil, bizarre non-human creatures had been seen, barking out orders in a language never heard before.

Now it was only too clear. An invasion from outer space was being prepared. The world, our beautiful earth, was in acute danger. All the great powers announced that the only hope for the human race was to co-operate to defend us all from this terrible threat. This was no time to fight others of our own race, however disagreeable. We all had to rally round to repel the invading aliens.

Huge popular demonstrations supporting this theme were held first in Central Park in New York and Hyde Park in London, and then all over the world. Public hatred was concentrated on the unspeakable aliens; bishops, rabbis and imams all preached on the duty of crushing your enemy. An elderly lady of unusual appearance in Western Australia was lynched.

The World Defence Force was formed, with comfortable quarters overlooking the lake in Geneva. Appointments to the large international secretariat were eagerly sought. Powerful telescopes scanned the skies perpetually, seeking a trace of the invaders streaking through space on a killing mission.

Meanwhile, there were no wars on the earth itself. The planet had never been more peaceful.

François Trichet sought, and obtained, a hefty bonus. He has bought himself an elegant chateau in the Loire valley. To deter intruders, he has placed a notice on the front lawn.

It says, in several languages, 'Beware of the Snakes'.

As Voltaire recommended, he cultivates his garden.

At the Graveside

"I feel sure," said Miranda, as they drove towards the crematorium at Mortlake, "that we are all in for a bit of a shock."

"We have had the shock already," retorted her husband, Henry, in tones of mild reproof. "Bertie having that unexpected heart attack. Just after a round of golf."

"He was a good five years older than you, dear," said his wife. "And all that frenzied dealing on the Stock Exchange must have been a strain. Not to mention living with Judith all those years."

Henry did not quite care for the drift of this conversation. It verged on the unseemly. After all, they were on their way to poor Bertie's funeral. And Judith would now be left a widow without anyone to boss around. Admittedly, she had never been easy. But she was a member of the family and he couldn't forget the nice way she had visited him in hospital when he had his gallstones operation. The trouble with Miranda was that she never knew when to stop. Her sprightly wit and unbridled imagination could make her good company. But on this really rather sad occasion, he would have preferred a dignified silence.

"It's such a pity," continued Miranda, unabashed, "that Bertie and Judith didn't have any children. I wonder why that was."

"I never asked," said Henry drily.

"There was an air of mystery about them," added Miranda, almost gaily, narrowly missing a somewhat insecure cyclist on the bridge across the Thames. "Even you must have noticed that, Henry." She liked to think of him as an unworldly scholar, just because he had spent so many years as Curator of Hittite Archaeology at the British Museum.

"I don't know what you are talking about, dear," he protested mildly.

"Well, it simply doesn't add up, Henry. Your cousin had been beavering away in the city for years. He must have earned a packet. Infinitely more than you. And you can't say that dear Judith has ever exactly spent a fortune on dress. Where did it all go? The money, I mean. They never had good holidays, did they? A long weekend in Bruges was their idea of an adventure. And we never saw them at Glyndebourne. Even we got there occasionally on your meagre salary."

"What exactly are you suggesting, Miranda?" asked Henry, his patience beginning to wear thin.

"It's not only the money, dear. There is also the question of your cousin's unexplained absences."

"He didn't have to account to me."

"No, but you said yourself that when you used to ring him in the evenings and at weekends, he often wasn't there. Judith would answer, sounding rather disconsolate and offering to ask Bertie to ring you back."

"Which he usually did the following day."

"Exactly. I'm sure he spent a lot of time and money

somewhere else. It's the only possible explanation. We may well find out now at the funeral."

"What on earth do you mean?"

"They are bound to be there. The second family. They could hardly miss it, even if they have to appear in disguise."

"The second family! Have you taken leave of your senses, Miranda?"

"It's been my pet theory for some time now. That would account for the absences and the shortage of cash. Living with Judith, he would need to take time off with some less demanding female. He goes there on Sundays and she ministers to his every whim. You told me yourself that Bertie was highly sexed during his adolescent years."

"Everyone is highly sexed in adolescence," Henry almost snapped. "Bertie will have got over that long ago."

"The results may still be on show," said Miranda obstinately. "A sweet, dumpy little common-law wife who used to work in fast food. Bertie met her over a hamburger in Leicester Square. Two kids, of course. A snide, bespectacled boy and a big, expensive girl."

"Nonsense," said Henry decisively. "Judith would never permit it. At the funeral, of all places. All their smart city friends will be there."

For once, Miranda relapsed into silence, contenting herself with a small, secret smile. Time would show.

It annoyed Henry that Bertie could not have had a decent funeral in a Church with some nice, old-fashioned hymns. But Bertie and Judith had never been believers, and she had insisted on this miserable affair in the crematorium with its canned music and sinister slab with rollers for the coffin. Judith gave them a guarded welcome. Henry knew a few old family friends, but most of the other mourners looked like prosperous financial people who meant nothing to him. It was all so different from his own small, enclosed world of Hittite scholarship.

"I don't see the second family," whispered Henry with satisfaction.

"Who is that over there?" retorted Miranda. "Hanging around, just behind Judith. Looking awfully lost."

She indicated an expensively dressed young man, who did indeed seem strangely out of place.

"I think he's a dark horse," added Miranda, in one of her unfortunately audible whispers.

Judith came over to them.

"I want you, darling Henry and dear Miranda, to sit behind me in the second row. It's so good to have family at one's back at an awful time like this."

"Oughtn't we to be beside you, Judith dear?" suggested Miranda boldly. "You need support."

"I shall have support, dear. Lucius has kindly agreed to sit beside me and literally hold my hand. Oh, I forgot. You don't know Lucius, do you? He is simply the most helpful antique dealer in the whole of Wimbledon."

"Pleased to meet you," volunteered Lucius. "I've heard a lot about you over the years."

Miranda could contain herself no longer.

"Who the devil is Lucius?" she whispered to Judith.

"Shall we just say, dear, that Lucius is one of the family."

In The Piazza delle Erbe

Few would have suspected the fastidious, elderly couple of being Australians. It was not a nationality that Peter and Emily Shoesmith cared to advertise on their annual trips to Europe. Not that they were ashamed of their origins. On the contrary, they were deeply proud of belonging to that rare and now endangered species, the upper class Australian. In Melbourne they ranked indubitably among the First Families. Peter's people had acquired their vast sheep-holdings in the state of Victoria, well before the Commonwealth itself existed. They had, of course, been free immigrants, though nowadays a slight convict tinge in the remote ancestry was perfectly respectable. Emily, too, was of impeccable provenance. Her father, of sound English Somerset stock, had come out to teach English literature at the University. Seduced by the vast purple landscapes and bold, bright birds, they had never gone home.

The trouble for the Shoesmiths was that, outside Australia, nobody was aware of their exclusive background. They shuddered at the prospect of being bracketed with their loud, cheerful compatriots wearing shorts and garish shirts and drinking huge cans of beer. Oxford or Princeton was more their type of thing. This anxiety perhaps made them seem excessively genteel. 'Prissy' would have described Peter with his beautifully tailored grey suits, and Emily in her neatly laundered linen coat and skirt. These days, as everyone knew, real aristos tended to slop around in sneakers.

They were staying in Venice, as they did most summers. Water was such a precious commodity in Australia. It was good to have it all around you. And they loved the echoes of Henry James and Diaghilev, and even Peggy Guggenheim. You could reach the station by water too and, from there, make fascinating little excursions onto dry land. So much better than wasting time with those vulgar people on the Lido.

Today they were in Verona. Emily had insisted. She had studied *Romeo and Juliet* at school and had never been quite the same afterwards. With her warm, passionate nature, she had dreamed of amorous couplings on summer balconies, of worlds lost for love. Marriage to dear old Peter had not been exactly that, though it did offer some solid comforts.

Now they sat in the Piazza at a table under a red umbrella, consuming the cappucini which Peter had managed to order in his heavily anglicised Italian. With his floppy white hat, neat moustache and well polished brown shoes, he looked, thought Emily, like a character from E.M. Forster in those nice Merchant Ivory films they both enjoyed so much. Brandishing his Michelin like a weapon, Peter started to enlighten her. She didn't much care for his readings from the guide-book, but had never quite summoned up the courage to tell him so. Peter was easily hurt and then his moody silences could last for hours. Their marriage was solid, but it needed constant working on, especially from Emily's side.

"We are in the Piazza delle Erbe," proclaimed Peter.

"The Grass Market," said Emily. "Just like Edinburgh."

"The Square of Herbs, if you like, my dear. Today the vegetable market place. Once the Roman forum. Over there is the capitello, or rostrum, from which decrees were proclaimed. See also the fountain known as the Madonna of Verona with a Roman statue."

One good thing about Peter's readings was that he never seemed to notice whether or not Emily was listening. This left her free to gaze about, as she did now.

The Piazza was full of young people. They might have been older children, or junior adults. You could never quite tell in Italy, where maturity began so young. She felt captivated by their dark, lively faces and animated movements. There was one particular little group which seemed to be concentrated on their corner of the square. It consisted of a sprightly, pretty girl and three attendant boys. Emily amused herself by imagining their characters. One boy was quiet and dreamy, the second a talkative show-off, and the third an aggressive trouble maker. The boys had skateboards, on which they were performing athletically, to the danger of passing pedestrians. The girl had climbed up some steps and was egging them on from a height. In Emily's youth, girls had been gentler and less troublesome than boys. But not any longer. The little minx enjoyed making things happen.

Was it Emily's imagination, or were there two separate groups in the Piazza now? Rival gangs, you might call them. A bit like *West Side Story*. The atmosphere was hotting up. She hoped there wouldn't be any trouble.

"Note the Venetian column," continued her husband imperturbably, "surmounted by the winged Lion of Saint Mark." He broke off suddenly, as a dull thud hit the legs of the table. The aggressive boy had crashed into them on his skateboard.

"God damn it," shouted Peter, "you nearly went over my foot then. Haven't you got anything better to do?"

"I don't think he understands English," said Emily.

"He knows perfectly well what I mean," growled her husband.

The aggressive boy, quite unrepentant, just stared at them. The talkative show-off gabbled away, a saucy grin on his face. Above them, the girl giggled. Then the dreamy boy whizzed past them on his own skateboard. Far too close, as Peter was quick to point out.

"Bloody Hell," he exploded again. "This is no way to treat visitors. I'm sending for the café manager. It's up to him to get the police. I want this place cleared of hooligans. Verona could do with a period of zero tolerance."

"Hooligans, dear. Are you sure?"

"Of course I'm sure. Do you think I can't recognise a hooligan when I see one?"

"I think they're just high-spirited young people. Out to enjoy themselves, like us."

"They ought to be at work."

"Maybe they're on holiday, dear. As we are. Can't you see that they are rather special?"

"Special?"

"Remember where we are. Verona. The city of the Montagus and the Capulets. That girl is Juliet. The pretty boy is her Romeo. Over there, young, doomed Mercutio is shooting his mouth off. And the rough boy who crashed into our table is an obvious Tybalt. All happening before our very eyes. It's lovely."

"What does that make us then? You the Nurse and I Friar Lawrence?"

There was a gleam of amusement in Peter's eye. Emily knew now that she would be able to calm him. He had spotted the dreamy boy, the Romeo. That face reminded him strangely of Clinton, whom he had loved so secretly at school at Geelong all those years ago. The boy had turned now towards his Juliet. Yes, there was real love in those young faces. He remembered how Clinton had gone on to date girls.

"What are you thinking of, dear?" asked Emily.

Peter Shoesmith didn't answer.

"We ought to be getting on," he said calmly. "To the Scaliger Tombs and the Roman Arena. They do Aida there with real elephants."

The Nightcap

Most people considered Geoffrey Potterton to be a nice man. He had built his career on that. As a professional diplomat, you had to establish a friendly relationship with a wide variety of professional contacts, ranging from the alarmingly intelligent to the totally inane. Many of them, too, were foreigners, an additional handicap. Geoffrey had cultivated an urbane manner and a capacity to improve the atmosphere, where necessary, with the odd light-hearted quip. He was believed to be a safe pair of hands.

But some of those in authority in the Foreign Office had spotted another side to Geoffrey. Beneath that pleasant exterior, he was fiercely ambitious, with rather too sharp a cutting edge, a soloist rather than a team player. That was the main reason why he was ending his career as Ambassador to a country in South America rather than in Rome or Berlin, for which he had pined and intrigued.

It also explained the tendency of his wife Molly to leave him for fairly prolonged absences, as she was doing now. She was not exactly unhappy in their marriage, but she did need to escape from his dominating presence from time to time. Once she had heard someone describe her husband as a psychic sponge and she knew what that meant. It was if he sucked you in and then spat you out. Fortunately, there was no shortage of excuses for these very necessary returns to England. She had family obligations there, her elderly mother in a home, the boy at Cambridge, the two girls at boarding school. Molly was a very caring person.

Geoffrey found plenty to do while she was away. The country, though distant, was important. It had oil and natural gas, together with a considerable capacity to inflict damage. It was believed to be a haunt of drug smugglers and even international terrorists. Its government had to be charmed and stiffened. Geoffrey was good at all that. He had embarked on a series of lively exchanges with senior ministers of the Government to which he was accredited. These had been noted with interest in London where it had been decided that a British ministerial visit to Geoffrey's host country was long overdue.

He had brought it on himself, he wryly acknowledged. Why had he not sat back and done as little as possible, as colleagues were prone to do in their last post? It would have been so easy to coast gently towards retirement.

It had been an exhausting day. After meeting the visiting Minister at the airport that afternoon, Geoffrey had escorted him on a series of official calls to long-winded Spanish-speaking local potentates, where Geoffrey was frequently called on to interpret. Then there had been a dinner of stultifying boredom with the foreign Minister at a local hotel. Now, at last, they had been able to return to the Embassy Residence.

"Would you like a nightcap?" asked Geoffrey, hoping for a negative answer. He had two air mail editions of *The*

Times to read in bed and a possible telephone call to Molly in Cheltenham.

"I wouldn't mind at all," answered the Minister promptly. "Have you got any malt whisky?"

Geoffrey had taken an almost immediate dislike to the Minister. But this had not shown on his face, or affected the impeccable courtesy of his reception. He was far too professional for that. Francis Glen MP was a Minister of State at the Foreign Office. His official responsibility was for British relations with the supposedly developing nations which used to be known as the Third World. Among the more irreverent of his officials he was known as Minister for Outer Space or even Minister for the Odds and Sods. Not that they gave any hint of that to the Minister himself. Sense of humour was not his strong suit. Glen was a heavily built man, with a slow, ponderous manner and the demeanour of a person of importance. In the sub-tropical evening, he was visibly, and unattractively, sweating in his too heavy English suit.

The whisky was brought in by the Residence butler; a suave, deferential servant in late middle age.

"Aren't you the man who took my suitcase away?" asked Francis Glen brusquely. "What has happened to my other suit?"

Geoffrey interpreted Ramon's rapid flow of Spanish. The suit had needed some emergency repairs around the button-holes. Pilar, the housemaid, had taken it away for the purpose.

"I hope she won't be long about it," snapped Glen imperiously. "I know what these people can be like. I lost a good pair of socks in Bangladesh."

"It will be returned tomorrow," said Geoffrey with chilly politeness. Just occasionally his mask slipped. One could hardly be a perfect gentleman all the time.

"I should jolly well hope so," snapped the Minister. "You shouldn't tolerate any sloppiness here, Ambassador. After all, your whole establishment is funded by the British tax-payer." He waved a pudgy paw in the direction of the chandeliers.

It was at this point that Geoffrey decided that he very much disliked his visitor. Everything about Francis Glen was repulsive; his loud, bow-wow manner, his bold overconfident baritone voice, his heavy jowls denoting a lifetime of over-eating and drinking, his rudeness to servants who could not answer back.

"I think we managed pretty well today," said the Minister, gulping his expensive whisky and giving himself, metaphorically, a pat on the back. "You did the preliminary spade work, and I like to think that my visit added some much needed heavyweight political backing."

The Ambassador found this attitude patronising.

"It's a perfectly simple deal," he countered, perhaps a shade abruptly. "They try to crack down on their cocaine exporters and we lighten up on our immigration procedures. It was all agreed last month."

"Nevertheless," said Glen with a touch of menace, "I think today has been useful. Don't you?"

"Of course," agreed Geoffrey hastily, aware that he could not afford to push his visitor too far. Overt confrontation had never been his style, least of all with those who could do him harm.

Glen called for a second, then a third nightcap. It was

getting late. Geoffrey came to a decision at this point. Glen's arrogance must be punished. He had long contemplated a plan for just such a contingency. As an Ambassador, one could hardly be openly offensive to a visiting politician. But you did have the capacity to make their life very miserable. He had never yet put this project into effect. Most visitors could be controlled by gentler means.

But there was a first time for everything. A slightly manic glint came into the Ambassador's rather steely eyes.

"I ought to be tottering to bed," said the Minister, somewhat incoherently. "What time am I to be called in the morning?"

It was the perfect signal. "Six-thirty," was all the host had to say. A chance to hear the BBC overseas news. After all, there might have been a sudden Government reshuffle at home. Breakfast would be served at seven, followed by a brisk inspection of the garden. Staff meeting at nine. Official calls all the morning with lots of gabbling away in Spanish. Lunch at the Residence for important guests at two-thirty. In this Hispanic country, the locals always ate late. End of lunch, following brandy and liqueurs, five o'clock. Six to eight in the evening, further meetings. Eight to ten, attend three cocktails, including the National Day of Paraguay. Dinner at ten-thirty. One thirty, end of dinner. Two-thirty, sink into bed, too exhausted to sleep. Six-thirty, wake up call again. Two days of this routine, he felt sure, would sabotage the strongest constitution and send the Minister off, a gibbering wreck, to Bogota.

Geoffrey came out of his pleasant reverie to hear his visitor say, "As you press me, I will just take a final snifter."

The wretched Glen was far gone now. The floodgates

were down. He embarked on a lengthy description of the horrors of his private life. He was unhappy in his political career. His constituents were threatening to de-select him. His wife was on the verge of leaving him for a jazz trombonist. His children had never really loved him. The neighbours at their country place were deliberately growing a huge hedge which spoiled their view of the Downs. And he didn't dare to consult the doctor about that nasty, recurring pain which sometimes kept him awake at night.

As the Minister rumbled on and faint streaks of rosy-fingered dawn appeared over the mountainous horizon, the Ambassador listened with exquisite patience. Suddenly he realised that he was feeling sorry for the man. Francis might be a loud-mouthed bully, but he was also a human being like everyone else, at heart weak, feeble and afraid. He deserved not dislike, but pity.

At long last the Minister got up to go to bed.

"Thank you for a super evening, Geoffrey," he said. "I may call you that, may I not? It's been good to let my hair down. But you never did tell me when I have to be on parade tomorrow."

"You need a good night's sleep, Francis," replied Geoffrey. "Shall we say ... breakfast at nine? Or later, if you prefer."

William's Word

Lucy and her parents had first met William Pontifex in the Parador at Caromna. He was a small, dapper man with an air of composure, who looked as if he knew what he was doing. He had come there for the same reason as themselves. Sevilla and Cordoba were intolerable in the day-time heat of high summer. It was much more sensible to stay, between the two famous cities, in the parador on the hill with its large, tempting swimming pool. From the comfortably renovated old castle you could venture down into town in the evening when the Andalusian sunshine was beginning to lose its lethal power. Lucy's father was good at that sort of thing.

William was on his own. He seemed a bit lonely. Lucy's mother had invited him to sit at their table. She was that kind of woman. It turned out that William was in Spain on business. He was an art dealer. It was his profession to pick up unconsidered trifles. Lucy's family found him congenial. In Seville he explained that Velasquez had gone to Madrid and found royal favour, but El Greco had remained quietly in Toledo and became a master for all time. They allowed William to attach himself to their party. Together they all went on to Granada where William proved equally well informed about the Alhambra

Lucy thought of William as her parents' friend. He was of their generation; a widower, he explained, running a small exclusive business from his house in a Cotswold village. Lucy soon forgot him on their return home. She was busy with her nursing training at a London hospital. Her parents lived in the North. To her surprise, William Pontifex appeared in London and asked her out to dinner. It proved to be a very pleasant evening. In spite of the difference in their ages, they got on well enough when alone together. William proved to be rather interested in her paramedical studies. He was diabetic and the workings of the body were one of his major concerns.

Two weeks later they were engaged. He had subjected Lucy to a whirlwind wooing of gourmet meals, avuncular kisses and the best seats at the Opera. Lucy found him a refreshing change from the callow, overworked student doctors who normally took her out. There was something delightfully confident and secure about Mr Pontifex. He reminded her of her dear father, a pillar of British rectitude and reliability. The nursing training could be put on hold. There was an immediate need to look after poor, solitary, bereaved William with his expressive eyes and occasional twinkle. Besides, he obviously lived well and the nurses' home left much to be desired.

Lucy's parents were far from pleased. "Are you sure you know what you're doing, dear?" asked her mother. "It's been awfully sudden and we know nothing about him. Bedsides, he's so much older than you."

"That doesn't matter," replied Lucy, rather annoyed by

this interference. "We're kindred spirits. I know it will be all right."

"I made enquiries," said her father. "They know him at Sothebys. He's in quite a small way. Apparently he specialises in selling medium price stuff to the Americans."

"I hope he's got enough for them both to live on," said Lucy's mother, ever the pessimist.

"He wasn't stinting himself in Spain," pointed out her father. He believed in letting Lucy do her own thing.

They had a quiet wedding with Lucy's family in Yorkshire and a short, hectic honeymoon in Paris. William proved to be an enthusiastic and imaginative lover. He wasn't, she reminded herself, all that old. Some people got even keener on sex as other faculties declined. She liked the house near Lechlade, built of honeyed, Cotswold stone, with a manageable garden. William stored his paintings and received his potential purchasers in a commodious conservatory, nicely heated in winter. There was an air of quiet affluence about him which Lucy found congenial.

She had hoped to find some caring work in the locality, but nothing exactly right came up. The months passed. From time to time, William had to go away for a night or two. As a dealer, he needed to replenish his stock. Lucy offered to accompany him, but he thought she might be bored. Lucy didn't really mind. She stayed at home and busied herself with the garden. She knew she could trust her husband absolutely. He had such an open, English face.

Sometimes, with William's permission, she would potter around in the conservatory. She enjoyed looking at his store of art treasures, many of them British watercolours from the late 18th and early 19th century. That was how she came to hear William in action with Mr and Mrs Belluno of Palm Beach, Florida. She happened to be sitting quietly behind the large bookshelf when the three of them entered. It would make her look a bit of a snooper to appear now, she thought, so she just stayed silent and waited for them to leave.

"I say, honey," cooed Elinor Belluno, "look at this pretty little picture. Isn't it cute?"

"You've made a good choice there," William was heard to say. "An early pencil and water colour drawing by the great Turner."

"What's it supposed to be?" asked Joseph Belluno doubtfully.

"A view of Edinburgh from Saint Anthony's Chapel," replied William promptly. "He was there in 1801 when he was 26, so we can date it exactly. There's another not unlike it in the British Museum."

"It's beautiful," said Elinor, "and by Turner, too. Everyone has heard of him."

"It's very small," pointed out Joseph. "How do we know it *is* by Turner?"

"It has his signature," said William. "JWM Turner. Here in the bottom, right-hand corner where he always signed."

"It's sort of vague," said Joe.

"That's meant to be, darling. He's the man who invented Impressionism. We've been doing that in my Art Appreciation Seminar. I sure would like to show the girls a genuine Turner."

"I should part with it with regret," said William.

"How much?" snapped Joe.

"I could get twenty thousand pounds for it at Christies

or Sothebys," said William. "But I like you both. I'll let you have it for fifteen."

"Ten," suggested Joe.

"Fifteen or nothing," said William, unexpectedly firm.

"Come on, honey," said Elinor. "You know we can afford it. We can't delay here any longer, if we're going to catch that plane home tonight."

The deal was agreed for fifteen thousand pounds. Lucy felt disturbed. She had noted that little watercolour herself. It looked suspiciously like one she had seen William buy the previous month from an old farmer down the valley. She had seen him working on it since then. Putting in the signature perhaps.

If William's word couldn't be trusted, terrible thoughts swirled round her brain. Had he married her only as a nubile body for sex, and then perhaps as a nurse in old age? Perhaps her mother's suspicions had been right all along. She resisted the temptation to confront him on the spot. She would not let him know that she had listened behind the bookcase. She would do the same again, next time he received American visitors.

That happened two days later. Lucy was there to hear.

"I've got a wonderful Gainsborough here," said William seductively. "Wooded landscape with gypsies. About 1765 when he was at the height of his powers. Three years later he was a founder member of the Royal Academy. As you see, he uses his typical brown paper. A sure sign of authenticity."

"That forty thousand you mentioned, Mr Pontifex. Would it be pounds or dollars?"

"For you, sir, I am prepared to take dollars."

RODE HE ON BARBARY?

Lucy felt increasingly disturbed. Hadn't he acquired the so-called Gainsborough at a house clearance auction in Bath? It seemed too good to be true. But again she said nothing.

That evening after William said, "I have to go away tomorrow, my dear. Manchester, so tiresome. But it's only for two days. I hope you'll be able to amuse yourself while I'm away."

"I'll come too," said Lucy firmly. William looked taken aback.

"It's only business, dear. So boring. I'll be thinking of you all the time. You have my word."

"That's the trouble," said Lucy. "It's all I do have."

The Announcement

Rose was sitting in the garden, pretending to read a book. That should have been enjoyable. It was a glorious summer day and Timothy's lovingly tended roses were in rampant, almost vulgar, bloom. But Rose felt vaguely guilty. It was a working day and she had never been an idler. She took pleasure in her job at the Public Library where, among other things, she had managed to build up a nice little collection of books of local interest. But this week she hadn't been feeling too well. Something, she felt sure, was happening inside her. She hadn't bothered Timothy about it. He was so absurdly protective of her. But she had gone to the hospital for tests, the results of which were now awaited. And they had told her to take the rest of the week off. It was hard to read when you felt a clutch of fear at the heart.

Suddenly she sensed a change of mood. It was like a shadow passing away across the lawn, leaving the purity of sunlight. Rose was reminded of Andrew Marvell's great garden description, 'Like a green thought in a green shade'. Hadn't he been MP for Hull? How many MPs, she wondered, were in the Oxford book of English Verse? Rose had realised by now that she was no longer alone. Looking up, she saw a person standing in the middle of the lawn and now coming slowly towards her.

That in itself was a small mystery. How had this creature arrived? One moment there was no-one there, and now suddenly this apparition had appeared. What sort of being was this? It wasn't effeminate, and yet it wasn't quite a man or a woman. The clothes didn't help either. The visitor wore a sort of caftan which might have been appropriate for either sex. Rose was mystified and almost frightened.

"Are you Rose?" the strange newcomer enquired.

"Yes." The name was short for Rosemary, but nobody used that nowadays. "What do you want?"

"I must first apologise for coming unannounced and so startling you." It was an unusual voice, light of timbre; neither quite male, nor completely female; and mysteriously enigmatic.

"You were expecting news, I believe," continued the new arrival.

"Yes. From the hospital." Rose could hardly keep her eyes off the face. It was beautiful and compelling, like something from another world. Was this all a dream? Had she simply nodded off in the sunshine? And yet everything was real, the roses, the singing blackbird, the visitor's unusual robe.

"I have come to give you the result of your test, Rose. You are pregnant. You will bear a son."

Pregnant! Rose felt a surge of joy. She and Timothy had been married for six years. They had longed for children but so far, in spite of all their efforts, she had not been able to conceive. That was why she had feared cancer. She would break the news to Timothy that evening. How happy he would be. He might insist on opening champagne.

"Pregnant!" she echoed. "Are you sure?"

"Of course we are sure. These are tidings of great joy. Your son will be a child of god."

"Naturally," said Rose calmly. "We are all children of God, aren't we?"

"That is true. But not everyone understands that. It has caused misunderstanding in the past."

"It was kind of you," said Rose, "to take the trouble to come."

"I had a reason. This child will be special. May power and strength be with you."

The strange, androgynous figure raised its right arm in a gesture of salutation. Then it was gone. Rose did not see it go. She felt understandably bewildered. Suddenly, she detected a rush of air and then a very slight pressure to her head. It was as if she had been lightly brushed by the tip of an angel's wing.

Rose could almost feel now the warmth of human life within her. How deeply this child was going to be adored. It was going to do great things, to be remembered down the centuries.

Then a thought occurred to her. Rosemary's baby! Wasn't that a horror film about a woman who gave birth to a child by the Devil? It would be a child of God, she felt sure of that. But which God?

The messenger had been clothed in the overwhelming aura of divine beauty. She realised that now. She had been visited by an angel, alright. But the Devil could assume the fairest of forms. Might it have been a fallen angel?

The Making of a Duchess

"Will you have some more tea?" asked Georgiana Brandon-Smith.

"No, thank you," replied the Vicar's daughter. "The cup you gave me was quite delicious. And perfectly sufficient."

Georgiana thought of the woman as the Vicar's daughter because she had forgotten her name. Their guest was an unpretentious little person, not very strong in appearance, but with a slightly mocking look which Georgiana found disturbing. She was not, in fact, the daughter of the Vicar of the parish where they lived in Hampshire. That would at least have given her a certain local cachet. Her father had been Vicar of another parish in the same county. He was now dead, and his family were living in reduced circumstances in the same village as the Brandon-Smiths. They had felt obliged to offer her some hospitality. Georgiana and her sister, Adelaide, had been brought up to show compassion towards the less fortunate.

They themselves *were* fortunate. Georgiana knew that. Their own father had died in India while serving in the Army. But their mother, who had preserved her attractions to a relatively advanced age, had brought off a splendid coup by the grandeur of her second marriage. She had allied herself with an elderly peer of reclusive temperament, known in private by his step-daughters as the Baron. Georgiana and Adelaide had been the beneficiaries. They lived now in considerable comfort and ease of mind, moderated only by the consideration that they were not getting any younger and were still unmarried at the advanced ages of twenty-five and twenty-four.

"I must be going now," said the vicar's daughter. "I don't want my mother to become worried. Thank you so much for having me."

"We could send you home in our carriage," suggested Adelaide.

"No, thank you. I am happy to walk."

They were not sorry to see her go. There was something painfully buttoned-up about their visitor and yet secretly merry, as if she were laughing at them behind their backs. But neither of the sisters minded. They were used to doing good turns. They were very nice people. It cheered them to remember that.

"I do wish that Hester could have joined us," said Adelaide, as they settled again by the fire to discuss the departed visitor. "It would be so good for her to observe how we handle ourselves in society."

"I don't think she wants to know," replied her sister sadly. "She despises our friends, I think. I have heard her describe our recent visitor as a dried-up spinster."

"Well, she *is* a dried-up spinster."

"Yes, dear. But there is no need to say it. Mama is always telling us to be kind to people. And we do both try to be. It's in the Bible, you know."

"I expect Hester will be sitting in the kitchen, as usual," said Adelaide. "Chatting with the servants. So unsuitable for the daughter of a peer."

"I hate the way she monopolises the friends," agreed Georgiana. "With her toes in the ashes. The servants don't care for it either. I believe they call her little Cinders."

"Her father should have taken her in hand," said Adelaide. "The trouble is that she seems to have run absolutely wild after her own mother died and before our dear Mama took command. The only person who bothered with her was that tiresome old godmother who lives in Andover. Not quite gentry, you know."

Hester was only seventeen and exceedingly pretty. Unlike her half-sisters, who had long, sallow faces, Hester's was round, soft and fetching, as she was well aware.

"It's all a performance," said Georgiana. "Hester has been reading too many novels. She likes to imagine herself as a down-trodden poor relation whose father's love has been usurped by a hateful second marriage. That's why she puts on this act of being employed as a servant. In point of fact, she is an Honourable, being the daughter of a peer, and we are not."

"Some would call her a scheming little hussy," said Adelaide.

"Not us, dear," said Georgiana, smiling very sweetly. "We were brought up to see the good in everyone. Even the most unlikely."

When she rang the bell, the door opened and the servants entered to clear the tea things. Among them came Hester who proceeded to load the tray as if she were a parlour-maid herself. How seductive she looked, thought her half-sisters, bending over the tea table with her long, fair, curly hair, so much more manageable then their own straggly locks.

"You don't have to do that, Hester dear," said Adelaide in her most melodious voice. "Leave it to the servants. Why don't you come and walk with us in the shrubbery?"

"No, thank you, sister dear. I know my place," replied Hester pertly, sweeping abruptly out of the drawing-room with the servants.

"I don't think she cares for us," remarked Georgiana with suppressed fury.

"Of course she doesn't, dear. With the servants she even refers to us as the ugly sisters. I have heard the housemaids sniggering."

"We must obtain spiritual counselling, Adelaide. It is the only way to bear this cross. I shall consult the Archdeacon when he comes to visit Canon Mowbray."

Next morning there was another excitement. The Man of Business of the young Duke of Basingstoke made an unexpected call. The Baron and his Lady were unfortunately absent, so he was received by the Miss Brandon-Smiths.

"My errand is simple and far from disagreeable," said the Man of Business, as Georgiana rang the bell for coffee and cakes. "I come on behalf of her Grace the Dowager Duchess of Basingstoke. Her son, the present Duke, who recently celebrated his twenty-second birthday, has just returned from an extensive continental tour, taking advantage of the defeat of the unspeakable Napoleon. He wishes to marry and beget an heir to his vast estates. For this purpose, he has decided to make the acquaintance of the most eligible young ladies of the county."

"Like a cattle market," commented Georgiana, who could be spirited.

"Not in the least like a cattle market," countered their visitor, Mr Mackenzie, with a touch of froideur. "Her Grace the Dowager Duchess is giving a conversazione to which all suitable ladies are invited. I am deputed to check the proposed invitation list. Am I addressing Miss Georgiana and Miss Adelaide Brandon-Smith?"

"You are," said Adelaide promptly. "We shall be delighted to attend the occasion."

"Good. And is there anyone else in this mansion who should be invited?"

There was an awkward silence.

"We do have a step-sister," said Georgiana, recalling Canon Mowbray's insistence on absolute truth.

"But she is rather peculiar," put in Adelaide hastily. "She has not shared our up-bringing. You see, she was born long before our beloved mother married our stepfather, the Baron."

"Peculiar?" echoed Mr Mackenzie. "What form does her peculiarity take? Is she an enthusiast for the guillotine? Does she smash wine glasses? Is she improperly attired? The Dowager Duchess is a stickler for the proprieties."

"There is no real harm in Hester," said Georgiana, determined to be fair. "But she has this thing about being friendly with the servants. She spends a lot of time in the kitchen."

"The servants! The kitchen!" Mr Mackenzie almost shrieked. "I don't think that would please the Dowager Duchess. Can you guarantee this young lady, if invited, would behave herself in a manner appropriate to Ducal circles?"

"She is the daughter of our beloved stepfather," replied Adelaide with one of her ambiguous smirks.

"That is hardly an answer," said Mr Mackenzie reproachfully. "King George is King of England, and yet he is not noted for mental lucidity. I cannot take any risk with the Dowager Duchess's guest list. To be the recipient of her anger is an appalling experience. I shall omit this Hester. Pray do not mention the function to her at all."

"That is your decision, Mr Mackenzie," said Georgiana. "Not ours."

"Indeed," added Adelaide hastily, "we did tell you about her." They were very nice girls, as Canon Mowbray often remarked.

The invitations to the conversazione duly arrived. Georgiana and Adelaide were in a state of considerable excitement. They would be chaperoned by their mother and stepfather and all would, of course, travel in the family coach with the baronial arms. To give Hester her due, she did bestir herself to assist her half-sisters with the niceties of their attire, complete with chignons, tightly-laced bodices, face creams and powder and all the aids to beauty employed by a fashionable young lady.

"How exciting!" said Hester naively. "One of you may become a Duchess!"

"You could have come too," pointed out Georgiana, "if you were only willing to behave like everyone else."

"Don't worry about me," said Hester. "My godmother may look in for a quiet chat. She promised to lend me a new book of sermons. Until then I shall sit by the fire in the kitchen. I know my place."

Exasperated, Georgiana made a sudden move. A large

safety-pin held by Hester plunged deep into her fleshy bosom, causing her to shriek with pain.

"I'm so very sorry," said Hester.

"Don't worry, dear," replied Georgiana with a ghastly grin. "One is not unused to suffering." Two could play at that game of being a saint.

They arrived at the Duke's castle in a state of high hopes, but reality proved somewhat disappointing. Mr Mackenzie had forgotten to invite enough young men, so the guests consisted mainly of eager young ladies and their chaperones. The Duke circulated among them graciously but, unfortunately, the Brandon-Smiths failed to catch his eye, much to their chagrin. After supper, the dancing began and the Duke opened it with a young lady who had only just arrived. To the astonishment of Georgiana and Adelaide, this proved to be none other than ... Hester!

"How on earth did she get here?" asked Georgiana.

"It would seem that her godmother called and insisted on bringing her," explained their mother.

The sly minx, thought Adelaide, though she was far too well brought up to voice such a malicious thought. One had to admit that Hester looked quite radiantly beautiful, with her sweet young face, her appetising figure, her long yellow hair and her gorgeous silk dress which had apparently once belonged to her dead mother. She was not in the height of fashion, but then she didn't need to be. The Duke, clearly captivated, danced every dance with Hester, to the barely controlled fury of the other girls. At midnight she disappeared and the Baroness explained that the godmother was too infirm for late nights.

"That was a fine trick you played on us last night,

Hester," said Georgiana the next morning.

"It all happened so suddenly," explained Hester. "Aunt Penelope insisted and I didn't like to refuse."

"I hope you enjoyed yourself," said Adelaide coldly.

"It was well enough," replied Hester, "but I felt out of my depth with all the people staring at me. I am more at home in the servants' quarters, as you know,"

"Come and sit with us, Hester," suggested Georgiana. "Bring your embroidery into the drawing room and tell us all about the Duke. Is he a nobleman of advanced mental powers? If so, how did you manage to converse?" Nobody could accuse her or her sister of jealousy.

"I'm afraid I'm wanted in the kitchen, Georgiana dear. Somebody has arrived at the back door and is asking to speak urgently to me." Presumably some rustic swain, thought her half-sister dismissively.

Later in the morning, the Baroness had occasion to inspect the kitchen. She had done much to bring some order into the Baron's ramshackle establishment. To her astonishment, she found Hester and the Duke himself sitting beside the stove in the snuggery, peeling apples for the pudding that evening. She rushed back to the drawing room to inform her astonished daughters.

"Apparently His Grace has simple domestic tastes," she managed to gasp. "He has asked Hester to marry him."

"I suppose she refused," suggested Adelaide hopefully. "She does not care for high life."

"On the contrary, she accepted with the utmost alacrity."

Being very nice girls, Georgiana and Adelaide were quick to express their unalloyed pleasure. Duchess Hester, they felt sure, would be a great hit at the castle with her down-to-earth manner and sweet innocent face.

"Not all that sweet," muttered Georgiana.

"Nor all that innocent," whispered Adelaide. It was the nearest those dear sisters ever got to bitterness.

Not long afterwards, they discussed the matter with that other little mouse, the vicar's daughter. Georigana could still not remember her name. She seemed fascinated and demanded to know the full details of the new Duchess's sensational engagement.

"I must put this episode into one of my little stories," she explained.

"You write stories?" asked Georgiana, somewhat surprised.

"I dabble a little," replied the Vicar's daughter with one of her shy, superior smiles. "All my tales are on the same subject. The lonely, lucky girl who makes a wonderful marriage in the last chapter. I find that theme rather haunting."

"Why is that?" asked Adelaide.

"I suppose because it never happened to me. And never will."

Georgiana saw now that, beneath her slightly mocking expression, the Vicar's daughter had rather a sad face. At last she had remembered the name. It was Austen. Jane Austen.

A Sticky Meal

"Have something else, Jamie," I suggested. "Coffee perhaps?"

"No, thank you, dad," replied my son.

It had been a sticky meal. They always were these days. Glowering silences tended to be followed by almost hysterical outbursts of accusation.

I could understand his attitude only too well. That was the pity of it. In his position, I might well have felt the same. From his point of view, I had done everything wrong. I had allowed his mother to die. At least I had failed to get her expert psychiatric help in time to prevent her suicide. Then, after years of bereaved loneliness, I had entered into a happy relationship with another, younger man. Could you really blame him for thinking that I had no right to be happy? He himself was not.

"Is it all right?" I asked. "This place where you're working now."

"No, it isn't," he snapped. "But it's all I could get."

"I would pay for you to retrain."

"I'm too old for that. Just leave me alone."

"Sorry."

RODE HE ON BARBARY?

"Look, Dad, I'm not prepared for any more of this silly chat with you. You like to pretend that nothing has happened to our family. But it has. I don't want to go on seeing you unless you're willing to have a proper talk. A real talk. About Mummy."

"There isn't much to say, Jamie. Mummy had a terrible illness. A mental illness. It swept over her, that dreadful urge to live no longer. She didn't know what she was doing." The old soothing let-out, I thought – suicide while of unsound mind.

"I don't think it was only that," said Jamie.

Yes, it was, I longed to shout. Her mother was strange too. It was in the family. God help the unfortunate men who had the misfortune to love these beautiful, doomed women. But, in arguing with my own son, I was fighting with one arm strapped behind my back. If I emphasised the congenital weakness in his mother's family, I should only alarm him about the consequences for his own mental stability.

"What are you suggesting?" I asked cautiously.

"I need to know properly why Mummy … did what she did. You never told me everything. You prefer men to women, don't you? Why did you ever marry her?"

"I have the capacity to love men and women," I replied. "In my time, I have fallen in love with both. I did truly love your mother."

"But you had affairs with men, didn't you? Even when you were married."

"No, I didn't. It was a true marriage. A marriage of love. Human beings are infinitely complicated. This stereotyped division into gays and straights is a comparatively modern thing."

"Now you're trying to shift the blame, aren't you? Onto me and my sister. But you're the guilty one, Dad. We weren't responsible."

I didn't really go along with that. If I had a share in Betty's tragedy, so did Jamie and Cynthia. They had quite often provoked her to almost uncontrollable anger. Her only hope would have been a life of serene contentment – a quiet husband, a quiet home, no children. I had totally failed to understand her. Nobody had warned me.

But I couldn't tell Jamie that he must accept a share in the responsibility. He had suffered enough. I couldn't add to his agony.

"Look, Jamie," I continued, trying to keep my voice calm and friendly, though it wasn't easy, "haven't we had enough of blame and guilt? It was like a Greek tragedy, in which the protagonists are inevitably shunted along the road to disaster. Blame the Gods, if you like." Like flies to wanton boys are we to the gods, I quoted inwardly, they kill us for their sport.

"That's the trouble," snapped Jamie, "you're always trying to avoid the blame, but it *was* your fault."

"I keep telling you, it was nobody's fault. She went mad." An unfashionable word, but it did express reality.

"You're so cowardly, Dad."

"Very well, let's admit there *was* blame, if it will help you. In that case, we are all to blame. We should have understood the problem and done more to help her. Let us agree to accept and share the guilt. And then forget. It was years ago. We need a new life. That is what Mummy would have wished."

"I think you must have treated her very badly, Dad.

Marrying her when you shouldn't have married anyone. As a cover, I suppose, to safeguard your career. That's why you gave her children, wasn't it? To pretend to everyone that you were normal."

"That's not true, Jamie. We both loved the idea of having children, to create a family."

"I hate to think why I came into the world. It was all a pretence. That's why I am ... where I am now."

"You were conceived in love, dear. I give you my word for that."

"I want a full explanation, Dad. I need to go into everything in detail."

"That's not good for any of us, Jamie. It's the wrong approach. We all need to try and forget. Let's forgive ourselves and each other."

"I've told you, Dad. Unless you take me seriously, I don't want to see you ever again."

He was trying to torture me and I refused to be tortured. Consumed with his own sense of guilt, the unfortunate boy was trying to pass it on to me. It was human and understandable, but that way lay disaster for us both, I felt sure. My attempt to defuse the atmosphere by adopting a calm tone of voice was only maddening Jamie the more.

He was shouting now. People were staring.

"I must go now," I said.

"Go! Go!" he yelled. "And never bother me again." I longed to put my arms around him. He wasn't a child any more though, but an angry, estranged man.

I walked out. It was a clear night with a few stars. That was rare for the city. Perhaps, in some distant future, we would be reconciled. Perhaps he would hate me until his dying day. At least that might be a way of alleviating his own terrible feeling of guilt. Poor devil, my still deeply loved boy, could you really help a soul in agony by allowing them to hate you? If so, was that possibly, in a weird way, some small service? If he could really shift the blame, then I was willing to take it on.

Fathers were like that. They never quite gave up. Perhaps you only understood your father when it was too late.

In The Archipelago

"I don't know how you find the way," said Giles, as Anders swung the motor boat through the maze of islands. "How long does all this go on for?"

"Miles and miles," replied the deceptively solemn-looking Swede. "The Stockholm archipelago stretches half way to Finland."

For Giles, an ambitious young journalist, it was his first visit to Sweden. He had been working now for a year in the show business section of a popular British tabloid newspaper. This had disappointed his parents who had expected him to do something better with his Oxford degree. But, as Giles explained, the money was good and it was fun sniffing out the sexual peccadilloes of minor actresses. Now they had received this potentially exciting tip-off, and Giles had hastily bought a business class ticket to Stockholm. He had been met at Arlanda by Anders, the paper's local stringer. The two clever, but frivolous, young men got on at once. Giles had been warned that a sense of humour was not a great Nordic virtue, but he soon discovered a capacity for the absurd behind the poker-faced façade of his Swedish colleague.

"We hibernate for most of the year," explained Anders. "But now, at the height of summer, we eat crayfish and drink schnapps and become quite human. You will see for yourself, my friend."

"These islands are beautiful," said Giles, "but they seem to be mostly deserted, except for the odd red-brown wooden hut."

"They are not as deserted as you might think. Thousands of people own their own little island. They come out to spend the weekend. No lighting, no heating, no motor car, no lavatory. It is the Swedish idea of paradise."

"Paradise?" echoed Giles in surprise.

"We Swedes are lovers of the simple life. At least in theory. And not all the time. In Stockholm we have our modern conveniences. But, on the weekends of high summer, it's back to nature."

Giles could see what Anders meant. There was something idyllic about those Nordic evenings, those endless white nights when the sun hardly set and all was bathed in the clarity of that intense northern light.

"Christ!" shouted Giles suddenly. "What the Hell is that?'

A vast floating building of many stories seemed to be coming towards them at considerable speed.

"That's the ferry from Helsinki," replied Anders calmly. "Don't worry, we shall keep out of its way."

"But it's so huge. Isn't it in danger of running aground?"

"They have a very shallow draught. And the water between some of these islands is surprisingly deep. At least in the main channels."

"Do you know where we are going, Anders?"

"I hope so. As children, we came out here every summer.

RODE HE ON BARBARY?

And the information phoned in by some kind well-wisher was fairly precise."

It would be a big scoop, thought Giles. There was no doubt of that. No need to spare expenses, the Entertainments Editor had told him. The paper had a readership of several millions and every day they needed a new story to beat their hated rivals.

"Let's hope you're right," said the Englishman.

"Why should he come to Sweden?" asked Anders. "Ours is not a country where foreigners like to settle. Too cold. Too expensive. And quite a difficult language to learn."

"His third wife was Swedish," replied Giles. "One of your blonde bomb shells. He was married six times, you know. Of course he was strikingly good looking as a young man. One of the daughters was by the Swedish mother. She probably has family here."

"You think she may be with him?"

"If he's still alive. We don't really know. His disappearance is a complete mystery to this day. He was at the very top, our greatest classical actor for years. He did all the great Shakespeare parts and Ibsen and lots of other things."

"We knew him from the movies," said Anders.

"Yes, he had begun to conquer Hollywood too. A world film star. Not bad for a boy from the back streets of Ipswich. He was doing *Lear* at the National Theatre. A huge performance. The critics raved. And then one night, it didn't go too well. He was having trouble with his lines. After the performance, he simply walked out, abandoning the rest of the run. He has never been seen, or heard of, again."

"Clever of you to find him them."

"I haven't found him yet," said Giles cautiously. If he

did, he thought, it could be the making of his burgeoning career as a popular journalist.

Anders seemed to know what he was doing. He took the boat up to one of the larger islands and tied it up to an over-hanging branch. The two young men jumped ashore. Pushing their way through dense green bushes they saw, on the other side of the island, a fair size wooden hut of the usual red-brown colour. A girl came out to meet them.

"What do you want?" she asked in Swedish.

"We're just having a day out," replied Anders. "I hope you don't mind our landing on your island. Perhaps you could kindly let us have a little drinking water."

"I'll bring it out," said the girl, showing no inclination to invite them inside.

"You're English, aren't you?" asked Giles in English.

"I am both English and Swedish."

This was too attractive a girl to deceive, thought Giles. He liked her clear, blue eyes, the defiant tilt of her chin, the slight incipient smile.

"Please wait here," she continued. "I'll be back in a moment with a bottle of water."

"Who the devil is that?" shouted a male voice from the direction of the house.

"It is nothing, Father," called the girl. "Nothing to worry about."

A man in late middle age appeared. There could be no doubt about it, thought Giles with a thrill of satisfaction. He would have recognised that famous face anywhere, with its prominent nose and chin, noble brow and penetrating eyes.

"Good afternoon, Sir Dominic," he said.

"Smoked me out, have you? Who the devil are you then?

Bloody journalists, I suppose."

One had to be frank, thought Giles. He introduced himself and Anders. The daughter, it seemed, was Lisa.

'Well, now you've come," said the famous actor, "we'd better have a talk. Come inside, both of you."

The interior of the hut was simple, but clean and comfortable. There was a stove in one corner. It was obviously rather more than a summer cottage. Sir Dominic and Lisa must be living here all year round, thought Giles. There would be a generator and cylinders of gas. Here, on the outer islands, you could live for years, away from the public eye.

"I bought the place for Lisa's mother centuries ago," explained the famous Thespian. "We remembered it when we needed a bolt-hole."

"May I ask, sir, why did you need a bolt-hole?"

"That's a long story. You'd better have some refreshment first."

Lisa brought akvavit to drink with surströmming, a Swedish speciality composed, or rather decomposed, of fermented Baltic herring. Anders gulped down both without turning a hair. Poor Giles disliked the burning taste of the strong drink and the disgusting aroma of the rotten fish, both obviously an acquired taste. But he managed to conceal his feelings with professional aplomb.

Taking advantage of this unexpected audience, Sir Dominic embarked on his long story, refreshing himself liberally with the alcoholic liquor which he literally poured down his throat.

"You obviously know who I am," said the actor, "but you don't know what I've become. You have heard of my famous breakdown on stage at the National. But you don't know why. Well, I couldn't remember the lines. And why was that? Because I was drunk. Drunk as a lord. I had become addicted to alcohol. And still am. Aren't I, Lisa?"

"You're getting better, Father."

"No, I'm not. You know that perfectly well. My memory's shot to pieces. I shall never act on stage again. Just look at me now … not less than archangel ruined and the excess of glory obscured. Milton, not Shakespeare."

"They still want you for films, Father. What was that part they offered you? Something called the Beast."

"The Beast," roared her father contemptuously. "That's how they think of me now. A creature with four feet, huge teeth and a coat of fur. Don't the fools realise? I still have immortal longings inside me."

"Don't get excited, Father. You remember what the doctor said."

"I am fallen into the seer, into the yellow leaf," said her father, ever an actor to the core. Giles remembered that, even in its heyday, Sir Dominic's performances were said to veer between the Gothic and the baroque.

"But why did you just disappear?"

"I was mortified, ashamed. I said to Lisa, let's get the hell out of here. And we did. Afterwards, it amused me to become a mystery."

"Would you like to sell us your story?"

"Certainly not. I have not yet sunk to that. Now listen carefully, young man. This is my sad history. You can have it for nothing."

Anders continued to munch the decayed fish with obvious relish. Giles tried not to. Lisa watched her father with anxious care. He went on consuming the strong alcohol while pouring out the tragic details of his downfall.

"You might think that public performance becomes easier the more you do it," he began. "But that is not the case at all. The higher the rise, the greater the strain. Critics are interested in your failures. They take your triumphs for granted. No wonder I started to crack. It was the same with Maria Callas, with Laurence Olivier. Audiences never understand. They are quite merciless."

"You suffered from stage fright?"

"Worse than that. Complete memory losses. The terror of that filled me with a horror of going on stage at all. That's why I took to drink. Now I'm too far gone to recover. Isn't that obvious?"

"It wasn't your fault, Daddy. The doctors said so. They called you a trauma victim. Macbeth, Coriolanus, Tamburlane, all in the same season. It was too much for you."

"So you decided to hide."

"I wanted to bury my shame, my appalling fall. Sweden was the obvious places. I was still in touch with the family of Lisa's mother. Very discreet people. They fixed up this … rural retreat for us."

"You never go into Stockholm – with a false nose perhaps?"

"Lisa does. We have a small boat. I stay here. And drink."

"Doesn't it become boring? Nothing but the damned beauty.'

"It's boring for Lisa. I am beyond boredom. The bottle knocks me out quite early each day. That's one better than public shame."

"I'm sorry we intruded," said Giles. Anders nodded.

"What are you going to do now?" asked Sir Dominic.

"I really don't know," replied Giles. "We had better be going."

"You should try to forget me," said the famous actor. "I am a fallen star, a burned-out comet."

"I think your visit did him good," said Lisa, with a smile, as she escorted the young men to their boat. "You can come again, if you like."

"I should like that," said Anders in Swedish.

They boarded their craft and chugged thoughtfully away from the thickly wooded island.

"You can send an email from my place," said Anders. "To your paper, I mean."

"I'm not sure I want to do that."

"But surely you're going to tell them you have found Sir Dominic. It will be a huge triumph for you."

"I know," agreed Giles. "But I would have to betray them."

"Betray? That's a strong word."

"Not too strong. He has sought sanctuary. To let in the media would be terribly cruel."

"I think you're in the wrong profession, Giles. Besides, you forget one thing. That tip-off. A female voice in Swedish, talking to our switchboard. Don't you see, it must have been Lisa. She wants to be betrayed, to be rescued."

It was a point worth considering. Giles stared ahead. He felt, somehow, that this was a turning point in his young life. All around them were the myriad islands, the lonely little red-brown houses, the screaming gulls, the fearsome clarity of an afternoon in the Baltic summer.

Dedication

I had not expected a place on the platform. Oh no, there were too many Very Important Persons for room to be found for the likes of me. Mrs Rosalba Bossano had pulled out all the stops. These Italian-American women pack punches. We all know what organisation lies behind their huge financial resources and capacity to go straight to the head of any queue. This was Rosalba's day, not mine. There she was, chatting to the Cardinal Archbishop of Palermo, with the American Ambassador in attendance. I took my humble place in one of the back rows, seething with barely suppressed rage.

It was all so unfair. The whole thing had been my idea in the first place. My idea alone. Me, the unmarried Anglo-Italian woman, plain Joan Harrison. I had been brought up in the village and lived there for years before Mother and I moved to Palermo to be nearer the hospital for her sake. My totally English father was an importer of citrus fruit who paid regular visits to Sicily to buy oranges. One day he decided to retire there. The climate was better than Yorkshire. He married my mother, a local girl, and then sadly died. They bequeathed to me a dose of Yorkshire obstinacy while forgetting to add a helping of Italian charm. People here think of me as a cat who walks alone. I have never had many enthusiasms.

But one thing has always aroused my passion. My sad, lonely passion. The great ruined cathedral and monastery of San Vitale. The Normans had started it and then moved along the coast to Monreale. I had often wandered through its sub-tropical desolation, those great arches and tessellated pavements, the mosaic of Christ In Majesty, half Byzantine and half Gothic, a meeting place of two worlds, lost beneath the orange trees. I longed to see that building spring to life. A visiting architect from Denmark told me that it could be done. The foundations were structurally sound. Only one thing was needed. Money. Lots of money. I didn't have any.

Then I had a piece of luck. At least it seemed like luck at the time. This big, fat American woman appeared in the reference library where I worked in Palermo. She was directed to me, as her Italian was rudimentary and I am bilingual in English and Italian. She was the widow of a prosperous American businessman. Exactly what this business consisted of, she seemed reluctant to say. Mafia, I suppose. She still lived in the family residence in South Bend, Indiana. Her husband had left her all his money and now she was having the fun of spending it. He had been of Italian origin, Sicilian to be precise. Rosalba had endowed a trust fund with the object of restoring Italian works of art, especially in Sicily. Now she was looking for projects. It seemed like the answer to a prayer.

Of course I told her about San Vitale. We went out there the next day in Mrs Bossano's chauffeur-driven limousine.

RODE HE ON BARBARY?

She fell in love with the place. Give the women her due, there was no shilly-shallying. She would use a good part of the trust fund to bring San Vitale to life. We went ahead with true American élan. An architect was engaged, then a top firm of builders. I was appointed to the staff with the nebulous title of local adviser. It was a pleasure to give up my post at the reference library, telling Professor Mandragora, as I privately liked to call him, exactly what I had thought of him all along. Too much of my life has had to be passed as a small smoking volcano with only rare eruptions.

I was over the moon. It was like a dream come true, watching my beloved San Vitale slowly spring again to life. I kept a careful eye on progress, of course, and the builders did an excellent job. But I had reckoned without Rosalba Bossano. The woman paid us frequent visits, jetting in from the States whenever the fit took her. I suppose she had nothing else to occupy her tiny mind. Her strident, nasal voice could be heard on the building site from dawn to dusk, my own role being limited to interpreting her shrieks of encouragement into Italian for the benefit of the bewildered labourers. Any suggestions I ventured to offer were brusquely rejected. Rosalba stayed, of course, in a suite in the best hotel in Palermo and I would be obliged to act, without extra remuneration as her lady in waiting. There was never the slightest recognition of my key position as the originator of the whole scheme.

I had grown to detest Rosalba's invasions. And this one, possibly the last, was the worst of all. The work was finished; the restored cathedral and cloisters glowed mellow and gold in the sunlight. There would be speeches and then we would follow the Cardinal inside as he re-dedicated the cathedral. The keynote oration would naturally be delivered by Rosalba herself, lady bountiful extraordinaire.

Now I realised how deeply I hated this brash American female. She had stolen my idea and would take all the credit for it. I was nothing to her, simply a little stooge who had been useful and could now be dropped without compunction. I felt my face flushing with anger and frustration. Should I stand up at the end and make a public protest? It would be intolerable if they gave the old bitch some kind of Italian decoration. I would tear it off her neck myself. Hatred was making me feel ill.

Rosalba Bossano was on her feet now. She spoke inevitably in her ugly mid-western American English. At some length, she described the scene and what San Vitale had once been and could now be again. She referred to America's huge debt to Italy. After all, it might never have been discovered but for Columbus. Now it was payback time. She thanked everyone: the Cardinal and the Church authorities, the Mayor and his city, the Governments of Italy and the United States and her own beloved husband whose wonderful work had made possible this generosity. I could feel the nails sticking into the palms of my hands. Would the creature never stop?

"And now," she continued, "before I sit down at last, let me pay tribute to the originator of this entire project. The wonderful person who most adores San Vitale, who longed so much for it to arise again, who had the courage to inspire the scheme of regeneration which we see today. The friend who has been by my side throughout this whole happy period and to whom San Vitale, and myself, owes absolutely everything. I refer, of course, to our dear Miss Joan Harrison. Will she please stand up to receive a very well earned ovation?"

They pushed me to my feet. I should have cringed with shame and embarrassment, but somehow I rather enjoyed it. They were all clapping, fit to burst. Rosalba skipped down from the rostrum and rushed towards me, imprinting a watery kiss on both cheeks.

At the Mass of Dedication which followed, I naturally felt elated. But there was something missing. Something I had been nursing for so long and would never now be able to recover. My hatred.

Counselling

"Would you like some tea?" asked the old man.

"Yes, please," replied his visitor, "that would be very welcome." He remembered the advice they had given at the hospice when he did their training course for bereavement counsellors. Try to make everything as natural and everyday as possible. The recently bereaved need to be restored to normal living.

He had accepted this present assignment with certain misgivings. The old man, Edmund Penstone, was, it seemed, a writer of sorts. Not a famous writer, but at least a professional author who had given his life to churning out books. The counsellor, Bill Downham, was a retired soldier who made no pretensions to being literary. He didn't think he was the right man for the job. But they had nobody else available, and so he agreed to take it on. Apparently, Mr Penstone was absolutely desolate after the loss of his wife Sally, following many months of a slowly wasting illness. Like so many people these days, he wasn't interested in trying to obtain comfort from the Church. He had no near relation close at hand, and lived far from a town in that small house on the cliff overlooking a foaming Cornish bay. Help was badly needed.

Bill was a caring man who wanted to do good. That was why he had taken on this voluntary activity. The unexpected death of his own wife in a bus crash had taught him about the overwhelming anguish of losing the other half of your life. He hoped that this appalling episode could somehow be translated into comfort for others similarly situated. But at heart he knew one thing. His real aim was to help not others, but himself.

Bill looked round the room while Edmund was outside in the kitchen. It was full of memories of Sally. Two large portrait photographs, smaller photos of the two of them in Venice, Paris and Trafalgar Square. In due course, Edmund should be advised to put these away. But not yet. In dealing with the bereaved, you had to tread carefully.

"Milk? Sugar?" asked Edmund, balancing the tray rather precariously on a small table. He did not seem very good at managing alone.

"Yes, please. Both." The old man's hand shook a little as he passed the cup of fine porcelain.

"Where are we to start?" asked Edmund.

"Wherever you like."

"I'll tell you about Sally then. She believed in me. That was the main thing about her. She thought I was a great writer, possibly on the verge of genius. She was sure that I should be relieved of all anxieties and petty practical activities, so that I could concentrate on making use of my talent. Of course I did nothing to discourage that illusion. I'm quite selfish, you see, like most men."

Sally was a trained secretary. She could have held down a responsible job. But all she wanted to do was to stay at home and cook, and wash, and sew for me."

"Did you have children?"

"One boy. He doesn't come home often. For years I couldn't quite make him out. He used to talk about a friend called Lesley. It took me years to understand that 'Lesley' was a boy and our son had always been gay. It seems that Sally had always known, but hadn't liked to tell me."

"Mothers are often ahead in that area."

"It came as a shock, I don't mind telling you. I had been looking forward to the grandchildren. We're an old family. There were Penstones in this neck of the woods in the thirteenth century. Not rich or famous, but honourable and honest. Family history had always been one of my interests. But I gave it up when I discovered that our branch was to die out. We were no more than a genetic cul-de-sac. Sally and I will leave no monument."

"Does one have to leave a monument?"

"At the end of life, it is good to have a reason for taking up space."

"What about your books?"

"Third rate. I know that. There is still some interest in my Cornish local history. They're trying to revive the language, you know. Minorities have become fashionable, you see, in our so-called caring society. But I was finding it increasingly difficult to find a publisher for my novels. I write about men who stand up when a lady enters the room. And that's considered out of date."

"You had Sally."

"Poor soul, she wasted her time, didn't she? Spending her life looking after a supposed genius who couldn't deliver." There was no mistaking the bitterness in Edmund

Penstone's voice.

"For how long were you married?" asked Bill Downham. Get them talking, keep them talking, that was the official advice. Every bereavement brings its quota of barely suppressed guilt. Help them to get it out of their system.

"Forty-three years. The first forty-two were wonderful. Sally ran the practical side and let me spend my energies in my writing hut in the garden. I could have done nothing without her. But then a year ago, she got this awful illness. The doctors were perfectly frank. She could look forward to months of slow, but inevitable, decline. We should concentrate on trying to manage first the discomfort, and then the pain."

"You gave up your writing, I understand."

"I had to. The poor girl needed full time nursing. I wasn't going to send her away. We moved her bed so that she could see the cliffs and the seabirds, the wheeling and crying gulls that she delighted in. I abandoned my Polperro Chronicle. Eleven novels already published and the twelfth on the way. I was just getting to the Napoleonic Wars. Our last trip together was to the battlefield of Waterloo."

"Wasn't that hard for you, Mr Penstone?"

"No. It was my duty. I knew I wasn't exactly a Tolstoy. It was all much more dreadful for Sally. I never thought of her as an old woman, you know. For me, she was always the same laughing, nervous girl who was keen on tennis. Human partnership is very strange."

"At the hospital they said you were wonderful."

"Don't be silly, Major Downham. There was a job to be done. I was glad to do it. She would have been totally helpless without me."

"You must feel some ... satisfaction. At the way you managed to keep her at home. Right up to the last ten days?"

"Satisfaction? Not really. I feel guilt."

"Guilt! You of all people? Why?"

"Sally spent her life on something that was not worth doing. Fostering my work. She never gave up hope that I would produce a work of art."

"And didn't you?"

"You know I didn't. Critics have never thought anything of my work. It just brought in enough money to live on. I had a tiny spark of talent, but it didn't amount to much."

"I don't accept that," retorted the counsellor. "You had a long and happy marriage. For many years you accepted your wife's devotion, thus giving her something to live for. To accept can be a form of grace. And then, in that last year, you gave up your own ambitions and lived, in your turn, entirely for her. The life of love ... can that not, in itself, be a work of art?"

"It's a thought," said the old man softly, giving, for the first time, an unexpectedly gentle smile. "Have another cup of tea. Or perhaps a whisky?"

Reunion

"You really know this Caspar Cairncross?" asked Amanda.

"Oh yes," replied Michael, her boyfriend. "We were very close at one time."

Amanda was impressed. After all, Caspar Cairncross was the most famous classical composer of the day. His symphonies were played at the Proms, his operas performed at Covent Garden. She was beginning to learn interesting things about Michael. They had met only a few weeks before at a debate in the University Union. They had clicked instantly and now spent together as much time as they possibly could. In fact, they might now be described as an item. She liked his fair, curly hair and subterranean sense of humour. He was mad about her trim curves, and he also knew that she was more a giver than a taker. They felt at peace in each other's company.

She had agreed enthusiastically to Michael's proposal that they should spend a weekend visiting the fishing village where Mr Cairncross had lived for years. Michael had rung the house and had been told by the housekeeper that the famous musician was in residence and would be at home all day. That was enough for Michael. He was sure of a warm welcome from Caspar who had always been very kind to him. He would certainly offer them a meal and might well invite them to spend the night, as in the old days.

"How did you get to know him?" asked Amanda.

"He came to our school. He'd written a piece for boys' voices and wanted to recruit some singers. I was only twelve and had a good treble voice. In fact, I was the star of the choir, a regular little show off with one of those angelic looking faces that silly grown ups rave about. Caspar took me on at once. My parents were thrilled, and so was I. It was an exciting time. We performed in lots of grand places: Glyndebourne, the Albert Hall, abroad even – Germany, Italy. Naturally, I saw a good deal of Caspar. He became really fond of me. I often stayed at his house here on the coast. I think he was a bit lonely. He had a friend living with him, but he was a violinist and was often away on concert tours. Gideon Baxendale."

"*The* Gideon Baxendal?"

"Yes. It's not exactly a common name."

"Weren't your parents suspicious? Mr Cairncross getting so keen on you."

"Oh no, there was nothing like that. Caspar is very religious. He writes a lot for the Church. Dad and Mum were delighted. It was something to tell their friends."

"But you haven't seen him for a few years."

"That was inevitable. My voice broke. I lost my bewitching treble and wasn't all that impressive as a baritone. No question now of singing in public. Anyhow, I was busy at school with exams and trying to get into University."

"You could still have visited Mr Cairncross."

"I suppose I could. He had become a sort of extra uncle to me. But now there wasn't any need to bother him. He weren't going off on any more tours together, and he was awfully busy. I didn't like to intrude."

"He could have taken the initiative."

"He was often away with Gideon. Playing in America, Japan. It didn't worry me. I know he'll be glad to see me. He's like family."

As they walked towards the well remembered house by the sea, Michael felt his heart pounding. The place had meant so much to him in the old days. He recalled it all so well – the sessions by the grand piano, the cream teas, the bedtime stories, Mr Cairncross coming up to his room to kiss him on the forehead and wish him good night. It had been so comfortable, so secure, so loving. When his voice broke, it was like being driven out of this paradise by an angel with a flaming sword. He had never again met anyone as fascinating and talented as Caspar and Gideon. Now he was back. He was longing to present Amanda. They would see for themselves how well he had done.

The door was opened by Gideon Baxendale who looked as calm and dignified as ever. Seeing the young couple of University students, he seemed courteously perplexed.

"Don't you know me, Mr Baxendal?" asked Michael, amused at first.

"I'm afraid I don't."

"I'm Michael. I used to come here often. I called you Uncle Gideon."

"Michael? The boy with the marvellous voice?"

"Yes."

"My word, how you've changed."

"I suppose one does."

"I didn't recognise you with those whiskers. And who is this young lady?"

"I'd like to introduce my girlfriend, Amanda Rawlinson."

"Pleased to meet you," said Amanda.

"What are you doing here, Michael?"

"We're taking a day off from our University studies. We thought we'd come and see you."

"That was very thoughtful of you."

"I'd like to see Caspar, if he's free."

"He's got a lot on at the moment. A new commission for the Royal Opera. But I'll go and see. Just wait here for a moment please."

Michael looked with pleasure round the large hall, which served as a sort of extra sitting room. The choice had often gathered there before piling into their coach. He seemed to hear the voices of excited boys.

The violinist returned, looking rather awkward.

"Look, I'm sorry about this, Michael," he said unhappily. "But I'm afraid that Caspar isn't free to see you today. As I told you, he's awfully busy just now. Perhaps some other time."

"Oh," said Michael. He felt winded, as if he had been hit in the chest. He didn't know what to say.

"He sends you good wishes and is sorry you had the trouble," added Gideon feebly. "Would you like some tea?"

"No, thank you," replied Michael. "We'll be on our way."

Amanda would think him a liar and a fool. But that wouldn't last. It was worse than that, much worse. They

RODE HE ON BARBARY?

trudged down the darkening drive in silence.

"It doesn't matter," said Amanda loyally, taking his arm. She really did love this boy.

"Of course it matters," retorted Michael angrily. "What on earth did I do wrong?"

"You grew up," said Amanda.

Safe

It would be safe here. They had told her that. It was what, in the language of espionage, they called a safe house. There were guards at the gatehouse and then a long, monitored drive up to the mansion. They had given her one of the best apartments with a view over the well manicured lawn towards the azaleas. Beyond the bushes would be armed police, trip wires, burglar alarms, all the human and technological apparatus with which she and Raymond had been familiar ever since he became Prime Minister.

It would be interesting to meet the occupants of the other holiday apartments. Who on earth could they be? Fallen dictators, police informants, foreign spies, united only by their capacity to make dangerous enemies. She had not been encouraged to establish contact. It would be much wiser, the Chief Inspector had repeated several times, to let nobody know she was there. Except, of course, the small staff who had all been most carefully vetted and given the highest possible security clearance.

She had been taken back into the womb. That was the nearest equivalent. To some extent, that was comforting. But it was also unnatural, spooky, possibly frightening.

Already she was beginning to miss the hustle and bustle of Number Ten, with Raymond going out on the doorstep, hand stretched out, smile at the ready, to greet the most powerful people in the world.

She had felt obliged to get away. The doctors had ordered her to take a rest. She was becoming tense and tearful. She would have to go alone. Friends were not acceptable to the security authorities without a long period of clearance. Raymond was too busy to come and the children now had gone their own way.

It was different when she and Raymond took their annual holiday together, preferably somewhere warm where they could swim. Then they usually found someone to lend them a large secluded abode, to which Raymond could bring his whole security team. The rich, and especially rich Italians, were always happy to oblige the British Prime Minister. But, on her own, she did not quite rate such treatment, though she would certainly have to be protected. They had asked her to be content with this flat in an old country house in the wilds of Northumberland. At least it was a chance to catch up on her reading. She had thought, wrongly, that this would be enough to occupy her.

Earlier Prime Ministers and their wives had actually been able to go out and meet people. The public had even been permitted to walk up to the very doors of Downing Street. She thought back with nostalgia to the comparatively calm, peaceful days of the Cold War when the balance of mutual terror had kept the world in order. But now danger could come from every side, lives snuffed out in an instant without warning.

Raymond and his family were in a specially exposed

position. Their advisers were adamant about that. He had been so courageous about taking the country to war, feeling sure that God approved his policy of pre-emptive strikes. And so he was widely hated by ruthless killers. These had been lonely decisions, she knew better than anyone. But he had taken comfort from knowing that he was called by the Almighty to lead the nation through these dark and perilous days, striking at our enemies before they could hit us.

Sometimes she wondered, in her heart of hearts, whether her husband had been too confident. He had never been very good at studying the fine print, assembling all the facts or engaging in close-hitting rational argument. But he had a team who were supposed to do that. And he had the born actor's talent for making inspirational speeches which subdued opposition by the sheer force of personal belief. She thought they would have made a good pair if they had been allowed to do the job together. Meanwhile, she was encouraged to lie low and conceal the fact that, of the two, she had the better brain.

How exactly was she supposed to pass the time during this solitary week? She could walk alone in the extensive grounds. There was no swimming pool. She had been specifically requested not to go beyond the guarded perimeter. The Chief Inspector had been adamant on that point. He had been detached to supervise her security. He would always be available at the touch of the red panic button. She suspected that he might be staying somewhere in the house. No doubt he would come and chat, if she got desperate for company. Chat about what?

It would have been pleasant to meet others at meals. But there was to be none of that. Food would be served to her in her own apartment and she would eat alone, like the Pope. Often she felt she wanted to get away from people, when she had to rush around with Raymond on their highly protected tours, pressing the flesh of the well screened. But the solitary life was too much in the opposite direction. She missed the children too: Tim on his cattle ranch in Uruguay, and Elizabeth at University in Oregon, both living under assumed names.

When would they all be able to lead a normal life again? She knew the answer. Never. That was the price you paid for starting a war, even a just war. Too many had died, leaving the deeply embittered bereaved.

She should have brought something to do. There was no point in reading the medical journals again. She would never be able to go back to her old life as a consultant physician. Medical advances moved very rapidly these days. Once out of touch, you couldn't return. Improving books perhaps? She had never read Gibbon or Proust. Perhaps she should ring Raymond's office and ask them to send her *War and Peace*.

There was a tap on the door. She welcomed the sign of human life. The attractive maid entered, the one who had carried her bags.

"I've brought your tea, Madam," said the girl. "I thought you might like a piece of chocolate cake."

"Thank you very much. What's your name, if I may ask?"

"Alison, Ma'am."

"Have you been here long?"

"Oh no. I applied for the job some weeks ago, but there was a delay before I could be taken on."

"Of course. All applicants for employment here would have to be most carefully vetted."

"Shall I pour out the tea, Madam?"

"Yes, please. Why don't you sit down, Alison? It would be good to have a little talk. The girl looked surprised, but did as she was asked.

"I'm glad to have this chance to speak to you," said Alison, unexpectedly bold. "I'd like you to know that your husband has ruined my life."

"What on earth do you mean?"

"My partner was killed in your war. He was in bomb disposal, a lovely man. He was dismantling one bomb, but they had put in a second. He didn't have a chance. That's why I do this work. To keep our children going."

"I'm very, very sorry," she said.

"That won't bring him back."

"He died for the country. I hope that is some consolation."

"No, he didn't. And it isn't. He died for your husband. To help him pretend he was saving the world. And win the next election. Nobody cares about me. We weren't even married."

That explained it then. If Alison was still single, she wouldn't have applied under her partner's name. She had slipped through the net. It must be mentioned to the Chief Inspector.

"I'm very, very sorry."

"You said that before. It doesn't help. I wonder how the Prime Minister would feel, if he too lost people he loves. Don't you think he deserves to suffer that?"

The red button was, unfortunately, on the other side of the room. To reach it, she would have to pass Alison. The girl had strong arms and looked determined.

"These were very difficult decisions for my husband," she said. "But you have to see the broader picture. You can't make an omelette without breaking eggs."

"As Stalin said."

This girl wasn't a simple chambermaid. She was a political activist, perhaps a terrorist herself.

Was it worth screaming? Probably not. The walls would be thick and there might not by anybody in earshot.

"We couldn't just have stood idly by," she muttered, almost apologetically. "My husband was given the wrong intelligence. It wasn't his fault, you see."

Alison was moving towards her. Her lips were set in a fixed purpose.

"What's that you have in your hand?" she shouted at the girl.

"Will you have some more tea, Madam? I could pour it out for you. And another piece of cake perhaps?"

She sank back, exhausted with the tension. The Chief Inspector would have to get rid of Alison quickly. But there were plenty of other Alisons around.

Would it always be like this? She knew the answer. Yes, to the very end. Raymond should have thought that one through.

The Valley of the Shadows

"Oh, look," said Brenda, "lovely snow-capped mountains."

"The Alps," said her Uncle Jeremy. "Have you never seen them before?"

He had always found his niece's girlish enthusiasms rather tiresome. Unsuitable, too, for an unmarried woman in her mid-forties. He preferred the clipped delivery of her sister Vanessa. But Vanessa was too busy to leave her desk at a top city solicitor's. It had been agreed in the family for some weeks that Brenda would accompany him on the journey to Switzerland. The two nieces were the only family that Jeremy Underdown had now. Years of bachelor art-dealing had left him with a solitary old age. Brenda and Vanessa were marginally better than nothing. It would look strangely bleak to make such a journey on one's own.

Everything worked with characteristic Swiss efficiency. Doctor Charpentier had sent a large, comfortable limousine, with smartly uniformed driver, to meet them at Geneva airport. This conveyed them, with effortless ease, to the doctor's private clinic in a mountain valley of spectacular beauty.

"Please make yourself comfortable, Mr Underdown," said the welcoming nurse in spotless uniform. "Doctor Charpentier will be with you shortly." Her English was almost perfect.

"May I stay with him?" asked Brenda.

"Of course. Throughout the … procedure."

"This room is rather dark," pointed out Jeremy. "Would it be possible to move to a brighter one? Just for the few hours."

"I'm afraid not, sir. The rooms on this side are all equally dark. It is the high mountains, you see. At this time of year, sunset falls early. We call it the Valley of the Shadows."

"Very appropriate, I suppose," riposted Jeremy glumly.

Brenda hoped that her elderly uncle would not relapse into his customary gloom. She knew he was in permanent, incurable pain. That would have a deflating effect on anyone's spirits. But at least he might make the best of an occasion where he was to be the focus of attention. She herself did not get many foreign trips these days. One liked to make the best of them. And the valley, even if shut in, was breathtakingly lovely. Brenda inwardly felt quite cheerful, though of course she was too sensitive to let that show. She had always been quite fond of dry old Uncle Jeremy, though his kindnesses were somewhat unpredictable

"Is there anything special you would like, sir? Nothing is too much trouble."

"Well, as you ask, I could do with a bottle of good champagne."

"Certainly, Mr Underdown. I'll have one sent up to you." She glided gracefully from the room.

"Are you all right, Uncle Jeremy?" asked Brenda.

"Not exactly all right. But no worse than usual."

"It's very luxurious here, isn't it?"

"Jolly well ought to be, at this price. I shouldn't hang around here, if I were you, Brenda. When it's all over, go straight home. They will know here that you have money and may try to rip you off."

"I haven't got any money, Uncle dear."

"You will. I made a lot. Selling that El Greco to the Getty. And other coups. I'm dividing it between the three of you."

"Three?"

You and Vanessa and the Tate Modern. I couldn't think of anything else to do with it."

"That's very generous of you, Uncle."

"It had to go somewhere, my dear."

Brenda resisted the temptation to clap her hands with joy. Now, at last, she would be able to move out of her horrible flat in the wrong end of Kilburn. She forced herself to think compassionately of poor Uncle Jeremy with his horrid back pain. He seemed to perk up slightly as he took his first sip of champagne. Who could deny him this final pleasure?

Doctor Charpentier bounced into the room, a small, cheerful man with a bald head and a bow tie.

"Mr Underdown?" he enquired. "I am delighted to meet you. As you know, Auguste Charpentier is my name. It is a great privilege to welcome you to our little establishment. I do hope that you will have an agreeable stay here."

"Agreeable!" echoed Jeremy Underdown. "That is hardly the object of the exercise."

"Perhaps, if I may, I should give you a short explanation,

as I do to all our visitors. As you know, we operate with the full approval of the enlightened Swiss law. We receive only patients who have the misfortune to suffer from advanced and incurable illness, and for whom life has nothing more to offer. Can I be sure that you fall within that category? We need a medical certificate to that effect."

"Here it is," said Jeremy.

"Extremely satisfactory," commented Doctor Charpentier, pocketing the document with a cheerful smile. Brenda privately thought it an unfortunate phrase. "You will wish to know what we now have in mind. I will give you a couple of hours to rest and recover from your journey. Would you care for some lunch? We rather pride ourselves on our chef."

"I don't feel much like lunch. Perhaps a caviar sandwich or two to nibble with the champagne?"

"Certainly. I'll have it sent up. What about you, Miss?"

"I couldn't manage any food," replied Brenda, quite untruthfully. There was a certain decorum about these things. When it was all over, she would go somewhere on her own for a good tea. The Swiss, she had heard, went in for the most delicious pastries.

"Would you wish to be consoled by the attentions of a Minister of Religion?" asked Charpentier.

"Certainly not," replied Uncle Jeremy promptly. "That would add a new horror to death." Brenda was reminded of his awful row with Father Patmore.

"I shall leave you now," said the doctor, "to enjoy the amenities we offer. Here is the provisional account for our expenses. Perhaps you would be good enough to give me a cheque on my return. Sterling is acceptable. I am sure you will understand. It is best not to leave these details until ... it is too late. I should not wish your charming niece to be inconvenienced."

"Very well Doctor. This afternoon ... what exactly happens?"

"I shall return with my assistants. You will lie on that comfortable couch. I shall roll up your sleeve and give you a little injection. A tiny prick, no more. You will know nothing and your passing will be entirely painless. Your delightful niece will be holding your hand."

"I see," said Jeremy doubtfully.

"Is there any special music you would like to accompany your ... happy departure? We have an excellent stereo system here. Some of our clients like to have a little Wagner. Highlights from Götterdämmerung perhaps?"

"I have always detested Wagner. Make it Offenbach."

"Very well. We pride ourselves on meeting our patients' wishes. It can be quite an exhilarating experience, you know."

"Are you sure I am doing the sensible thing?" asked Underdown, when he and his niece were left alone.

"Oh yes, dear uncle," replied Brenda enthusiastically. "As soon as Vanessa showed me that bit in the Sunday paper about this place, I knew it would be just right for you."

"I'll bet you did," snapped Jeremy sardonically. You couldn't really blame the girls for wanting to get rid of him. It must be a chore for them, having to drive down to Eastbourne by turns each Sunday to have a rather miserable lunch with him at his expensive private old peoples' home. They could both use his money too. This was the civilised way out for all three of them.

"You won't feel any more pain," added Brenda seductively.

"Don't be too sure, dear. There may be devils with pitchforks waiting to escort me straight to Hell."

Brenda laughed unconvincingly.

"That's what I always liked about you, Uncle dear. Your lovely sense of humour."

The champagne sent Uncle Jeremy to sleep. He looked so peaceful. Brenda wished she had brought a book to read. You could not spend all the afternoon staring at the mountains. The room suddenly flooded with cheerful music. She detected a Can-Can. It was almost a relief when Doctor Charpentier returned with two mild-mannered assistants. But then Brenda recollected what they are there for, and her heart missed a beat. Uncle Jeremy, she suddenly remembered, had always been generous at Christmas with his quirky presents. He had once given her a tame guinea pig with a sweet little tail.

"How was the champagne?" asked the doctor.

"Not at all bad," replied Jeremy, slightly slurring his voice.

"We'd better get going," said the doctor. "It won't take a minute.""All in the day's work for you, I suppose," suggested Jeremy, with a tinge of irony.

"I shouldn't put it like that," replied Charpentier reproachfully. "We take our responsibilities very seriously here. We are very conscious of the individual humanity and importance of all our clients."

"What do you do with the bodies?"

"Cremation is the usual method. For a small extra fee,

you can have your ashes scattered on a mountain top. Is that the signed cheque? Oh, thank you. Now, dear sir, under the rules, I am obliged to ask you just one question."

"What is that?"

"Are you quite sure that you wish your life to be ended this afternoon by mutual consent?"

"No."

"No ... what?"

"I am not quite sure."

Doctor Charpentier's cheerful smile faded.

"What exactly do you mean, Mr Underdown? Are you having second thoughts?"

"Yes. I'm beginning to think that I'd like to go on a bit longer."

"But, dear Uncle Jeremy," said Brenda, almost tearfully. "You thought it all over most carefully. You were so keen to end that nasty pain."

"It was the champagne that did it. And the Offenbach. They made me feel ... almost jolly. And the pain has eased off a bit."

"It is, of course, entirely your decision, Mr Underdown," said Charpentier, his voice heavy with disappointment. He motioned to his assistant to put away a large and menacing syringe. "But I am obliged to point out one consideration. My clinic has been obliged to incur considerable expenses in preparing your welcome today. To accommodate you, we had to postpone the visit of a client from Japan who was very keen to bring his grandmother here. But, as you have already given us a cheque, I will examine the possibility of offering you a slight refund."

"You needn't bother, Doctor. If you examine that

cheque, you will see that it is signed by Micky Mouse."

Charpentier's benevolent features crumpled into incipient rage.

"You have been fooling me, sir," he shrieked. "Wasting my time and money. I could sue you for this."

"I shouldn't do that, if I were you. Your activities are not viewed with approval by everybody."

"Just look what you have done to your poor niece. She is awfully upset."

"It wouldn't have taken long, Uncle," said Brenda painfully. Vanessa would blame her dreadfully, she knew. There would be no question now of that nice cruise to Antarctica to see the penguins.

"I'm sorry, Brenda. But the world still seems rather good. At least from the Valley of the Shadows. Don't look so disappointed. I'll try to make it up to you tonight. We'll go into Geneva and have a slap-up dinner. No point in saving money now. I can't take it with me."

Brenda gave him one of her ghastly smiles.

Carnival

It had been Major Tremain's idea. That in itself might have been enough to put Phyllis Nugent off. She did not care at all for Major Tremain. He represented masculinity in excess, with his tall figure, red face and over manly baritone voice. It was only when Guy Longworth supported the project that Miss Nugent began to see something in it. She had liked Mr Longworth from the first. He had not been in the village long, but he was very affable and they were glad to welcome him on the Parish Council. He was about the same height and build as Major Tremain, but he was younger, better dressed and had a much more sensitive and intelligent face. A more foolish woman might have felt tempted to fall slightly in love with Mr Longworth. But Phyllis Nugent was not a foolish woman. She was not the type to be carried away by passion. Sometimes she thought that this had given her a rather sterile and sad life, redeemed only by singing for the local Madrigal Society.

The two men, however dissimilar, had one thing in common, a slightly obscure marital status. Neither could actually produce a wife. But Guy was rumoured to be a widower. Perhaps that helped to explain the attractive melancholy to be glimpsed occasionally in his dark brown eyes. Widowers, as Phyllis knew, were usually unable to manage for themselves and were perpetually in need of a well cooked hot meal. Whereas Major Tremain, as he frequently boasted in the snug private bar of the Live And Let Live, had divorced at least three unfortunate women ("traded them in" was how he put it) and was presumably now sniffing around for a fourth victim. In the old days, men of that sort had, not infrequently, tended to end up on the gallows.

"I know you all mean well," said the Vicar, Harold Porchester, "but I think we must consider everything very carefully. It is certainly a splendid plan to try to raise money for the Church Organ Restoration Fund, a cause very dear to my heart. I am not sure, however, that a Carnival would be quite right for our village. We must do nothing to discredit the Church. And, thank God, we have a lot of quiet, retired people living round the Green. A carnival sounds rather noisy, perhaps even a trifle louche. Isn't that the kind of function they used to have in Venice in its most degenerate days? Byron and Browning and all that." Mr Porchester had never cared greatly for abroad.

"The Church has always taken a kindly view of Carnivals, Vicar," said Major Tremain in his know-all voice. "You must be aware of that. They still have them in Venice, held on Shrove Tuesday, or Mardi Gras, the day before Lent begins. In New Orleans too, and Rio de Janeiro, and other lively places like that."

"Lower Didlington is not exactly New Orleans," protested the Vicar. "Nor even Venice, except for the flooding."

"The idea is to let off steam before the rigours of Lent begin on Ash Wednesday," explained Guy Longworth. "A highly therapeutic concept."

"What rigours of Lent?" enquired Mr Porchester drily. "I detect few rigours in our modern pagan society."

"I once tried to make a sacrifice for Lent," said Major Tremain, "to please a woman, of course. I decided to give up malicious gossip. But then I had nothing at all to say. As I sat silent in the Mess, night after night, they began to worry about me. I was forced to take it up again."

The others smiled. Major Tremain was a well known original, rapidly developing into a regular village character. Phyllis alone looked at him sourly. He responded by giving her a decidedly suggestive wink. She turned hastily away, trying not to blush.

"Enlighten me," said the Vicar. "Exactly what form will this carnival take?"

"There will be food and drink," explained Mr Longworth in his attractive, light tenor voice which, not infrequently, gave Phyllis the goosebumps. "Music too, and dancing. Food and fellowship."

"That sounds like a perfectly normal party," said Mr Porchester. "There is nothing special about that."

"Oh, but a carnival does have an additional attraction," said the Major. "Everyone wears a mask. Animal, historical or grotesque, or whatever you like. Nobody knows who they are talking to. That's the point of the whole thing."

Phyllis wasn't very happy to hear that. Surely the masks would give people the chance to behave even worse than they usually did?

"Won't these masks be rather hot?" she asked.

"Only if you get excited, Miss Nugent," snapped Major Tremain. She was mortified to see the others smirking, except for that nice Mr Longworth who was always so gentlemanly. Almost too gentlemanly perhaps. She remembered how he had pointedly looked in the other direction when she was climbing down the rope ladder from the bell-ringing chamber in the church tower.

"The masks will make it more authentic," added Guy. "We will promote it as a Venetian Carnival. That should bring in the younger crowd. It's not the kind of thing you get every day in the heart of the Cotswolds."

"Very well," conceded the Vicar. "We will have the masks. My dear wife and I might come as Darby and Joan. Or perhaps as Anthony and Cleopatra."

"You mustn't tell us your character in advance," piped up Lady Bosanquet, knitting at the end of the table. "That would spoil the fun."

"I'm not sure I can offer the Church Hall," said the Vicar. "It sounds a thoroughly secular affair, though for a good cause. We usually end our functions there at ten o'clock for the sake of Doctor Curtis next door, who has to commute to Oxford."

"Don't worry about the Church Hall," said Major Tremain breezily. No doubt, thought Phyllis, this was the kind of abrupt disposal of difficulties which had earned him the MBE. "I'll talk to my friends the Melniks at the Grange. They'll lend us their Rumpus Room. Just right for a carnival."

"Rumpus Room?" echoed Miss Nugent. "What precisely is a Rumpus Room?"

"They have turned their whole basement into a large

cellar," explained the Major. "Like the kind of beer parlour they have in Munich, where the NAZIs got started. The Melnik kids use it for their rave parties."

"Rave parties!" exclaimed the Vicar. "I can't allow the Church to become associated with rave parties."

"Don't panic, Vicar," said the Major. "A carnival is not the same as a rave party. It is classy and continental, just the kind of thing they are encouraging in the European Union."

"And nobody will recognise you, Mr Porchester," added Guy Longworth. "Or Mrs Porchester, even as Cleopatra."

"Very well," said the Vicar with the firm smack of decision. He had once played rugger for his college. "The Rumpus Room at the Melniks it shall be, if they agree. Any objections?"

Miss Nugent pursed her lips, but remained silent. It would not do to seem a spoilsport. And the Organ Restoration Fund really was in dire need. The Vox Humana had made an awful noise in the Faure Requiem. But she did not care for the sound of the Melniks. They had made a lot of money rather too quickly. These days you couldn't be too careful.

The day of the carnival arrived. Phyllis dressed with special care. She took a long bath first, so that she would not feel hot and sticky, and put on her best silk underclothes, inherited from Aunt Mildred in Cheltenham, who had lived in Africa. It could well be uncomfortably hot in the basement at the Grange. She had always disliked the idea of being compulsorily brigaded at close quarters with other revellers. That coach trip to Assisi had been bad enough. One valued one's privacy and one's personal space. She left off her carnival mask until the last moment. Indeed, she was pulling on her Lucrezia Borgia face, with its long fair curls and seductive leer, as the taxi drew up to the door and the driver started to hoot. Thank God she would be unrecognisable.

Her arrival at the Grange confirmed Miss Nugent's worst suspicions. She was surrounded by gibbering fellow guests in carnival masks. The noise and the heat were intense as she felt herself swept down to the Rumpus Room. The Melniks' idea of interior decoration seemed to verge on the baroque with a nasty, indigestible touch of the rococo. So different from the traditional style favoured in the staid old days by Colonel and Mrs Worsley-Taylor. In one corner, a masked band were belting out rhythms emanating, apparently, from the Heart of Darkness.

The floor was crowded with jigging revellers engaging in a series of semi-athletic contortions, which Phyllis could hardly dignify with the name of dancing. In some of the darker corners, she suspected, these activities would verge on the unseemly.

In normal circumstances she would have flung herself upon the protection of the Vicar and Mrs Porchester. But who were they among the masked party-goers; Charles the second and Nell Gwynn or perhaps, even more improbably, Adonis and Aphrodite? It was all most confusing. Phyllis felt bewildered and a little faint. Where was comforting Lady Bosanquet? Surely not that robed figure, with the face of a satyr, which seemed to be attempting the paso doble? It was all so unlike their quiet, well behaved village.

Suddenly she felt herself seized by strong arms and whirled onto the floor. Her partner wore a grinningly jovial wild boar mask and, of course, she didn't recognise him.

At first she felt shocked. No opportunity to refuse had been given her. She had taken this for rudeness, but now she thought that it might be in accordance with the anarchic spirit of the carnival. The unknown man dragged her into a lively quick-step.

After a moment's hesitation, Phyllis began to try to enter into the atmosphere of the occasion. At least she was not doomed to sit along the wall, as the matrons and spinsters used to do at dances in her youth. She remembered now that she had once been considered quite a good dancer when the girls danced together in the sixth form. After all her trepidation, she was beginning to enjoy herself.

But who was her partner? She longed to know. Someone who had spotted her, she suspected, and who was acquainted with her already. Suddenly, in a flash, it came to her. This must be Guy Longworth. It would be typically kind of him to choose this as a way of assuaging her loneliness. He hadn't wanted her to feel like a fish out of water. Perhaps he had been waiting by the door and had got in a quick word with the taxi driver. There could be no doubt about it now. She was being whirled round the floor in Guy's strong arms. It was a delicious thought and she was determined to make the most of it.

Now he was holding her tighter than ever, grasping her closer to his body. The pressure was increasing. She could feel the swelling behind his trousers. She felt sure about that. After all these years, Phyllis had been able to arouse a man. And Guy Longworth too, a lonely widower she knew she could love. It was all too wonderful. She began to imagine the future. Honeymoon in Italy perhaps. Or possibly in that nice hotel in Torquay with the deferential staff.

RODE HE ON BARBARY?

For Phyllis, this was a supreme moment of joy.

She was being steered off the dance floor now to a small, dark area in one corner, no doubt a popular venue for the Melnik kids. He still held her very closely, pressing his mouth against hers. Phyllis found herself responding. They were as one. Darling, thoughtful Guy, she thought, I really do love you.

Suddenly, with a wild impulse, she put out her right hand and snatched off the man's mask. She felt such a longing to stare into Guy's beloved face and gaze into his dark eye's, now aflame with the passion of mature love.

Her heart skipped a beat. It wasn't Guy's sensitive face she saw in front of her. It was the brutish countenance of Major Tremain.

"Naughty, naughty," he said with one of his coarse laughs, as he also tore off her mask. "You're not meant to do that. However much I excite you, my dear."

"Disgusting!" she gasped.

"Disgusting? You enjoyed it well enough."

"It's not what you do that is disgusting," riposted Miss Nugent. "It's the person you do it with."

The Night Carnivore

"You want to be careful in Australia, sport," said the yellow-haired Herman, as they settled down in their twin beds. "Stick your toe out at night here in the outback and you could get nipped by the redback spider. We're very close to nature here at the Top End."

Clive, the boy from England, shuddered, as he was meant to do.

"I've always hated snakes," he said. "I nearly stepped on an adder once in the New Forest."

"We have one hundred and forty different species of snake," whispered Herman ghoulishly. "But only twenty of them are poisonous. Be careful of the mozzies, too." He enjoyed making the handsome pommie's flesh creep. "Especially at night," he added with relish.

Clive was conscious of the presence of danger. Night carnivores were the least of them. This backpacking lark was not proving as enjoyable as he had hoped. To begin with, he was not sure that he had enough money to get home in time for the start of the University term. His cash was coming to an end, and his debit card would be no use when his bank account ran out. The obvious thing would have been to ring his parents in Sussex and ask for more. But he hated the idea of doing that. He had flounced out in fury when Dad had tried to get him a job in the bank for his gap year. Clive had expected to obtain work in Australia, but this had not proved easy.

This is what had brought him up to Broome, an old pearl fishing town on the turquoise-coloured sea of the far north-west. They had told him in Perth that the area was enjoying a tourist boom because of its proximity to the wild gorges of the Kimberlies. Polite young Englishmen were apparently popular as waiters in the better hotels. But nothing had materialised so far. Perhaps he seemed too eager, too desperate. They had sensed something wrong.

He had liked the look of young Herman when the two met in the friendly semi-darkness of the bar in Broome. In tropical Australia it was a relief to escape from the merciless sunshine. Herman had volunteered that his aunt and uncle were away in Bali for their holidays and he was alone, looking after their homestead in the outback.

"Have you got a sheila with you?" he asked.

"No," replied Clive. He had been long enough in Australia to know that this meant a girlfriend.

"Nor me neither," replied Herman. He grinned.

Clive did not know what to make of that. He hoped it did not mean that the good-looking Australian was gay and was making advances. He liked to think that he himself was straight, though he was not entirely sure. There had been boys at school, but that was some time ago and, since then, he and Tracy had been pretty close, though not close enough to become permanent. It was all rather confusing and he didn't think he could cope with more entanglements.

He remembered that Sunday morning on the Downs and the scene she had made.

"If you've nothing better to do," Herman had said, "come back with me to our station. I'll get you some grog and tucker and you can stay till the old folks come back. You never know, they might take you on as a jackaroo. That's what the farmers say when they have a new boy for training."

Clive felt tempted. Broome had proved a disappointment work-wise, and he did need to earn.

"It's great in the outback," continued Herman seductively. "The freedom and the space. We have lots of Abos around. They could teach you the didgeridoo. That's the weirdest noise. Something to shake them when you get back home."

"I'll come then," agreed Clive. "But no funny business."

"Too right," said Herman placidly. "I've got my pickup outside. Just throw your swag into the back. We'll get away from these larrikins here." Did all Australians have to talk in that folksy way?

It had been pleasant, that evening with Herman at the homestead. They had both drunk far too much, and at last had tumbled into their twin beds in Herman's room.

"We'll go walk-about tomorrow," promised Herman. "I'd like to show you the cattle."

"Could snakes get in?" asked Clive nervously. It seemed a long way from Hayward's Heath.

"Don't worry, sport. If you feel anything tickling your toes, it's more likely to be me."

"It's very lonely out here," said Clive apprehensively. "Suppose somebody broke a window. We could be murdered in our beds."

Herman pointed to a heavy stick in the corner.

"I keep that for self defence," he said grimly. "Now let's pack it in. We mustn't be late in the morning. I've put grandfather's old ticker here to be sure of the time."

He showed Clive a magnificent gold watch which he set beside his bed.

"That must be worth a fortune," said the English boy.

"Dad says so. But I wouldn't dare to sell it. Family heirloom. The only one I've got."

Herman turned out the light. Both young men tried to sleep. But neither did. Both were in the grip of the same strong emotion. Not lust, but fear.

Herman knew. It was going to happen again. He would lose this boy as he had almost lost all the others. They were willing enough to come out to the farm, these lonely, homeless drifters. He was glad of the company. It was a lie, what he told them about his uncle and aunt being away in Bali. The truth would have been harder to believe, that his parents had been killed in a motor crash, leaving him the station and the thousands of acres and all the cattle. That he had lived there alone for months, icily lonely with only the locals coming in to help with the livestock. From time to time, he had picked up a boy in the bar in Broome. But most of them did not want sex, and those that did were not in the market for love, or for anything that would last. They would all have gone away in the morning if he had not taken steps to prevent them. There was only one way to do that.

This pommie boy would be the same. Herman liked him, wanted him to stay forever. The fear of losing him made it impossible for him to sleep. He had to take action now, while Clive was asleep.

But Clive wasn't asleep. The fear gripped him too, the fear that he wouldn't have the money; that he wouldn't be able to get home in time. His father would have won then. That gold watch was the answer, it would fetch a lot of money. It couldn't be sold in Broome, of course, but he had just enough to get down to Perth and it could be disposed of there for the price of the air fare to London.

He was sorry for Herman. He had quite liked him. But this had to be. He couldn't miss Cambridge.

In the dead hours after midnight, the time of the night carnivores, one of the boys crept out of bed and put on his slippers. You couldn't risk the spiders, or possibly the snakes. There was just enough moonlight through the cracks in the curtains to be able to creep across the room without making a sound. He seized the heavy stick and moved across to the other bed. The young head, so peaceful on its pillow, made a perfect target.

The Beggar

I'm old now, and I sit most days in the kitchen by the fire. The master doesn't expect much from me any longer. I was afeared that he would turn me out of the castle, now that I'm no use to anyone. But he takes no notice of me and just lets me be, old Antoinette, once the nurse and confidante of the adored young lord, his eldest son. Perhaps the master is simply being merciful. Or does he think I know too much?

I adored the boy from the first. He depended on me when his mother got took ill. He was a fine, upstanding lad, but he was never like his school fellows. There was a look out of his dark eyes, as if he dreamed dreams and saw visions that others missed. We would walk together in the poppy fields below the castle, where the great river runs down to the bridge at Avignon. His father was always cold and he turned to me for love. He seemed to love everything – the village people who weren't always very clean, the little frightened rabbits, the old bear that came down from the mountain in winter. I knew he would always be different from the rest.

Then he started to give money away. Not only money, but precious objects he took from the castle without permission. A silver goblet much prized by his father, the Count. A necklace taken from the bedside of his now permanently sick mother. A pony that belonged to his younger brother. Naturally, the poor flocked to the castle gate, waiting for the next handout. We didn't care for that.

His father was understandably furious. His bitter rebukes to the boy could be heard throughout the castle.

"What does this mean?" he shouted, raising his stick, "Am I to be reduced to abject poverty?"

"Poverty is a blessed state," replied the lad brazenly. "That is the clear teaching of Our Lord as expressed in the Holy Scriptures."

"Nonsense," yelled the Count. "You are living in the past. Holy Poverty may have been embraced in theory by the church a thousands years ago, in the years following the death of Christ. But all that has long gone out of fashion. Don't forget, we are living in the thirteenth century."

The arguments continued, but the young man would not give up. His father called in the priests to remind him of the respect due to parents. But he claimed that he had to carry out a higher duty. There was another young man, far away in Italy, who had pointed out the way. Somebody called Francis, also a great pain to his father; or so our boy said. We had to love the poor, even if they did smell a bit. I don't know where he got that idea from; perhaps from that Francis person.

"You may intend to become a saint," shouted his father. "But I do not wish to become a beggar."

"There is one simple solution, father," said the boy, very cool and determined. "I will renounce my inheritance and go far away. For ever. You will not be burdened any more with my presence."

"What will you do?" asked his mother. "Where will you go?" Her poor eyes looked wilder than ever.

"I will go where God leads me, Mother. My task is to succour the poor, the bewildered."

"What is to happen here, boy?" asked his father. "Who will be the master of the castle and the lands and the villages after I am gone?"

"I have a younger brother, sir. He will take my place."

By now they were frightened. They didn't want to lose him. But he wouldn't listen. Next morning, very early, he left the castle, dressed humbly with nothing but a small pack on his back. I was the only person waiting at the gate to bid him farewell. He kissed me. I knew it was too late to plead. He was leaving Provence for ever. The thought made me weep, but he told me to dry my tears, for he was summoned by a higher Master.

I was kept on at the castle to look after the younger boy. He was much more obedient and he felt no need to give anything away. Gradually the Count came round to looking upon him as his heir.

The years passed. I got old. Sometimes the lords and ladies visited us from Aries or Tarascon, or the citadel at Les Baux. We were living in a land of troubadours and goliards. Sometimes nobody came and the count looked bored.

And then one day, many years later, a vagrant was brought up before the Count for punishment. He claimed to be a religious mendicant, begging for alms to use for charitable purposes. The Count refused to listen to such excuses. He ordered the man to be whipped and locked up in chains in the castle dungeons. I am told that is a fearful place. The water runs in from the great river by day and night. Most prisoners there do not live for long.

As the man was taken away, I caught a glimpse of his face. And then I knew. The eyes were the same, glowing with compassion and love.

I was about to shout to his father. But then I looked at the Count and I realised something terrible. He knew too.

Why had he done it? At first I could not understand. Why not come down from the magisterial chair and embrace the prodigal? And then it came to me. One day quite soon, my boy was due to inherit the castle and the title and everything they owned. If so, he would give it all away to save his immortal soul. It would be the end of a great family, a nobility that had survived for centuries.

The younger brother, an ordinary Provençal lord, would be a much safer custodian of their ancient family treasures.

I was tempted to shout, in protest against the outrage. But then I saw the Count darting me one of his sternest glances. I knew what that meant. If I betrayed him, I would be thrown out of the castle. Starving, I would end in the river, floating down to Avignon. So I kept silent.

I could not get into the dungeons. I think he would have died there quite quickly. At least I hope so.

They hail him now as a saint. The pride of our family. Saint Roch, one of the glories of Provence. Sometimes I feel ashamed.

Brinsley

I am worried about Barbara. We haven't been all that close for years but she *is* my wife and, as a top city accountant, one hardly wants trouble in the family.

Barbara is an actress. A famous actress, as she frequently reminds me. No harm in that. These days, she brings in a lot of money. She has never been very bright, though I suppose many actors are like that. Their intellectual powers are devoted to learning their lines. I wonder how many members of the present Cabinet she could actually name.

Barbara has never been beautiful. But she has other assets. She is invariably cheerful, perhaps even jovial. That is not a quality one values at breakfast, but it does come in useful at those sticky dinners of the better Livery Companies. They say I have a rather dry manner, whereas Barbara's is as liquid as her kisses. And her large, mobile face is brimming with character and emotion, unlike mine. We complement each other rather well. When I married her, she was a struggling beginner. She was offered parts like the Fairy Queen in the annual pantomime at Barrow-in-Furness. But now she has left all that behind her. For some time she has been starring in a television sitcom about a preposterously snobbish female who devotes her life to a quest for upward mobility. It is mildly amusing, and they have a large audience at a peak viewing hour. I have even heard myself described as Barbara's husband.

That does not really disconcert me. Behind the scenes, she remains very much in awe of my superior mental powers. I think she was really meant to be a mum. She regrets that we have no children, though I sometimes think that is just as well. The poor little creatures could well have inherited my charm and Barbara's capacity for lucid thought.

My dear wife is not really a good actress, but she does throw herself into her roles, heart and soul, and identify's herself completely with the character she happens to be playing at the time. That is the secret of her success. But it does have a snag; she finds it hard to leave her part at the stage door. We get a lot of it at our home, an elegant executive mansion in the best part of Wimbledon. It seemed incongruous when Barbara insisted on slopping around in carpet slippers for her role in a revival of *Love On the Dole*. As Lady Bracknell, she even ordered *me* to stack the dishwasher. And, when she was playing the suicidal Hedda Gabler, I had to hide her bottle of sleeping tablets. That is surely carrying professional enthusiasm too far.

In her current show, Barbara has a rather feeble husband, very unlike myself, and she also does a good deal of telephoning to their fictitious son who lives in Australia. This wretched young man, whose name is Brinsley, never actually appears on the screen, but he is obviously the apple of Barbara's eye. Although *she* dotes on him, her husband does not, as he is continually demanding remittances. One suspects that Brinsley is of bohemian lifestyle and dubious morals.

Unfortunately, Barbara has begun to believe that Brinsley really exists. Only recently I found her at my address book, in a befuddled state, trying to find his location in Melbourne. I tried to calm her, but I am really concerned now about her mental stability. If she had to leave the show, that would have an adverse effect on our cash flow and, therefore, on my ability to service the mortgage on our chateau in the Gironde.

This evening has been the final straw. I came home to find Barbara chatting enthusiastically to a young man in tight jeans.

"Hello, darling," said my wife. "I want you to meet Chet. He's a great friend of Brinsley, and he's been telling me all about him. Isn't that lovely?"

"Brinsley doesn't exist," I said coldly. "He is a figment of your scriptwriter's imagination."

"Don't be silly, dear," retorted Barbara. "Chet has brought all the latest news, haven't you, dear?"

"Happy to oblige," said our young Australian visitor, with an oafish grin. I could see that he was rather wary of me.

"Brinsley is doing very well," continued Barbara happily.

"As you might expect. He's taken up painting in a big way. Of course he was always talented, they said that at school. They've just had a show of his landscapes at a rather smart little gallery. Thirty-five views of Ayers Rock. A good idea to keep doing the same thing. Like Monet with all those water lilies."

"Is Brinsley married yet?" I asked sardonically.

"Not exactly," replied Barbara evasively. "But he isn't alone, I am glad to hear. He and Chet are sharing a loft apartment near the Park in Melbourne, within easy reach of the Arts Centre."

"Oh, indeed?" I said nastily. Chet had spotted my reaction and had at least the grace to look somewhat abashed. "What exactly do you do, Chet?" I probed.

"Chet works in the domestic cleaning industry," burbled Barbara. "But now that Brinsley is taking up nudes, Chet will be well placed to do some posing for him."

"Sounds ideal," I retorted, with heavy irony.

"Chet is flying home tomorrow," continued Barbara. "He has very kindly agreed to take messages from us to Brinsley. Isn't that nice?"

"I'm sure glad to be of service," said Chet expansively. "Now I must leave you good folks. It's been a great privilege to meet Brinsley's mother. And father too," he added impertinently.

He left rather quickly and I heard him slamming the front door. By the time I looked out, he had gone already.

"Wasn't that lovely, dear?" said Barbara. "Talking to Brinsley's friend. Such a handsome boy, too."

A thought had suddenly occurred to me.

"You didn't give him anything, did you?" I asked. "Our silver ashtrays? The Herend porcelain?"

"Of course not, dear."

"Money?" I snapped.

"Well, since you ask," replied Barbara," I did make a donation. To take back to Brinsley, not for himself. I was quite clear about that."

"What did you give him?"

"I found that big old envelope, stuffed in the back of your desk drawer. I felt sure you wouldn't miss it."

"Wouldn't miss it!" I shrieked. "That contained twenty thousand pounds. In used, hundred pound notes."

"What on earth for?"

"It was my getaway money," I replied evasively. "In case I ever had to leave in a hurry. There have been investigations in the city and you never know."

"I should have consulted you, dear, I know," said Barbara serenely. "But Chet is so sweet. And Brinsley will use the cash wisely, I feel sure of that. They want to build a sun lounge for their pedigree cats."

"You are an exceedingly silly woman," I trumpeted. "I want you out of that show at the first opportunity. It's driving you round the bend. They'd fix it easily enough. You can crash your limousine, or something like that."

"I've been thinking of that too, dear. I'd like to widen my range of roles. So important if one hopes to become a Dame. They have offered me Lady Macbeth at the National."

Lady Macbeth! Wasn't she the awful female with the daggers and all that sleepwalking?

The Woman on the Moor

I didn't go straight up to the front door, of course. Oh no, I'm too well trained for that. I asked around a bit first. As I expected, the locals were suspicious of the woman. She hadn't lived long in that little cottage on the edge of the moor, and she kept very much to herself. They didn't take easily to strangers and this woman had done nothing to make herself known, to come alive for them as another human being. She only visited the shop for bare necessities, and she never entered the pub. They wondered why she had come, why she wanted to live there of all places. It was at the head of the valley, the back of beyond, a road that led to nowhere. People appeared in the summer for walking on the heather-clad hills. But the winter was bleak.

In the pub, they soon decided that I must be a journalist. One of the investigative types who like to stir up the dirt.

"We know why you're here," said one old grey-beard, as I sat drinking my lager. "We thought it wouldn't be long before someone ferreted her out."

"It's horrible what she did," commented another. "She deserves all she gets."

"How can you be so sure," I asked, "that it is really her?"

"It stands to reason, doesn't it? She comes here all alone and keeps very much to herself. She doesn't mix with us, and she doesn't have any visitors. Something to hide there."

The murmur ran through the bar. "Something to hide." I felt a little stab of satisfaction. I had been given the approximate locality, of course. Otherwise the job would have been impossible. But now it did look as if I was on course for the target. That was exactly what I was looking for, a woman who was trying to forget the past and move to a new life.

When I rang the doorbell, she answered almost at once. She wasn't very young, but still quite attractive. There was something haunted about her face and her staring eyes, as if she had been through an ordeal, that was what I had expected.

"Come in," she said, not very cordially. "I know you want to. I saw you prowling around outside."

"Thank you," I said. She offered me coffee and biscuits and I accepted. There wasn't much furniture. Perhaps she only intended it as a stopping place on the journey.

"All right," said the woman, almost smiling. "Let's be honest."

"I'm all for honesty," I agreed. That wasn't true, but it sounded good.

"You've been snooping, haven't you?" she said. "Asking about me in the village. I heard them talking in the shop. Which paper do you work for?"

"That would be telling," I replied, with one of my enigmatic smiles, the fruit of long practice in front of my bedroom mirror.

"I know who you think I am," she said. "But her picture

was in all the media at the time. Look at my face. It's not the same."

"Faces can be changed. There's such a thing as plastic surgery."

"Would that be worthwhile?"

"Oh yes. To get away from that identity!" She had been the nation's hate figure. Those pathetic little children, and the way they died! I could see now, there was a mark on her jaw.

"There was never a prosecution," she said.

"That was what enraged people," I said. "The guilt was so obvious. Who else could have been responsible?"

"But they didn't have the proof. Nothing that would stand up in court."

"They might re-open the case, you know," I said. "Now that they have developed these DNA techniques."

"Indeed?" she replied coldly.

"May I ask you frankly? Are you in fact Norah Musgrave?"

"I am under no obligation to answer that."

"Norah Musgrave is in danger. You must realise that. There is still a very strong popular feeling against her."

"I read that the police have had to hide her away and invent a new identity for her."

"You ought to know, Madam. They seem quiet people in this village, but it wouldn't take much to get up a mob from the town."

"Are you threatening me, sir? Lights on the moor at night, banging on the front door, bricks through the window? A portable gallows perhaps?"

"Anything is possible," I said. "This country is reverting

to barbarism."

"You are planning to expose me, I imagine. A hot scoop in your filthy tabloid. So typical of Fleet Street."

"You're behind the times. The press haven't operated from Fleet Street for years."

"Have another biscuit?" she suggested.

"Thank you. They're awfully good. Do you make them yourself?"

"I do most things for myself."

"I think you're making a mistake," I said. "It doesn't make you safer to hide yourself away like this. Norah Musgrave would do much better in crowded city streets. They don't stare at faces there."

"Perhaps that is exactly where she is."

"You're trying to tell me that you're not Musgrave?"

"I'm not trying to tell you anything. You're making all the running. But I will say this. You won't frighten me away from here so easily. I've been through a hell of a lot. The moors bring me a kind of peace. The purple of dawn, the rose of sunset. The everlasting birdsong. A private place."

"The Wuthering Heights syndrome," I suggested.

"You could call it that."

"So you won't move?"

"Not unless I have to."

I made a mental note. That's how I do my job, picking up vital pieces of information.

"Are you really going to write me up?" she continued.

"We'll see." Keep them guessing, my old chief always said. Without mystery you don't have power. "I don't dislike you, you know. On the contrary, I think you could be rather nice. Those biscuits are delicious."

"You're not a fool," she said. "You must know perfectly well by now that I'm not Norah Musgrave."

I smiled. I wasn't telling.

"You'd better go now," she said. "You won't want to be caught with me when the lynch mob arrive." Was she making a fool of me? Two could play at the game.

I mulled over that interview on the road to Newcastle. The woman was in danger. But it was something quite different. I roughed out mentally my report to Mr Templeton. He had threatened to murder her, I knew. That was why she was hiding away. Men could be terribly bitter about their ex-wives. He was perfectly capable of coming to get her. Why else should he be so desperately anxious to know where she was, regardless of expense?

Was I going to do her immense harm then? That was not my intention. But one has to earn a living and Mr Templeton was paying good money. One is not responsible for the use made of one's information. It's morally neutral, being a private detective.

Rode He on Barbary?

It all looked so different now, thought Philip. The walls of the large drawing room seemed almost bare without the English watercolours collected so lovingly by Cressida's parents – the Bonington sea pictures; the David Roberts views of the Alhambra; the small, precious Constable sketch. Cressida had made our Embassy Residence so warm, so welcoming. Even the stuffiest residents of this prim northern capital had succumbed willingly to the blandishments of her unforced smile. But now he had retired from the Diplomatic Service and Cressida was dead, slaughtered by that fool of a doctor in Lyme Regis who failed to spot her tumour early enough.

It had been an effort to return. The place held too many memories. But time hung heavily on his hands these days. And the Baltic cruise was free, provided he came as a guest lecturer. Out of sheer politeness, he had written to tell his successors that the ship would be there for this one night. They had responded with an invitation to a cocktail party they happened to be giving for a group of visiting back-bencher Members of Parliament. That was typical of Harold and Melanie; kindly colleagues, though not exactly sparkling. With a certain dread he found himself reliving the past.

Jan, the familiar hired butler, rushed up to greet him and offer him a large whisky, as in the old days. The old man prided himself on knowing the favourite tipple of all the Heads of Mission. That tended to give visiting VIPs the unfortunate impression that you were a dipsomaniac, but that couldn't be helped. Philip was politely, but not effusively, greeted by Harold and Melanie. They were a quiet, low-key couple, he thought, and they had managed to downgrade the Embassy only too successfully, so that it now looked like a villa in Surbiton. He knew he was a bit of a snob. It had done his career no good. But tonight he could not help aching for his incomparable Cressida and the haven of beauty she had created in these high, spacious rooms overlooking the river and the dark woods.

He saw a few familiar faces, whose owners waved politely in his direction. Friendly acquaintances, but no more than that. He was in no mood for diplomatic chit-chat. One had to put up with enough of that from the old people on the cruise ship. He could see now that there were still slight stains on the walls where his own pictures had been taken down. The whole place should have been redecorated, but there was never quite enough money available when you worked for the British Government. He had hoped to move into well-paid directorships in the private sector after his retirement, but these had mysteriously failed to materialise. Perhaps he had spent too much time in Scandinavia hunting elk with the reclusive local aristocracy from their crumbling castles in the south.

In no very gracious mood, Philip decided to bypass the

British MPs, making the most of their freebie by swilling down the free drinks at the tax-payers' expense. They were supposed to be investigating nuclear waste disposal, or cervical cancer treatment, or some other worthy cause. But, to Philip, they looked suspiciously like pigs with their snouts in the trough. He had never been very good with politicians, as the Permanent Secretary had mentioned in dismissing his plea for Rome or Madrid.

He pushed his way through the crowd to the door leading onto the terrace. This feature, he had always thought, was the glory of the Embassy residence. It ran along one side of the house and overlooked the river, which wasn't really a river at all, but an arm of the Baltic. At least his successor had not, so far, been able to damage the roses, seen so clearly in the bright glare of this northern summer evening where it was light till after midnight.

On the terrace, he was pleased to run into Sven, a musician friend and one of the most civilised of the regular Embassy contacts. Sven gave him a cordial greeting. Like most people in this urbane city, he spoke almost perfect English.

"I was sorry to hear about Cressida," he said.

"Thank you, Sven. You're still coming to the British Embassy, I see."

"Naturally."

Philip reined in his tongue. It was bad form to criticise your successors. He himself had seen a good deal of Sven during his days as British Ambassador. Cressida had been a great music lover and Sven was one of the leading local cellists. He found it hard to believe that Sven would have much in common with Harold and Melanie whom he suspected of taking little interest in the arts. But the British Embassy was a respected social centre, and Sven would be happy to be seen there. Perhaps an Ambassador was inevitably respected more for his position than for his personality.

"How are you, Sven?" he asked casually.

"I have had a disappointment, Philip. You may remember my cello, the joy of my life. A seventeenth century Ambrosini from Cremona with the tone of an angel. Quite outside my financial range, of course. I only had it because my rich uncle left it to me. Amazing luck for a string player."

"You certainly made a gorgeous sound. Cressida was mad about your Elgar concerto."

"Well, I had to sell it. The boys are extravagant and we ran into difficulty. I found a handy purchaser in the patrons of our orchestra. As you will remember, I am a co-leader of the cello section. The idea was to use it for one of the principal players. Of course I thought they would lend it to me, so that I could go on playing it. But they didn't. They passed it on to Heinrich, that pushy young German who's supposed to be my co-leader, I heard them say that he had a longer future. You can imagine what it means to me every time I see him. The brute hugs my beloved instrument between his bony knees and puts on an angelic smile. I would rather he did that to my wife."

"I know exactly how you feel," said Philip sympathetically. "Just look around and see what my successors have made of this lovely house. It may seem foolish, but I still feel the place should belong to me."

"I understand," said the disappointed cellist with a

sympathetic smile.

The two ageing men stared unhappily across the water towards the little wooded hills, still ablaze with summer. Between them there was a deeply felt silence.

"Rode he on Barbary?" quoted Philip with sudden bitterness.

"I don't understand."

"Shakespeare. Richard the Second. The perfect part for the young Gielgud. The King has been deposed and is cooped up in a dungeon of the castle of Pontefract. There he learns, to his horror, that Bolingbroke, the usurper, has been crowned King in London as Henry the Fourth. And, supreme insult, he rode to the ceremony on Richard's own favourite horse; his beloved Barbary. For Richard it is the final straw. His humiliation is complete."

Neither man spoke for a moment.

"Yes," said Sven at last. "That's the feeling exactly. Rode he on Barbary?"

The Madonna of Saint John's Wood

It was remarkable, thought Teresa, how easily you could get around these days. A winter weekend in Florence cost so little, and the comfortable small hotel was within easy walking distance of the Ponte Vecchio. She could, of course, have travelled in style; first class to the Excelsior. Bruce was a rich man, having devoted his life to making money as an asset stripper. You only had to buy up small businesses in good locations and then sell off their freeholds, leaving their disgruntled employees to move elsewhere. Their own house in leafy Grove End Road, just up the street from Lords, was worth millions. But Bruce was keener on adding to his fortune than spending it, and Teresa was of a peaceable disposition. She had naturally invited Bruce to accompany her, but he had claimed an early meeting on the Monday. In any case, he said, he preferred to spend his weekend on the golf course where there were useful insider tips to be picked up. Teresa was not entirely sorry. Bruce was not good in picture galleries and besides, her trip had a rather special motive which she had not revealed to him.

Doctor Tettamanti had kindly agreed to receive her at the Uffizi on the Saturday morning. Teresa had done her research and established that he was a world authority. She had brought the photographs with her. It had been worth getting in a professional to do them. They had come out with marvellous clarity. You could see every detail of the Madonna's robes, the Bambino's chubby legs, the Tuscan country scene in the background. Theo Upminster at the National Gallery in London had been fascinated and was quite sure that the picture was an important work of the Florentine late Quattrocento. But he had modestly suggested that she should seek a second opinion from his Italian opposite number. Hence Teresa's little private mission.

"You are very kind to receive me at the weekend, Doctor," she said politely. It was partly for her innate courtesy that Bruce had married her. This was not one of his own qualities and she made a refreshing change from some of the other city wives.

"Not at all, Signora," replied the distinguished curator in his perfect English. He had taught at Cambridge. "It is always a joy to look at pictures. And especially yours."

He gazed with appreciation at the serene, beatific faces of the Madonna and the happy mischief to be seen on that of her gurgling baby. Could this, thought Teresa, really be a representation of God incarnate as an infant, the birth of the Man Of Sorrows? What stupendous, divine impertinence you would need to try to put such a scene on canvas!

"This is indeed a very lovely painting," said Tettamanti after a lengthy inspection. "About 1480, I should say.

Obviously by one of the very greatest masters. By then they had acquired all the technique and had not yet lost the spiritual momentum. The golden age of Florence and of Italy. Since then it has been downhill all the way. May I ask, how did you acquire this marvellous work?"

"It was left to my husband recently, by an old aunt. She lived in the back of beyond. Way north of Hexham. We used to go and visit her. A long, tedious drive."

Bruce had been furious when Aunt Hester put out one of her periodic appeals for his presence. But he had never refused to sacrifice his precious weekend. Aunt Hester had let it be known that she was leaving him something in her will. He had expected money and was enraged when the legacy proved to be nothing more than the Madonna. The investments and the substantial house had gone to the Stray Dogs Home in Newcastle. Bruce had petulantly hung the Madonna in the spare bathroom, where he sometimes shook his fist at it. But, for Teresa, the picture had always held a mysterious, almost compelling, fascination. She longed to know the painter's name.

"Your husband's family must have had money," said Tettamanti.

"They once owned a family bank," replied Teresa. "In the days when such organisations existed."

"I expect one of them did the Grand Tour. Probably in the eighteenth century. In those days, English milords could pick up Italian pictures for a song. Is there no record of the painter?"

"I don't think so," answered Teresa. "Aunt Teresa became rather vague towards the end, and seems to have burned a good many family papers to keep warm. She never got round to central heating."

"Ghirlandaio, I thought at first. Perhaps Domenico himself. But on reflection, I think it is even better than that. Just look at the Bambino's smile. And the folds of the Madonna's blue robe. My dear Madam, this is by one of the very greatest Masters." The curator's long, sensitive face glowed with the excitement of discovery. "I feel in my bones that this is one of the lost Molinellos."

"Molinello?" echoed Teresa.

"Bartolomeo Molinello. He's enormously rare. Even more than Giorgione. We have one here at the Uffizi. There's nothing in the Louvre, or the National Gallery. He died at twenty-six, you see, probably of the plague. His greatest love was Simonetta Vespucci, the prettiest girl in Florence. This could be her. She also modelled for Botticelli. My dear Madam, this is absolutely marvellous."

"Are you sure?"

"Of course I'm not sure. These are splendid photographs though, probably easier to study in detail than the canvas itself. But I shall need to consult my mentor, Professor Chieti-Lucera, who has written the definitive monograph on Molinello. He lives in the country on the road to Siena. I will invite myself to lunch with him tomorrow. Then, in the evening, I will telephone you at your hotel with his verdict."

"That will settle the matter?"

"Not completely. I shall be obliged to visit you in London to inspect the original. But that will be a pleasure, dear lady. Fortunately, I have a trip already planned for next month."

Teresa sensed that he was certain already, in spite of

his words of caution. The Italian's face was beaming with delight. This could be the apex of his career as a scholar and a lover of beauty.

"We shall be glad to welcome you," she said warmly. He would not have much in common with Bruce, she thought. But that would hardly matter. Bruce could be very pleasant when money was involved.

"I know what you are thinking," he said, "but are too British to ask. Will this attribution make much difference to the value of your painting? The answer is simple. Yes, it will. Italian religious art does not attract the great prices that it once did. So many of today's purchasers are Japanese, Arabs and other non-Christians. A Madonna by an unknown Master would not go for a lot. There are plenty of them around. But a genuine Molinello, authenticated by Chieti-Lucera and myself, would command big money. He is so wonderful and so rare. You could easily sell it to the Getty in Los Angeles for two million pounds. Probably more. Your own National Gallery could not afford it."

Teresa felt a little faint. It was all so hard to believe, like something out of a fairy tale. She thanked Tettamanti warmly and adjourned to a nearby restaurant for a stiff whisky.

On the following day Teresa took a taxi up to Fiesole and went for a walk. She had not slept well. That evening Doctor Tettamanti telephoned, as he had promised.

"You are in luck, dear lady," he said, bubbling over with scholarly enthusiasm. "The Professor is entirely satisfied. The excellent photographs are enough for him. He is perfectly sure that you own a Molinello of enormous value. But I still need to come and authenticate the picture itself next month."

"My husband and I will be delighted," said Teresa warmly. Bruce, she knew, would be over the moon. Money meant so much to him, as a symbol of power and success, and this was real money.

"In the meantime," continued the Florentine scholar, "I advise you to be very careful. Don't tell a soul, except your husband. You don't want to encourage burglars. Then you'll have to think about the insurance."

"My husband will want to sell the Madonna as soon as possible."

"Oh, will he? That is understandable. But perhaps a little sad."

"We are most grateful to you, Doctor Tettamanti. You have been very kind."

"I was only doing my job."

Teresa wondered about that. Would he expect a fee? Or perhaps a hefty percentage? She must find out the form. Berenson, she remembered, had done a profitable trade with Duveen, but then he was a private connoisseur.

She found it hard to read on the short flight home. Bruce would be thrilled, she knew, and that would put her, for once, in a favourable position. He had nagged her so often in the past, and not only about money. Now he would have to be grateful.

As soon as she got back to Grove End Road, finding her husband still in the City – as she might have expected – Teresa rushed to the spare bathroom. She was avid now to feast her eyes on their Madonna and Child, worth two million pounds at least, a superlative example of the finest Florentine art. To her horror, she saw only a blank wall.

The Madonna had disappeared.

"The Madonna?" she almost shrieked, when Bruce at last came home. "What on earth has happened to it?"

"I sold it," replied Bruce calmly.

"You what?"

"I got rid of it. That little firm in Saint John's Wood High Street took it off my hands. You know the people, they do a lot of house clearance sales. They came here early this morning."

"You had no right to do that, Bruce."

"Yes, I had. It was left to me. That bloody old Hester was my aunt."

"But I was away. You chose the moment on purpose."

"I suppose I did, dear. As a little surprise. I thought you'd be pleased. Now you can have a new vanity mirror with all the trimmings."

"Did you get a good price?"

"Not bad, for what it was, only old religious junk. I was glad to see the back of it."

"What have you done with the money?"

"I've bought another picture. From a nephew of a chap in the office. One of the best of our younger painters, they say. He's been a runner-up for the Turner Prize."

"Let me see it," said Teresa coldly.

Bruce went out to collect the new picture from the car. He unwrapped it slowly. Teresa felt faint with horror.

"This will be a much better buy in the long run," said her husband complacently. "I don't know much about art, but they say these young British brutalists are all the rage. Just the thing for Tate Modern."

"What on earth is it meant to be?" The picture, in vivid

oils, was incomprehensible to her.

"Elephant Shitting, he calls it. So right for a bathroom."

"The Madonna was worth at least two million pounds."

"What?"

"You heard, Bruce. Two million pounds." Her voice was chilly.

Her husband's fleshy face, highly coloured most of the time, was beginning to grow pale. At that moment Teresa made up her mind. She would file for divorce as soon as possible.

Remembrance of Things Past

Laurence Pemberton felt a small stab of pleasure. He knew the handwriting at once. The card was indeed from Ben Hudson, a boy he had once loved. But Ben wouldn't be a boy any longer, or even a young man. He must now be in early middle age. It had all happened so long ago.

Laurence himself had long since retired. He was an old man now, a former schoolmaster who had never married. He had enjoyed his lifetime of teaching. He had a gift for explaining things, and he had been fond of many of his pupils. On leaving the school, he had never bothered to move away from his small house in the village. He lived in peace with his neighbours, respected as another Mr Chips. The school did not forget him. Occasionally they invited him to a prize giving, or a concert. His pupils had, on the whole, done well. One of them ran the Bank of England.

Inevitably, Mr Pemberton was fraying a bit around the edges. He forgot new names too easily, though he had almost total recall for the remote past. His moustache had grown a little ragged, and his hair was thinning on the top. He often dropped asleep after lunch. But these developments did not worry him too much. They were all part of the long process of fading out of life.

The school took girls now but, in Mr Pemberton's heyday, it had been single sex. He kept up with some of his old boys, but only a few. From time to time, one of them would pop in to see him and there were cards at Christmas. But most, he assumed, would have forgotten him, and he felt no resentment about that. If he had been able to give a little help to the vulnerable young, that in itself was enough reward.

Recently, he had been feeling the occasional pain in his chest. Indigestion, he thought. He really must cut down on those buttered muffins. He had made an appointment with his doctor for the following week. No doubt they would put him through some troublesome tests.

All this was forgotten in the pleasure and surprise at receiving Ben's postcard. He had not heard from the boy since he left school. His family did not live nearby, and Mr Pemberton had been unable to discover what had happened to him. So this bolt from the blue was totally unexpected. Ben simply said that he had a present for Mr Pemberton, and would deliver it in person in two days' time. A present! How kind and thoughtful of him, mused the old schoolmaster.

It was good to know that Ben still had some affection for him. He had always worried a little about that. In the old days, unlike now, you were allowed to show the boys a bit of avuncular kindness. You could, on occasion, ruffle their hair, or put a hand around their shoulder. But Mr Pemberton had always been intensely aware of the danger of going too far. Especially as a lifelong bachelor. You simply could not afford the slightest whiff of scandal. Thus, he had ended his teaching career in an atmosphere of honour and respect.

With Ben, however, the most promising and the best loved of all his pupils, it had been a bit different. It had happened on that last evening at Interlaken. Discipline tended to be relaxed on the school skiing trips in the Christmas holidays for the senior boys. They had been allowed to drink the local wine and perhaps had overdone it, even austere Mr Pemberton. He had tumbled tipsily to bed at the end of a long, happy evening, and somehow young, beautiful Ben Hudson had been with him. It was only a vague memory, and Mr Pemberton did not think they could have done very much in that condition. But he was left with the distinct impression that on that occasion, quite exceptionally, he had gone too far.

He was worried about the boy after that. But Ben had left the school soon afterwards, bidding him a polite, correct, farewell. Since then, no word. So this lone postcard brought a particular joy. It showed that Ben cherished no ill feeling, and perhaps even retained a little affection for him.

On the day of the visit, Mr Pemberton dressed with special care. He wore a clean shirt and his best sports coat. He had prepared a cold lunch, in the hope of tempting Ben to stay for a meal. He must not get too excited though. He did not want a return of those chest pains, which seemed to be worse when he got worked up.

There was a click at the front gate. Someone was coming up the path. Surely this could not be Ben, that scruffily-dressed, middle-aged man who looked as if he could do with a bath and a good haircut. Why couldn't time stand still?

"I'm Ben Hudson," announced the apparition. "You remember me, Mr Pemberton?"

"Of course I remember you, Ben. Come in and sit down. Will you have a cup of coffee and a piece of cake?"

"Thank you, sir."

There was something distant about the man's manner. Mr Pemberton could not quite place it. The eyes were still a bright blue, but they had a sort of haggard stare. Obviously, all was not well.

"How are things with you, Ben?" he asked.

"Not too good. I've been in a spot of trouble. But you wouldn't be interested."

"Oh, but I would," said Mr Pemberton with great sincerity.

"You look pretty good to me," said Ben. "Enjoying a serene, respected old age?"

"I should like to think so."

"Look, I haven't come to talk, Mr Pemberton. I just wanted to give you this." He produced a document and handed it over. "Read it now please."

The old schoolmaster read, first with astonishment, then with mounting horror. The paper was addressed to the police and contained a detailed account of how Ben had been seduced in Switzerland by Mr Pemberton as an underage schoolboy.

Mr Pemberton finished reading and sat silent. His chest had begun to pound.

"You wanted to see me reading this," he said at last. "And then to look at my face."

"Yes."

"Why, Ben?"

"I've always hated you."

"But what for? It was so long ago."

"It made me feel unworthy. Ashamed. Dirty. I blame you for everything. The way I could never settle to anything – a job, a place, a person. Even for my drug habit."

"I loved you, Ben."

"You lusted for me. It's not the same."

Outside they heard the police sirens. "They asked me to arrange this," said Ben. "To make sure you would be in."

There was a smirk of bitter satisfaction on his ravaged face. Mr Pemberton clutched at the agonising pain in his chest. Then it all went dark.

In the South

They didn't want me to go to their headquarters. Instead, I was invited to call at a small flat in Ebury Street. I was received there by a man called Porteous, whose hair was just starting to go grey.

"You have my sympathy," he said.

"It's not your sympathy I want," I replied. "It's protection."

"I can well understand that."

It had all begun to go wrong so quickly. For years we had been used, as a family, to the very best of treatment. Dad had been Prime Minister for ages, and we were accustomed to receiving every possible assistance from the police and the security people and the numerous lobbyists who wanted to get something out of him. Mum, too, had been a power in the land, receiving top people at Downing Street with magnificent aplomb. A far cry from the early days when we all slummed it in that little house in Muswell Hill.

Then Dad was defeated in the General Election and the Nasty Party, as we called them, came into power. Mum and Dad just wanted to get away, so they accepted an invitation to stay with this Green ship owner in his comfortable house on Mykonos. They didn't know that it was a trap. Some damned international lawyer put in an application to the Greek Government to have Dad arrested as an alleged war criminal. To everyone's astonishment, this was agreed. Dad was now in prison in The Hague, awaiting trial before the International Court of Justice. Mum was fluttering around there, taking him special food.

Lots of people believed this was a travesty. Surely the Court had been set up to try dictators from Balkan, Asian and African countries, not a former British Prime Minister. But others thought that Dad was only getting what he deserved. The War had bitterly divided public opinion. It was all a big surprise. Dad and Mum had gone to church every Sunday and were quite religious.

I was between jobs and rather at a loose end. I suppose I had become a bit spoiled. Inevitably, I had got used to people doing things for me. Now I was living in a hostile world where you had to pay for things.

Then the death threats started to come in. They had found out where I was living. They wanted to get me, as a way of revenging themselves on Dad. So many innocent people had been killed in his last war. I had to ask for help.

"I have arranged everything for you, Jimmy," said Porteous calmly.

"Thank you."

"You are going to die this afternoon."

I sat up in astonishment.

"You will be killed in a road accident," he continued placidly. "Not really, of course. Just one of our deception plans. We want to get them off your tail and buy a bit of time."

RODE HE ON BARBARY?

"But what happens then?"

"We can't afford squads of police officers. You're not in public life yourself, so we are giving you a new identity. It's the best way to protect you. I hope you will agree."

"Who am I to be?"

"Your name is Guy Somerville and you're becoming an estate agent."

"Estate agent! I've never done that."

"It's not a difficult job. You only need a convincing manner, the capacity to jolly people along. Your father always had that. Until the very end."

"Mum and Dad will think I'm really dead."

"They have already been told the truth."

"And where do I do this new job, Mr Porteous?"

"In Dunedin."

"Dunedin! Where the hell is that?"

"New Zealand. The South Island."

"That's a dreadfully long way from anywhere else."

"It's quite near the Antarctic."

"And what about my girlfriend?"

"I'm afraid she has to be written off. We made enquiries. She's a bit of a talker."

"Suppose I don't agree?"

"You don't have much option, do you? It's your only hope if you wish to stay alive. There are girls in New Zealand too."

"Will I ever be able to come back?"

"Perhaps some day. When your Dad is simply part of history."

"When do you think that might be?"

"We can't tell now."

RICHARD PARSONS

I knew the brute was right. Without him and his people, I should be a dead duck. I wanted to break down and cry, but then Porteous would have sneered. It had all begun so well, with Mum and Dad so keen to improve the world. Now he had fallen like Lucifer. And I was Lucifer's child.

Mrs Patel's Cat

Everyone in our office had known for some time that old Mr Jardine was due to retire. Slumped at the supervisor's desk, he had been getting sleepier and sleepier, especially after lunch. Then one day, a circular came round inviting applications for his position. That's one thing abut working for the council. Everything is supposed to be above-board and preferably on paper.

Of course I applied straight away, emphasising the long years of service I had already put in. My husband encouraged me.

"You'd be ideal for the job, Maureen," he said. "Being a supervisor means bossing other people around. And you're very good at that. By all accounts, that old Jardine has been far too soft. You'd be a breath of fresh air, getting a grip on all those silly women." It's true that most of our operatives in the Complaints Department are female, and some of them do need a good shake up. This side of our work is a growth industry these days, the council being very strong at generating complaints.

I was called for an interview with the Deputy Assistant Chief Executive or DACE as he is known in the office. He is a white man, which you can't take for granted in our Council, as our employees are all colours of the rainbow. He motioned to me to sit down and gave me a long, cool stare. I thought that a bit unnecessary as I was not competing to become Miss Hoxton.

"I'd like to ask you a question, Mrs O'Brien," he said at last. "As you know, we in this Council are committed to being a full racial equality employer. That means being true to the spirit as well as the letter of the law. We are proud of having many employees whose families originated outside Western Europe, many from Asia and Africa. You yourself are from Ireland, I notice."

"That's not my fault," I snapped.

"Indeed not. But we have to be careful because the Complaints Department is a highly creative, and indeed expanding, area of our work. Do you think you could show generous sympathy and understanding towards subordinates of totally different backgrounds?"

"They're all human beings, aren't they?" I retorted. "I expect they all look much the same on the lavatory seat."

I thought of that interview a few days later when the name of our new supervisor was announced. They hadn't appointed me. The job had gone to Mrs Patel. I was frankly gobsmacked. It was astonishing that I would now have to work under a dim little Indian woman who wore saris and old fashioned spectacles, and spoke in a quiet, squeaky voice like a bewildered mouse. She certainly would not have my talent for putting the fear of God into the shirkers.

I wrote to the DACE to complain and got a short, snooty reply, suggesting that I take the matter up with Mrs Pinkerton-Jones, our Staff Ombudsperson. My husband encouraged me to have a go, pointing out that I had a natural ability for controlling others and should make sure this was recognised.

I knew about Mrs Pemberton-Jones. Her husband is a barrister, and they have moved into the upmarket Islington end of our council patch.

"You have something to say, I understand, Mrs O'Brien." she began graciously.

I launched into one of my speeches, explaining how good I was at the job, and how Mrs Patel was a little nobody who wouldn't impress anyone. I demanded to know why she had got the promotion and not me.

"I'm sure you are very forceful, Mrs O'Brien," said Mrs Pinkerton-Jones, "and would no doubt make a good supervisor. But, in deciding on these appointments, we have to take everything into account."

"What exactly does 'everything' mean?" I asked.

"Balance, for example. Remember that we are committed to inter-racial policies."

"Oh, I see," I said triumphantly. I had caught her out there. "You mean I would be better at the job, but Mrs Patel has to be appointed because she is an Indian."

"I didn't say that," retorted the Ombudswoman. "But we are not ashamed of our policy of reverse discrimination. We have to remember that our friends in the immigrant communities have been through difficult years. We have to help them to improve their socio-economic conditions. My husband has just taken a very charming girl from Sri Lanka into his Chambers."

"I hope he enjoys that," I said nastily. A glint entered Mrs Pinkerton-Jones's big blue eyes.

"No doubt these liberal policies are splendid." I added.

"But please remember one thing. They are paid for; not by the likes of you, but by the likes of me."

I flounced out, rather pleased with myself, but it hadn't done any good.

We had a farewell party for Mr Jardine, and Mrs Patel moved into the supervisor's desk. She looked bewildered, as I knew she would. It's a shame for anyone to be promoted above their proper level, as my husband points out. He's a wily old bird. Mrs Patel must have felt that herself. She tried to suck up to me in the canteen.

"I hope we can work well together, Maureen," she said in that soft voice of hers.

"We'll have to see," I replied cautiously. "We'll soon know, won't we?" She realised I was a potential troublemaker and I'm not ashamed of that.

I did rather egg the other girls on, I will admit. We overwhelmed her with questions and kept referring the difficult decisions to her. By the end of each day, she looked a bit worn, and once I caught her wiping away a tear. But I didn't feel sorry for the woman. Why should I? I had been the victim of a monstrous injustice.

My husband agreed that my Human Rights had been infringed. But he warned me to go carefully with my protest campaign.

"You might get the sack," he said, "and then I should have to go out to work myself."

"Nobody ever gets the sack from our Council," I replied. "They wouldn't know how to do it." All the same, I did tone it down a bit after that. It might not be all that easy to get another job. My husband says that I'm not everyone's cup of tea.

RODE HE ON BARBARY?

Then suddenly one afternoon something unexpected happened. I encountered Mrs Patel in the female rest room. She was crying as if her heart would break.

"What's the matter, Mrs Patel?" I asked. I had never known her first name, though she used mine.

"Terrible news," she gasped. "They've just rung me." She was speaking with difficulty between her sobs.

"Your husband?"

"No."

"The children?"

"No. It's Englefield."

"Who is Englefield?"

"Our cat. My husband took him to the vet. He's been breathing badly. Old age, you see. The man said he would have to be put down. So they did."

"Without consulting you?"

"My husband thought it would be kinder that way. He was only an ugly old moggy, but I loved him. The cat, I mean. He used to sit on my lap and cuddle up to me. I think he was very wise. He had the most beautiful eyes."

"Why Englefield? It's not an Indian name."

"We used to live in Englefield Road."

"You must get another cat," I said.

"No, I couldn't, Maureen. There will never be another."

"Oh, come!"

"Please try to understand. We had an arranged marriage. The children have left home. I am not liked in the office here. Englefield loved me. He was the only one who did."

I put my arms round Mrs Patel's thin shoulders and patted the grey hair on her head. Somebody told me later that Asian people don't care for that. But she didn't seem to mind.

Symposium

It would not do to make a fuss. Aubrey knew that from experience. It was his long suit. He was no longer young, but he still had youthful feelings such as emotional longing and physical desire. For years he had enjoyed himself as a robustly heterosexual, but unattached, bachelor; a phenomenon well understood in the Victorian and Edwardian eras, but rare in modern times. He liked the company of women, but he did not need them with him night and day. Besides, he was polygamous by nature and he had never greatly cared for children.

Then one evening, at a private view at the Royal Academy, he had met Sally. She was tall, slim, vibrant and a good deal younger than he was. He had invited her out to dinner and then he found he had fallen for her. That was no unusual experience. But this time, from the very first, he had known that it would all be quite different. He needed to live with this woman for the rest of his life.

To his surprise, Sally was pleasantly responsive. It had been no uphill struggle. In early youth she had been choosey and boyfriends, discouraged, had faded away. Her job at the museum did not occupy all her attention. She was content to give it up and settle for married life with Aubrey in his fine house in Holland Park. He ran a successful publishing company, no easy feat in modern times. What Sally needed now was financial and emotional security. Aubrey was well placed to provide both. They married quickly and privately and then honeymooned in a small palazzo with a pool near the Ducal Palace in Urbino.

Aubrey was respected in his publishing world though not loved. The damaging phrase 'asset-stripper' was sometimes levelled at him. He had moved his firm out of the eighteenth century house in Mayfair, inherited from his father, into an anonymous modern building, selling off the old mansion to a Russian tycoon of dubious provenance. Some of his distinguished stable of old novelists found that their work was no longer acceptable. Instead, Aubrey had done well out of the ghosted memoirs of popular celebrities. He had been blackballed at the Garrick Club.

Aubrey very much enjoyed his sex with Sally. She had a delicious body, smooth, curvaceous and tactile. But there was one slight snag. A woman could just lie there and be adored, but more was expected of a man. Aubrey's Viagra pills were a help but, in spite of them, he did sometimes experience problems of arousal or, as one of his new young female novelists bawdily put it, 'getting it up'. Perhaps, he thought, he was working too hard at the office. He started to delegate more and to come home earlier. Sometimes, too, he lured Sally into taking a 'siesta' with him on a Sunday afternoon in their Wiltshire cottage when the libido seemed to be friskily rampaging. Sally made no objection to this, but sometimes, he thought, she did just lie there passively like an early Christian martyr about to be roasted.

Occasionally, he did rather miss Georgina's prying fingers and Daisy's outrageous jokes.

Aubrey loved to slide his hands gently over Sally's slim thighs, her delicious breasts and deliciously moulded buttocks. But she showed no corresponding interest in his own body, and it was extremely difficult to excite her. For how long, for God's sake, was one supposed to rub the female clitoris?

Aubrey was not a fool and it did not take him long to realise that their lovemaking did not give Sally the same pleasure that it did him. It was only something that she accepted as part of the package.

Matters came to a head on that Sunday in April. It was raining outside on the Downs and the cottage seemed snug and welcoming. After tea they would drive back to London. They had lunched well, with a good bottle of champagne.

"Come upstairs, darling," he suggested. "Just time for a cuddle." He tried hard not to leer.

"I don't feel quite like it today, dear," replied Sally in her small girl voice. "I must be a bit squiffy. If you agree, I'd like to rest in this chair. You don't mind a lot, do you, dear?"

"Of course not," he replied urbanely, inwardly raging. He must control himself; he mustn't let her see how desperately he did care. He had been all set to perform. Another chance might not arise so easily. He was silent over the *Sunday Times* at tea. In the Bentley, she caught him scowling.

Aubrey longed to have a real talk with Sally, to let her understand his passion, his vulnerability, his fear of old age. But somehow, he didn't think that would be the right way to manage this younger woman. She looked up to him as a tower of strength. It wouldn't do to let her see the feet of clay.

The next morning, at the office, he received Felix Moberly; one of his veteran novelists. Moberly was still on the books, having successfully negotiated a transfer to this freer, more liberated, modern age. His works were much in demand among lascivious old ladies. With Felix, a man of the world, he knew he could speak freely.

"It's not going well with Sally," he said.

"What's the matter? Has she got someone else?"

"I don't think so. But I don't believe she really loves me. Not in the way I love her."

"In a different way perhaps?" suggested Felix.

"I know she appreciates the security I give her. I'm a sort of kindly uncle to her, a sugar daddy."

"You probably each bring something to your relationships. But something different. Does that matter?"

"I want her to be in love with me, Felix."

"In love with you? That could be asking too much. Do you remember your Plato?" Felix had once taught Greek and Latin before discovering the financial rewards to be derived from Restoration romps.

"You're thinking of the Symposium, aren't you? His discourse on love. A drinking spree down at the Peiraeus on a summer evening."

"Exactly, my dear Aubrey. An intellectual piss up. That's what symposium actually means. As you will recall, Socrates thought that erotic love can be sublimated in a way that draws a person to aspire to philosophical truth. Or, as we would say, to God."

"I haven't quite got to that, Felix." He suddenly had a vision of Sally's naked breasts.

"Don't worry. In *Phaedrus*, Plato admitted the pull of the flesh. You see, he saw a loving relationship in terms of the lover adoring the beloved. Isn't that what you have got?"

"It was different in ancient Athens, surely. Grown men lusting after adolescent boys."

"Maybe, but the principle is the same. The lover and his beloved. Two different, but inter-dependent emotions. You're lucky to have a beloved, Aubrey. You should be content to be the lover. The French have a phrase for it, as usual, don't they? There is always the one who loves, and the other who turns the cheek. You'd better get that straight if you want to be happy."

Aubrey smiled, waving Felix to the door. He picked up the phone and dialled home. Sally would be up by now.

"Hello, darling," he said, with a little spurt of joy.

The Head of Personnel

David Sharman felt a small stab of pride as he fitted his little legs under the imposing executive-style desk. At first he thought the furniture would be too big for him. But then he decided that he would grow into it. The same could be said of the job. This was his very first day as Head of Personnel. He was nervous, of course, but he was determined to make a go of it. The office sent people all over the world. The selection of officers for specific postings was essential for the success of the entire organisation. It was a key position, at the very heart of the management. If David did it well, he would go on to higher things. His predecessor, Hugo Taverner, had arranged to post himself to Brussels.

David had joined the office twenty years before. From the first, he had felt himself to be at a disadvantage compared with most of his contemporaries. He had envied them for their accents, their wardrobes and their loud bow-wow voices. Most of them had been to famous public schools and to the ancient universities. His own school had been undistinguished and his university was of recent civic origin. But he had worked hard, developing a talent for networking and an ear for gossip. Now he had his first real reward, a foothold on the ladder of advancement, even a finger on the wheels of power. Back in Blackburn, they were justifiably proud of his modest success.

Phyllis Pereira, his new secretary, wheeled in a trolley containing a formidable pile of personal files.

"I've brought you these as a first instalment," she said cheerfully. "They cover all the people due for a move in the near future."

"I can't read all those," expostulated David. "It would take weeks."

Phyllis was an old hand. "Of course you don't have to read them all," she said soothingly. "Just glance through, to get some rough idea. The school and university reports, right at the beginning before they first joined us, are often the most revealing Mr Taverner used to say. He thought they showed what the subjects were really like before they had time to grow a public face."

"Some of the files are much thicker than others."

"The best people have the thinnest files. Nobody ever complained about them, so they just sailed on from promotion to promotion. The weaker officers have pages of justifying their behaviour and asking to be moved to another post where their talents can be better appreciated. When in doubt, simply promote the thinner file. That was Mr Taverner's advice."

"Am I allowed to see all the files? Even my superiors'?"

"Of course. All except your own."

His own file! Yes, that would make disturbing reading. It would be like having a glimpse of one's obituary and taking note of the date.

"Mr Bulstrode is speaking to the new entrants at twelve o'clock," said Phyllis. "He invites you to be there to support him."

"Very well." The idea of Simon Bulstrode needing support made him give a small smirk. Bulstrode, the Chief of Administration – his immediate superior – was a bold, confident man, given to wearing Savile Row suits with waistcoats. "Now I had better get my teeth into these."

"Do you take tea or coffee, Mr Sherman?"

"Tea please. And I think you might call me David."

He settled down to the task in hand. He had always been interested in people, unlike some of his loftier colleagues who concentrated grimly on policy. That presumably was why he had got the job. It was a great help to come to the post well briefed on the current gossip. But that was no substitute for a careful study of the files and particularly the annual reports filed on every officer below the most senior ranks.

As David read, strange new thoughts entered his mind. So many of the files did not fully tally with the men and women he had known, and actually worked with, for years. Phyllis had been wise to direct his attention to the early reports. These revealed, with startling clarity, how everyone had started. David began to realise that many of them had artificially created the personality he knew and admired today.

There were some striking examples. The smooth, urbane Fitzpatrick, who had done so well with all those Duchesses in Madrid, had often been heard to speak of their family place in Lincolnshire. David had enviously imagined an impressive mansion with ancient oaks and a home farm.

Now the file revealed that his colleague's father had been a dentist in Grantham. Then there was Sylvester Brandon-Smith, a cultured bachelor, whom they had off-loaded on San Salvador. It was generally known that he had left Harrow at the premature age of sixteen, supposedly to study renaissance art in Florence. But it became apparent that he had, in fact, been requested to leave for offering his person to the Captain of Cricket. Only his uncle, a member of a Conservative Cabinet, had got him taken on at all. And so on.

"You'd better get going, David," said Phyllis, bouncing in. "Mr Bulstrode doesn't like to be kept waiting." The Head of Personnel wondered whether he had made a mistake in encouraging the girl to adopt a familiar approach. He must try, from now on, to think of himself as a dignified figure.

In the large conference room, Bulstrode waved him to a seat and prepared to address the ranks of well-scrubbed neophytes. David knew what he would say. It was all so obvious. He switched off his attention for a few minutes, rapidly returning to consciousness when he saw his superior's beaky eyes switching towards his direction.

"The great thing in our job," pronounced Bulstrode, "is to be totally transparent and honest. Conceal nothing, manufacture nothing; show yourself to be a totally transparent person of complete integrity. That is the way to get on. And, more important, to advance the great causes we have in common."

No-one could have put it more clearly, thought David. And more disastrously. Bulstrode had given exactly the wrong advice to those unfortunate innocents. The path to success, in fact, required you to forget your disadvantaged background, your early struggles, your limited capacity for foreign languages. You needed to develop cheek, cockiness, bravura. And a thick skin.

He could hardly wait to get back to his own office and send for Bulstrode's personal file. That might be worth reading.

East of the Khyber

Several flights were delayed that morning at Heathrow. Something to do with a go-slow by the baggage handlers. I felt thoroughly frustrated, but brightened a bit on seeing the rubicund face of old Oliver Hughes. Oliver is far from being among the most prestigious members of the club to which we both belong. But he is certainly one of the jolliest and most hospitable. We had lunched together on several memorable occasions at the long table. But I never felt that I had got to know him well. There was something of the dark horse about him. That amiable smile had become a kind of protective carapace.

"This is bloody Hell," announced Oliver cheerfully. "I've got at least two hours to wait."

"So have I," I said.

"Come and have a stiff whisky then. There's a little bar upstairs."

I gladly agreed. One could hardly have a better companion to dispel the gloom.

"Where are you off to?" I asked.

"Moscow first. Then I pick up my flight with Genghistan Airways. I'm treating myself to Club Class on that leg. It seems that their World Traveller section is mostly filled with dogs and goats."

"Where on earth are you going, Oliver?"

"Timurgrad. Capital of Genghistan. Formerly a jewel of the Soviet Union, now an independent Islamic State. It's a long way into Central Asia, well east of the Khyber Pass."

"How exotic! Not the usual holiday resort."

"Indeed. But I won't be on the usual type of holiday, Luke. I have a special purpose."

"I thought Genghistan was a perfectly dreadful country," I said in astonishment. "Mostly desert, isn't it? Ruled by mad mullahs. Kept afloat only by the Americans and Russians, competing for access to its oil pipeline."

"That may well be true," replied Oliver in measured tones, "but social life in Timurgrad, though restricted, does apparently offer something ... well, you might call it almost unique. I feel I know you well enough to be perfectly frank, my dear Luke."

"Thank you, Oliver."

"How do you think I have spent my life?"

"Something diplomatic, wasn't it?"

"You could say that. Actually I was in MI6, our foreign intelligence service. That's always made me a bit cagey at the Club. The actors there talk about their shows and the lawyers go on about their cases. But I couldn't say a thing about my secrets. It had to be a closeted life."

"But in a good cause. Our national security."

"Thank you, Luke. As a matter of fact, the requirements of the job fitted in well with my main leisure time activity. Both called for ... the utmost discretion."

"You mystify me."

"That was my intention. You may perhaps be aware that I have always been a bachelor."

"I *had* assumed that." He seemed far too carefree to be a family man.

"The truth is, Luke, I am as queer as a coot ... gay as a bird ... call it what you will. Lots of us are, in the secret world. I suppose the way of life attracts a certain ... temperament. I'm a bit of a hunter, I do admit. Long ago, in my very early days, it was illegal. You faced shame, even prison, if you got caught."

"Ghastly," I said sympathetically, thinking of my own happy years of married love.

"Ghastly?" echoed the old reprobate. "Not at all. I enjoyed every minute of it. An exchange of expressive glances in the pub ... or even in a public lavatory. A quick fumble in the park. Or, better still, inviting the boy back to my digs in Half Moon Street. Smuggling him out in the early morning before the milk floats appeared."

"But the danger! Surely you couldn't have enjoyed that."

"Don't you see, Luke? It was the danger that really turned me on. The awful thrill, the sick feeling of apprehension ... when a policeman gave me a threatening glance, or I received one of those prim little notes from some young man asking me for money. I lived in a perpetual state of terror. It was absolutely divine. I needed something to fear. The Metropolitan Police, or the KGB ... it was all the same to me."

"You're a very odd man, Oliver."

"That has indeed been said. I had a very exciting youth. But then the bleeding-heart liberals muscled in and legalised my little hobby. That took a lot of the fun out of it.

RODE HE ON BARBARY?

But for years after that, you still had to be pretty careful if you worked for the Government. I was in deep cover in Embassies abroad. You couldn't appear with your gorgeous Berber boy at the Ambassador's soirée. So I liked to think it was all a bit hole and corner."

"Not any longer, Oliver. Gay and Lesbian rights are publicly recognised."

"That's the whole trouble, Luke. Cabinet Minister are overtly gay. Bishops too. The steam has gone out of the whole thing. What's the point of picking up a Ukrainian muscle man on the seafront at Brighton if the fuzz simply wish you goodnight? Britain is now a miserably dull country in which to be gay. There's no danger, no thrill, no frisson of fear. You are stuck with an ill-educated youth, often with spots in unfortunate places, who doesn't know the difference between a Manet and a Monet."

"My heart bleeds for you," I said with heavy irony. "But there isn't much to be done about it."

"Oh yes there is," retorted Oliver with an expression of lip-licking satisfaction. "That is exactly why I'm off to Genghistan. Its devoutly Moslem rulers have never heard of gay and lesbian rights. Under their penal code, homosexuality isn't just a sin. It's also a dreadful crime, incurring the severest punishment. They have a full-blooded Islamic penal code. Even for unseemly suggestions, or lewd winks, you can have protruding parts of your person cut off. In public too!"

"But, Oliver, you can't possibly want to have anything like that happen to you."

"Of course I don't. But don't you see, Luke? There will be awful danger all the time. It will make little activities

... indeed, my whole life ... so terribly thrilling. I shall re-capture the illicit raptures of my licentious youth. Did you know that I was once known as the Beast of Balliol?"

"You won't find any partners in such a benighted place."

"Don't be too sure, my dear boy. I have consulted the World Cruising Guide. There is a handy little park, pleasantly dark at night, just behind the office of the British Consulate. Sounds like the local equivalent of Hampstead Heath."

"Well, Oliver, I wish you luck. And a safe return. With everything you started out with. I think you're taking a big risk."

"That's the whole point, old man. I'd better get along now to the check-in. Genghistan Airlines are notoriously haphazard, they say. They may have made up a bit of lost time. The one-way flight to Timurgrad was pleasantly inexpensive, you know. They want to encourage tourism."

"One-way flight?" I said in astonishment. "Didn't you book a return?"

"They said there would be no need for that," replied Oliver happily. "I could decide to stay on. The FO might take me on as Honorary Consul. Their last one was eaten by a bear."

"You remind me of the old days," I said, "when hunting people used to argue that the fox rather enjoyed the thrill of the chase."

"Perhaps they were not far wrong, Luke. Well, good luck to you. By the way, I never asked you. Where are you going yourself?"

"Only to Malaga. To visit my daughter and her family."

Oliver gave me one of his urbane leers.

"How awfully dull," he said with a kindly wave.

On the Fields

Andrew Thwaites sensed that something unpleasant was going on behind him. He could hear the whispering, the scuffling and the small yelp of pain. One of the weaker pupils was being tormented. He knew he should turn round briskly from the blackboard, where he was drawing a map of Australia, and face the culprits boldly. They would be some of the louts at the back of the class, who should long ago have been booted out of the school to join the swelling ranks of the unskilled unemployed. He nerved himself to make the effort. It was apparently the Head Teacher's policy not to notice bullying, but Andrew could not agree to that.

He was an idealist. He wanted to do good. That had got him where he was today, geography master in a sink school in Hackney. Saint Cassian's, so-called from the Patron Saint of Schoolmasters, had been founded long ago by an evangelically minded local vicar, but had now been subsumed into the state system where it was on the list of unsatisfactory establishments ripe for the chop.

The desolation of the school had actually attracted Andrew. The whole point of life, he believed, was to put your shoulder to the wheel in the area where you were needed most. That was why he had taken up teaching in the first place. His father had been a stockbroker and, in those happily nepotistic days, could have got him a well paid job in the city. But Andrew preferred to adopt one of the caring professions. He had deliberately decided to take up the challenge of teaching in a state school in a deprived area. At heart, he was rather vain. He cherished the belief that he personally could improve the career prospects of these disadvantaged young people. But it had not worked out well. He was middle-aged now and his hair was greying. He was single and he was poor. He was beginning to lose heart.

Even in that tough part of London, some of the other teachers seemed to manage to keep some kind of order. They had a sort of aura that commanded respect. But poor Andrew, with his mild manner and his posh voice, was a natural target for the young thugs who tyrannised the rest of the class in this urban jungle. Some of the girls, with their snide malice, could be even worse. He could explain, he could encourage, he could sympathise. But he could not keep order.

Nevertheless, he still had some vestige of self respect. Some things had to be faced head on. With a sudden gesture, he whipped round to confront his unruly class. It was as he had expected. Little Ryan was in tears. Somebody had been pinching, or punching him, or worse. Ryan was just the sort of child to attract the malevolent attention of the bullies. He was small, gentle, bad at sports and … horrors … known to be fond of classical music. Andrew spotted at once who the guilty parties were. The oversized Callum with his tiny brain and incipient moustache, and his girlfriend; the more intelligent Chloe who did the thinking for him. He had privately christened them the Macbeths.

Andrew stared fixedly at the offending couple. They giggled offensively.

"I'm reporting you both to the Head Teacher," he snapped.

He would try to get them excluded from school for at least a week. Even that mild, though public, punishment might not be approved by the timid Mrs Akure. Nobody was ever expelled permanently from Saint Cassian's. There was no more degraded school to sink to.

"We didn't do nothing," grumbled the brutish Callum.

"It's against our human rights," commented the more astute Chloe. "There's a new law about that. You could get sent to prison."

Andrew was shocked to see the naked hatred in their young faces. He dismissed the class as soon as the bell rang and walked pensively home to De Beauvoir Square across London Fields. He wondered whether he should give up teaching. There was no real evil in these ruffians, of course, since everyone was born in the image of God. But he wasn't doing them any good. The daily confrontations were bad for his own nerves, too. Perhaps he could retrain as a librarian. He liked the idea of quiet hours spent cataloguing shelves of books. They wouldn't answer back.

Next day, Andrew was not surprised to hear that Mrs Akure had declined to exclude the troublesome pair. She lived in fear of offending the Governors. Callum and Chloe were back in their usual places, grinning at him with looks of gloating glee. They had gathered beside them, in support, some of the other overgrown pupils; boys and girls bulging with testosterone more suitable, in Andrew's private opinion, to a chain gang hewing rocks in a quarry than to an establishment ostensibly devoted to learning. Little Ryan looked terrified. He knew now that Andrew would be unable to protect him.

That afternoon, Andrew walked back again across the fields. It was getting dark. He hurried on. In London these days you had to be careful. Ahead of him, blocking the path, he saw a small group of young people. To his surprise, they consisted of Callum and Chloe with a few of their cronies from school.

"Good evening, Mr Thwaites," said Chloe pertly.

"Good evening," replied Andrew, with a slight sinking of the heart. "What are you doing here?"

"We was waiting for you," replied Callum.

"I'm afraid I'm in a hurry," said Andrew, this unexpected meeting was not a pleasant experience. He wanted to get home to tea. There were jam doughnuts.

"We've got a bone to pick with you," continued Callum.

"My Dad knows a solicitor," said Chloe with a smirk. "He wants to take up my case. He says I've been victimised, and we'll get damages out of you."

"Don't be silly," said Andrew, forcing a smile. He must appear cool, at all costs. These were only big children. But inwardly he felt tempted to panic.

The gang, for that was how Andrew thought of them now, had gathered menacingly around him. The lights had gone on around the edge of the fields. But here, in the grassy centre, it was now almost dark.

"Ever heard of Saint Cassian, Mr Thwaites?" asked Chloe.

"Of course. He gives his name to our school. My patron saint, in fact."

"Know what happened to him?"

"He was a schoolmaster, wasn't he? And a Christian martyr."

"Do you know how he died, sir?"

"I'm not sure that I do."

"Hacked to death by his own pupils," riposted Chloe gleefully. "I've been reading it up. They used their pens. Little pagans they must have been."

Andrew was shocked to see that the children had brought out their biro pens and were flourishing them in front of his eyes.

"You won't get far with those," he said dismissively. It was only a silly joke, he thought. He must hang on to that.

Callum pressed a tiny catch on his pen and the others did the same. To Andrew's astonishment, small, sharp knives protruded from the ends.

"It's the latest gimmick," explained Chloe happily. "Just arrived from the States."

They had only meant to frighten and humiliate him. But Andrew's sudden expression of terror somehow touched a feral nerve. He just had time for one last feeling of despair, a black glimpse into the pit where there was no God.

Callum struck the first blow, well aimed at the heart. Andrew's bleeding body was found shortly afterwards. They took him to Homerton Hospital, not far away. He was pronounced dead on arrival.

The police made an investigation. But nobody gave them any information. And the victim did not fall into one of the specially vulnerable categories which interest the media. No prosecution was ever brought.

The head teacher spoke movingly at Andrew's funeral. It

was well attended.

The school has been renamed. It is now called Saint Jude's after the patron saint of hopeless cases and lost causes, though that is not emphasised in public.

Something Understood

Joshua Gillespie was an impatient man by nature. He had even started life by being born slightly prematurely. At the wheel of his Ferrari, he had been known to honk rather rudely at slower drivers. This constitutional inability to tolerate obstruction had contributed to the breakdown of several relationships. Now, in his early forties, he was footloose and fancy free once again, though not without some enjoyable objects of diversion. Socialite and bon viveur, with a practised eye for the main chance, he earned a good living as editor for the society gossip pages of a big English daily newspaper. He was in Venice now for the wedding of the year, the flamboyant nuptials of the Duke of Catanzaro and Ellie Southwold, the Hollywood starlet. He was, of course, staying at the Cipriani. One needed to rub shoulders with the rich and famous, and the paper generously recognised that. It was a worldly life, but then Joshua Gillespie was a worldly man.

He was flying home that afternoon, but he had some three hours to kill before then. Venice was not a bad place to do so. Joshua suddenly remembered that he had never been inside the Cathedral of Saint Mark's, though he had spent many hours in Harry's Bar and on the Lido. This was surely an opportunity to "do" the great Byzantine-style Basilica. Not that Joshua was a great man for church-going, though he found funerals more fun than weddings. He liked to think that he had vaguely spiritual feelings, especially when drunk, but he had never quite been able to swallow all that business about Jesus Christ being the son of God. Besides, sermons always went on too long and made him want to cough. But San Marco was surely rather special.

On arriving in the Piazza and brushing off the pigeons, who seemed to have designs on his nice grey suit, Joshua was annoyed to find a long queue of patient sightseers waiting to secure admission to the Basilica. He was not accustomed to waiting in queues and he did not have the time. There were two doors for those going in and one for those coming out. Joshua boldly presented himself at the exit door and made as if to enter. Not surprisingly, his way was brusquely barred by a uniformed attendant who put out an arm with a majestic gesture worthy of a medieval Doge. Joshua scowled. This was not how they treated him at the Ritz, or the George Cinq.

He tried to argue, but his Italian was not up to it. He even put his hand into his pocket, as if to offer a bribe. Italy was surely a great country for bribes. But the flunkey dismissed the idea with a lordly wave of disapproval. A neighbouring party of Estonians started to snigger. For once in his charmed life, Joshua Gillespie began to feel somewhat at a loss. Then he had an inspiration.

"Voglio pregare," he hissed. "Orazione urgente."

He made it sound as if he expected a heart attack and needed to make an emergency act of contrition in order to avoid the fires of hell. The doorman was clearly impressed.

"To pray," he repeated in almost perfect English. "Why did you not say so before, sir? Go round to the left and you can enter by the little door reserved for those who come to make an act of penitence and attend Mass."

Joshua thanked him and made his way round to the modest entrance he had mentioned. There he had no difficulty in securing immediate admission. With a purr of satisfaction, he found himself kneeling in a pew, looking up at the great image of Christ In Majesty. He had promised to pray, so he must do so now.

He was not used to praying and it did not come easily. Besides, he felt uncomfortable on his knees. So he sat back and just gave himself up to the thoughts that came into his head. He hardly noticed the throng of noisy tourists. There was something quite magical about the great dim Basilica with all its flickering lights and golden frescoes. You couldn't help being carried away by the atmosphere of spirituality. For once, Joshua forgot his usual concerns, the crippling mortgage on his mansion flat behind Claridge's, his mother's querulous phone calls from Edinburgh, his own thinning hair. There was something about this cathedral that seemed to grip him with its immense power. You didn't have to worry about whether you believed in Jesus Christ the Son Of God. All you had to do was to surrender to this huge presence, to the Everlasting Arms, to the notion of a planned creation that would see you through to the end, if you would only allow it to do so.

Joshua was aroused by the tinkle of a bell in one of the side chapels. A priest was saying Mass. He moved over to the chapel. The priest was offering Communion.

Joshua suddenly felt an urge to join the faithful who were coming up to the altar to receive the host and drink from the chalice. Did it really matter whether or not this was the body and blood of Christ, as the church claimed? It was at least an opportunity to attempt union with the Divine. The only opportunity he had ever had. Joshua succumbed to the longing, the hunger. Meekly he joined the small queue of communicants and moved forward behind the others.

With reverence, he returned to his seat. From now on, he thought, he would be a changed man. He would give up his silly job and his frivolous lifestyle. He would even abandon alcohol. He would eat sparingly and bite back the witty, malicious comments that came so easily to his lips. He knew of a monastery in the north of England. A Bavarian nobleman, whom he had once interviewed, had sent one of his sons there to be discreetly dried out. The monks were compassionate men of the world. Joshua would present himself there. He would ask to stay in the monastery and share the modest meals of the brethren. He would rise each day well before dawn, in order to attend the numerous daily services. He would perform manual work for the benefit of the community. He drew the line at mucking out the pigs, but he could certainly mow the lawns. He would go to bed early, exhausted and sober, and sleep like a baby. Above all, he would enjoy the delicious and unusual luxury of possessing a good conscience. Many years later, he would achieve a saintly death with the grieving community around his bedside, like an edifying scene by Fra Angelico. It was a delightful prospect.

With a new spring in his legs, Joshua joined the tourists flocking out into the piazza. With the sudden access of emotion, he suddenly felt tired. That was hardly surprising. A complete change of lifestyle would be enough to exhaust anyone. He decided to pop into Florians for a little sit down. Mimsy Saxe-Coburg was lolling in the corner with a couple of daiquiris, but he pretended not to see her. He was putting aside malicious gossip forever. The waiter approached. Joshua wanted to order something very modest, in keeping with his new austerity policy. Perhaps a small plain wafer and a cup of weak tea. To his disappointment, he heard himself asking for one of those huge chocolate dishes laced with mountains of cream. He was very partial to chocolate, and he liked cream too.

Worse was to come. The sight of Mimsy's opulent and well-explored torso reminded him of his programme for the following evening in London. He couldn't help thinking of that come-to-bed smile, those soft lips, the long smooth legs, the unflawed skin so soft to the touch.

It was all going to be the most dreadful effort.

The Treasure

Elspeth Macgregor was an absolute treasure. Everyone in the Hospital agreed on that. She had worked there for many years and had become something of an institution. At first she might look a bit dour, with her big spectacles, buttoned-down mouth and straggly grey hair. She was thought to derive from some remote island in the Hebrides where they believed you went straight to hell if you smoked a cigarette on a Sunday. But when you got to know her better, and especially when trouble loomed, you realised that nurse Macgregor had a warm heart, as well as a capable pair of hands.

No wonder she was greatly valued. Not only was she content to work in the geriatric ward, one of the least popular in the hospital since it involved prolonged close contact with incontinent and crotchety aged patients, but, in addition, she was happy to take on night duties; another unpopular chore with the younger nurses who valued their social life. It was assumed by the administration that nurse Macgregor's willingness to shoulder these responsibilities derived from a highly developed sense of duty to the community, but the reality was rather more personal. The truth was that, in the lonely midnight hours, as sister in charge of the large geriatric ward, with only a couple of young probationary nurses to help her, Elspeth Macgregor felt herself to be monarch of all she surveyed. At this time of the night, there were no tiresome consultants or administrators to interfere. The slumbering, toothless ancients were at her mercy. She enjoyed that feeling – the responsibility, the need for sudden decisions, the sensation of power over life and death.

The geriatric ward was one of the success stories of the hospital. The patients looked relatively clean, in spite of their disabilities, and the atmosphere was friendly. Of course, some of them died from time to time. That was only to be expected with patients of that age. It was just as well, thought Mr Rivers, the Chief Administrator. He was a tall, melancholy man who had once tried in vain for the Foreign Office. This regular pull-through among the elderly, as he put it, enabled fresh patients to be frequently introduced into the ward, thus cutting down the waiting lists to the satisfaction of the men from the Ministry. Death, one could hardy deny, was a valuable ally at the cutting edge. One hardly wanted the ward to be clogged with too many patients in a state of prolonged, and often articulate, dissolution. Mr Rivers could cope with the comatose, but he did not relish the complainers.

On this particular evening, nurse Macgregor stalked her ward as usual, examining each patient with her customary care. They were supposed to be sleeping, and most of them were. She believed in dishing out sleeping tablets where these seemed necessary. It was like a spaceship in the dimly lighted ward, thought Elspeth. Outside, the night lights of the great city twinkled. They might have been cruising through the galaxies with herself at the helm. Caring for patients at night might seem a soft option, but it called for special qualities. Most of the deaths seemed to occur at that vulnerable point in the human cycle, shortly before dawn. You needed to be constantly on the watch.

At the other end of the long ward, Elspeth noted, her new assistant was bending over a patient. She had only been with Geriatrics for a short time, but already she had cottoned on to the routine and seemed to be taking a keen interest. Too keen perhaps, thought nurse Macgregor. She was used to trouble from young reformers who tried to change her well-tried methods. Up till now, she had managed to get rid of them, preferably to Uro-Genitary. This one might prove trickier to shift. There was an unpleasantly stubborn look in those youthful blue eyes. Nurse Macgregor gave one of her formidable snorts which had tamed more than one famous consultant.

She continued her progress down the ward, noting the appearance of the sleeping patients. Old Mr Sylvester was sucking his thumb as usual. He had reverted to second childhood. Perhaps he had never really left it. She had heard that he had once been on the stage, a funny man, noted for his appearance in pantomimes. That's the end of your japes and jollities, she thought. It was a mixed ward, though for the sake of decency the patients were provided with curtains round their beds. At the farthest end of the room, the one most remote from her prying assistant, the curtains were drawn around poor, miserable Mrs Porlock. Nurse Macgregor peeped in and noted with relief that the venerable sufferer was asleep. So often Mrs Porlock had tried to detain her with innumerable petty complaints. Nurse Macgregor found these hard to bear. Admittedly the woman was in a good deal of chronic pain, relieved only by drugs, but she would be made to realise that this was not an expensive private clinic. When you were nothing but a nuisance to others, you should be made to lie low.

And nurse Macgregor knew just how to achieve that. The great thing was to avoid a silly mistake. Nurses had been caught before now, using syringes or altering the drugs. That could all be traced at the post-mortem these days. Simpler methods were best. All you had to do was to put on a pair of gloves and use one of the pillows. Of course, the patient's DNA would be on the pillows. That was where you expected it to be. You didn't have to exert much pressure, certainly not enough to leave bruising. Breathing was so feeble in these very old people, life so tenuous. It didn't take much to stop it altogether and let them go to heaven, as the Minister had explained during her childhood.

Mrs Porlock went quietly. Just a sad little gurgle and then silence. Nurse Macgregor's strong hands had done the trick with the minimum of effort. She stuffed her gloves away into her capacious pockets, having already smoothed down the pillows. With a small smile of satisfaction, she passed through the curtains into the body of the ward. She would allow her pushy assistant to discover the body in due course. Then nurse Macgregor could institute the usual procedure, the emergency call for the doctor on duty, followed by a summons to the porters to take the body away to the mortuary. Everything should be cleared away by the time the day staff came on. One must not upset the other patients.

Miss Macgregor felt sure that she had done another good job. Poor old Mrs Porlock had been liberated from her pain. She had been spared possible weeks of suffering and apprehension. Death had been almost instantaneous, bestowed with the minimum of fuss. Now the bed would be vacated for a new patient. Another name to be struck off the waiting list. It was just what Mr Rivers, the Chief Administrator, would have wished her to do, had he been officially consulted. But that was not acceptable as yet, so you had to use your own judgement. That is exactly what she had done.

How funny, she had been thinking about Mr Rivers and there he was in person, at the other end of the ward, talking to her eager new assistant. You hardly expected the Chief Administrator to visit the Geriatrics in the middle of the night. Elspeth felt sure that her assistant had been making trouble. The girl had that sharp look. Nurse Macgregor saw the assistant pointing her out. With them were a man and a woman, both in dark clothes. What on earth were they doing? What could it all be about?

The group advanced up the ward towards her.

"Nurse Macgregor?" asked the man.

"Yes."

"Inspector Ottaway and Sergeant Glebe," he said, flourishing a warrant. "We'd like to ask you a few questions."

Elspeth felt strangely unworried. She knew she would be able to explain all. There would be strong support. Everyone at the hospital considered her to be a perfect treasure. Perhaps they would all like a cup of nice strong tea.

Just Friends

The occasion was sad enough, thought Toby, and now it had started to drizzle. He had travelled by train to the suburban station in South London which seemed, from the map, to be nearest to the crematorium. There should have been a short walk across a park. But the grass was poor and fouled by dogs. And the drizzle was now turning to quite heavy rain. Toby wished he had brought his heavy mackintosh. But he had wanted to wear his smart dark overcoat for George's funeral. George, the love of his life, to whom he had never felt able to speak of love.

He could see now his friend's open, youthful face as it had been when they first met in the quadrangle at Oxford. They were both eighteen, coming up to Oxford, to the same college, for the first time. It was a hearty, sporting college where men were manly and played rugger. For one golden year, they had shared digs together down the Cowley Road. George had been one of the games-playing majority. Toby had taken up with the acting crowd. He had played Rosencrantz in a once memorable *Hamlet*. But there was always something between them. Something unspoken and, of course, never acted upon. That was the pity of it, thought

Toby, as he walked across the park, becoming increasingly sodden.

Toby hated funerals at a crematorium. But hardly anyone now had a church where they worshipped regularly. At least there was to be a short service before the coffin shot through to the flames on those ghastly rollers. Staring at the coffin, Toby thought of George's body, not sapped by drink and late nights as it was now, but in its youthful strength and athletic beauty, as it had once been. Toby had occasionally seen George naked in those distant days. They had travelled to France together long ago, and done a lot of swimming at La Ciotat. But he had never touched that body, as he had longed to do. In those days of penal sanctions, that would have been unthinkable. One ill-judged move could have wrecked that precious friendship.

Neither man had ever married, but their lives had taken different directions. Toby, longing for a true partner, had spent many years trying to find one. There had been the pretty boy from Hong Kong, the boy with the long eyelashes from Penang, the tough young fellow with the weird accent from Glasgow. None of them had really fulfilled his need. It was not that any of them had actually taken him for a ride. He had never been desperate enough to pick up the truly heartless. But they had treated him, at best, as a kindly uncle with an open purse. He did not blame them. The penniless young had to make the best use of their only assets. At the end of the day, he had always been left alone.

He often dreamed of the life he might have enjoyed with George. They could have pooled their incomes to buy a decent house. They would have given little dinner parties, gone on wonderful holidays together. They would have shared a bedroom, given each other a cuddle in the night. Above all, there would have been a meeting of their two minds, somebody to share the joys and sorrows of the long pilgrimage.

But that was nonsense, thought Toby as he padded through the now drenching rain. He had reached the main gate to the crematorium now, but there was still some way to reach the red brick building itself on the other side of the manicured lawn. George had always been rigidly heterosexual. That had been clear from the start. He had often spoken to Toby about his various girlfriends, though Toby had never actually met them. George's principal partner, he understood, was a mature widow called Emily. At least he had taken up with her in his later years. He looked forward to encountering Emily after the funeral and swapping reminiscences of the dead man they had both loved. Emily could tell him a lot. She had shared her holidays with George, and he often stayed at her cottage in Wiltshire.

A car stopped. The driver offered him a lift to the crematorium which Toby was glad to accept. There were two other men in the back seat. They were all going to the same funeral service. It turned out that they were regulars at the same bar in the same pub. They met there nearly every night, and so did George. They had obviously spent many hours chatting and drinking with George but, even so, they did not seem to know a great deal about him. Saloon bar conversation, thought Toby, must be ideal for those who did not wish to expose surface. In his solitude, when Emily was elsewhere, George must have been driven to the hearty fellowship of the pub and to the whisky and cigarettes which had ruined his health and shortened his life.

The crematorium chapel was not very full. Toby greeted George's two sisters, Lucy and Holly, and their husbands, all of whom he had met. There were a few other people, somebody who had been at school with George and a couple who proved to be his neighbours. The men from the pub sat near the front and motioned to Toby to join them. He found himself sitting next to a warmly dressed middle-aged woman.

"I'm Emily," she whispered. "You must be Toby. I've heard a lot about you."

"Yes. And I've heard a lot about you, too."

"We must have a good talk. Lucy has invited us all back for tea afterwards."

After the sad little ceremony, they adjourned to the sister's house. The few other guests seemed quite cheerful. Toby wondered whether any of them secretly shared his sense of desolation. He and Emily secured a quiet corner in which to talk.

"You were at Oxford with George, weren't you?" she said. "He often used to talk about those days. I think they must have been his happiest times."

"Wasn't he happy later?" replied Toby.

"He enjoyed himself sometimes. It's not quite the same as being happy. As you may remember, George didn't give much away."

"I'm sure that you meant a lot to him," said Toby politely.

Emily seemed mildly surprised by this remark.

"Well, I don't really know. George was a regular old bachelor at heart, I always thought."

"You went on holidays with him.

"Oh yes. George hated travelling alone, and it's not much

fun for a single woman either. Besides, on these cruises, you have to pay extra if you're not willing to share a cabin."

"But I suppose he came to stay with you in Wiltshire."

"From time to time. George wasn't really a country person, you know. I could see him getting bored. He liked me to stay in his London flat, but I couldn't take much of that. The place is a proper pigsty.

"You must miss him very much," said Toby, continuing to probe. Again Emily gave him that unexpected look of surprise.

"Won't we all?" she replied casually. "George was always such good company. One of my more intelligent friends. But I think you probably were more important to him than I was."

Now it was Toby's turn to look surprised. He had assumed that Emily was a kind of partner to George. But obviously she wasn't, and never had been. They were just friends, perhaps a useful element in George's heterosexual façade. If façade it was.

So George might perhaps have been with him all along. They could have shared a life together. George would never have made the first move. But Toby could. He remembered that night in Avignon, when they arrived late at the hostel and had to share a bed. He could have held George's young body in his arms all that night.

But he had not dared. It seemed too great, the risk of losing him altogether. That was just what he had done now.

Toby made his excuses and trudged out into the rain. Emily felt sorry for the lonely old boy. She had expected something more from George's brilliant friend.

Death in Moscow

Humphrey Bannister was dying. He had expected to die in Somerset, in Clumber, the old family home he had been due to inherit on his mother's death. He had envisaged himself ambling among the chestnut woods, feeding the ponies in the paddock, dozing in his father's library. But that was not to be. It seemed to be strange to end his life in Moscow in this small apartment in a high-rise block looking down over the frozen river. The women came in twice a day to see to his needs. He could not have managed otherwise.

Angela had left years ago and taken the children with her. He had heard that she had re-married and was living in Toronto. The boys had changed their names. He could not blame them. His own name was one of infamy. He was notorious throughout the world as the British spy who had defected to the Russians in the most dangerous phase of the Cold War. His whole family had suffered terribly as a result. His parents had been ostracised by their neighbours. His brother had been obliged to leave the Navy. And he had never really taken to life in Moscow, with its chilly winters and hectic summers. The place had improved a little with the collapse of Communism, but not all that much.

Had it all been worth it? He sometimes wondered. When he had fled, he had known intellectually that he would never see England again, but he had not taken that in emotionally. He often thought of his home country now, with all the frustrated longing of an exile. He dreamed sometimes of the daffodils in Saint James' Park, Mozart at Glyndebourne on a summer evening, a night with the climbers at Wasdale Head. Foolishly sentimental of course, but you got like that when there wasn't much time left.

He had long ago reconciled himself to being generally regarded as a vile traitor. That was part of the deal. They had made that clear to him from the start. There was no hope that his true motive could ever be made public. It would make the Russians look foolish, and that was something the British Government could not afford to do. He had not even been allowed to tell Angela. That seemed cruel, but she tended to talk too much after her third whisky. He would take the secret with him to the grave. Did that really matter? In the end, the only judgement worth having was one's own.

It seemed but only yesterday that he had been summoned to see Molyneux at that quiet office in Ennismore Gardens. Molyneux seemed like an old-fashioned family solicitor, but Humphrey knew at once that he was the real thing: a master of spies.

"We've got a rather special mission for you, Bannister," the older man had said, motioning him to an easy chair. "But first you must give me your solemn promise that you will keep this entirely to yourself. To describe this as top secret would be something of an understatement."

Humphrey had readily agreed. As a promising, but still only middle-rank official in the Foreign Office, he was used to practising discretion.

"As you know," Molyneux had continued, puffing at his pipe, "we live in a highly dangerous world. There exists a state of very considerable suspicion between ourselves and our Free World allies on the one hand, and the Soviets on the other. We can't let that continue, at least in its present state of intensity. One side could make a false move, the other might feel obliged to react, and we could be in for a Third World War, a nuclear conflict this time that might destroy life on the planet. We have an obligation to mankind to take what steps we can to avoid that. There has been some serious thinking about that at the very top of Government."

"I don't see where I come in," Humphrey had said.

"You will," Molyneux had snapped, impatient of interruption. Humphrey had remembered every detail of their conversation to this day. "Our assessment is that the Soviet Union do not really present an immediate threat to us at the present time. They still make noises about exporting Communism worldwide and promoting international revolution. But that has become something of a pose. The truth is that they are desperately occupied, trying to keep down their satellites in Eastern Europe and making their rickety economy work. They've got more than enough on their plate as it is. But the danger is that they may misread our intentions in the west. If they thought we were about to attack them, they might launch a strike, so as to get in first. That would be a terribly tragic misunderstanding. As you know, Stalin put the Kremlin into a state of paranoia and they see themselves as surrounded by enemies. They have never recovered from Stalin's dreadful misreading of Hitler's intentions in 1943, and they still fear it might all happen again."

"That isn't helped by the bellicose statements of some of our Cold War warriors," pointed out Humphrey. "Especially in the States."

"Agreed. We've got to get away from words. The problem is to find some way of assuring the Kremlin that they can trust our peaceful intentions. It has to be done by an emissary they will really believe, not some overt diplomat, or politician. The job is to show them that we genuinely want peace, so we have hit upon a plan. We're going to send someone who will pretend to be a communist sympathiser, fleeing from people like me, joining the Russians because he has been on their side all along and is bringing them valuable secrets. Once they have accepted him as a trusted adviser, he will be perfectly placed to carry out his mission."

"Ingenious," admitted Humphrey. "But what sane man, or woman for that matter, would want to live with the odium of appearing to be a Russian spy?"

"A very courageous patriot," countered Molyneux simply, "who cared about the future of the world."

"It would be so awkward when he came home." He imagined the unpleasantness at the club.

"That will not arise. He won't be coming home."

"Poor sod. Why are you telling me all this?" But he knew.

"We want you to do it."

"Why me of all people?"

"You're the best we have. We've looked very carefully

through the files. You are highly intelligent and promising. You had an extreme left wing background at Cambridge."

"Only to annoy my family."

"They won't know that. You also have an unstable streak, which would be just right for the role. I'm thinking of that bust up in a bar in Tokyo."

"I was drunk."

"Perfect. Will you do it?"

"I shall have to think."

"Very well, Bannister. We'll give you twenty-four hours. But don't talk to anyone. Not even your wife.

In the end, he had agreed. The bizarre proposition had appealed to his vanity, to his underlying belief that life was given us for some kind of purpose, and perhaps to his anarchic sense of humour. Molyneux had explained the details. The whole thing had to be made convincing enough to deceive some sharp minds on both sides of the divide. Humphrey would be supplied with relatively harmless secrets to offer to the Russians. He was to present himself to the Russian Embassy in London as a high-minded potential agent, acting for ideological motives. His early background would support that. Then an incident would be staged. In Britain, he would find himself in danger of discovery. He would have to ask the Soviet Union for emergency asylum. They couldn't refuse, and in Moscow he would be welcomed. The British would disown him, of course, and threaten prosecution if they ever laid hands on him. He would be branded irreparably as a traitor.

"Let us be quite clear about that," Molyneux had said. "We shan't be able to do anything to help you. You will be out on your own, Bannister."

Yes indeed, thought Humphrey now, so many years later. He had been out on his own for half a lifetime. But he had helped to calm the Kremlin, even in the Cuban Missile Crisis where they had enjoyed the huge advantage over the Americans of not having to respond to public opinion. The Cold War had never escalated into nuclear war, once so greatly feared on both sides. Now it was supposed to be over.

Something special was supposed to happen today. He tried to recall. Memory, once so sharp when he had secured his First in history, was unreliable these days. Then he remembered. His nephew in England was sending out a doctor to see him, an eminent heart surgeon. It was too late, of course, but he would go through the motions.

Donald Lamsley duly appeared, oozing professional competence and unflappable self-control. The Russian authorities had made no difficulties. His credentials were in order and, in any case, things were much easier now. All they wanted of Humphrey Bannister was an unobtrusive death.

"It's awfully hot in here," remarked Lamsley after the examination was over and he had produced some new pills which Humphrey was to take at once.

"That's the central heating, always so fierce. One thing I can't abide about the Russian winter is … the heat," laughed Humphrey.

"Is there anywhere else we can go?" murmured Lamsley.

"Let's pop up to the roof terrace. I can just about manage to totter up there. We'll have to be well muffled up."

Humphrey had taken the point at once. Lamsley wanted to tell him something, out of reach of the ubiquitous listening devices which the Russians had never abandoned. He must have been briefed by the Embassy.

The view from the chilly terrace encompassed much of central Moscow, but Lamsley didn't seem to notice.

"I can't do much for you professionally at this stage," he said quietly. "You will know that already. I was mainly sent to bring you this." He handed over a small black box. Humphrey opened it cautiously. It contained the ribbon of a decoration to be hung round the neck, together with a little note of explanation.

"The GCVO," continued Lamsley. "Knight Grand Cross of the Royal Victorian Order. The only British Order that can be awarded without publicity. As you may remember, it is a personal gift of the Sovereign. She sends you her very personal good wishes too."

Humphrey's eyes brimmed suddenly with tears. He thought of Angela and his lost boys; of his mother in the woods at Clumber.

"This has to be strictly between the two of us," continued Lamsley.

"I'll only wear it in the bath. Perhaps you brought the wrong Order for that."

The decoration gimmick had worked well, thought Lamsley. It shouldn't take long now with the new drugs. He would stay in Moscow for the necessary day or two, then ask to examine the body. He had strict instructions to bring the medal home. They didn't want any fuss.

The Night Auditor

It was the last evening of the cruise. Ruth Kesselring had carefully locked and labelled her suitcase and placed it outside her stateroom door, in accordance with the instructions. It would be collected during the night and she would see it again in the morning on the quayside at Fort Lauderdale, Florida. She had kept out enough clothes to wear the next day and a small overnight bag. There was something psychologically soothing about being reduced to so little, like an ascetic in a hermit's cell. Next morning there would be no need for the usual agonising decision about what to wear. Ruth had never had cause to worry much about big issues, so she tended to fret about little things.

That night, she suspected, she would not sleep well. It was often like that when she had to be up early the next day. You had to vacate the cabin by eight-thirty. And she never entirely trusted her travelling alarm clock. There was so much to think about. Going over the events of the last fortnight when she had cruised the Caribbean. Making sure that everything was in order for the next day, which was bound to be a busy one. She was due to fly directly from Miami to Boston. Picking up her car at the airport, she would drive to Pleasant Vale near Lexington, Mass, to the apartment above the Emerson bookshop which she had shared with Naomi for the past eighteen years. But, this time, Naomi would not be there.

Looking back, she could see that the skids had been under their relationship for some time. Naomi had started going out with younger women. There had been that designing little bitch from Vasser and several others, like the minx with the squint. Naomi, too, had taken to giving Ruth strange disconcerting glances. That was the trouble about getting to know another human being so well. You could read their thoughts, and sometimes that could be painful. Ruth had always been in the habit of holding forth at some length about literature and politics. When a subject interested her, she liked to share it. In the old days, Naomi would simply have smiled at these flights of eloquence, but now she often looked plainly bored. Ruth had seen it coming.

But, when it did, the shock was appalling, all the same.

Naomi, one spring evening, had poured out for Ruth her usual Bourbon and water and then calmly informed her that she had sold the bookshop. The apartment would go too, but Ruth could stay there for a few weeks until she had found somewhere else. Naomi herself would be moving to California in search of the sun.

"Who with?" gasped Ruth, stilled stunned.

"That's my affair, honey."

For the first time, Ruth noticed what long, cruel nails her friend had. Like the talons on a bird of prey.

"What's going to happen to me?" she asked miserably.

"That's up to you, dear. Come on, Ruth baby, don't look so glum. We've had a good run for our money. My money in fact. It was bound to end some time."

Ruth had thought it would be for life. That was certainly the impression Naomi had given her when they happened to sit next to each other at the Philharmonic. There had been that delicate pressure on her hand, possibly casual but perhaps infinitely exciting, during that long piece by Mahler. Even today she could not hear Mahler without emotion.

From then on, Ruth had not had to do a lot of thinking for herself. It was Naomi's family money that bought the bookshop and the apartment, taking the profits and paying the expenses to this day. From the whole operation, Ruth had received nothing but a little pocket money. That hadn't seemed to matter. Naomi had her family food-chain behind her, while Ruth's father had only been a Professor of Moral Philosophy at Harvard.

Now, at forty-one, Ruth found herself ditched, friendless, penniless, homeless and unemployed. She had to get out of the apartment, and she didn't want to work in the bookshop even if the new owners were willing to take her on. The place was too full of memories. She remembered so many of those private jokes with Naomi. That new assistant who stacked a copy of *She Stoops to Conquer* under the heading of 'Gymnastics'. The dear old State Senator who always made straight for 'Erotics' which he pronounced 'Exotica'. There had been so much to savour in their little world together.

She had pleaded, of course, even sobbed and screamed. But that had proved totally counter-productive. It only hardened the bleak, dark look in Naomi's big eyes. Ruth soon realised that there could be no appeal. At least she had her degree in literature and her secretarial training. She would leave Pleasant Vale. It should not be too difficult to find a job and a small apartment in Boston. She would remain in New England, of course. Middle America did not appeal. She knew London and Paris far better than the United States.

"I'm sorry about this, Ruth," Naomi had said at the end, when the taxi was waiting at the door and there would be no time for a last minute reprieve. "I really am, honey. But that's the way the cookie crumbles. I'm six years older than you, and not getting any younger. I owe it to myself to make hay while the sun shines. We'll always be buddies, won't we? We did have some fabulous times."

Ruth had been too upset to speak. Naomi had kissed her on the lips for the last time. Then she was gone and Ruth, stunned with grief, had heard the taxi drive away.

Naomi had left her some money, so there was no immediate hurry about getting a job. She sought resolutely to make herself independent. She had seen an advertisement for a Personal Assertiveness Course and thought that might help. As might have been expected, the other students looked like fragile weaklings. But this could not be said of Amanda, the course director, who seemed to have developed personal assertiveness into a fine art. One evening she invited the still moping Ruth to a pasta and confession session in her snazzy modern penthouse apartment. Then she revealed that her day job was in a vibrant Boston law firm.

"We could help you, Ruth," she said enthusiastically after the latter had poured out her troubles. "My firm specialises in personal claims, and we have had some remarkable successes. At first sight, it looks to me as if we could get you a heap of dough out of Naomi. There are all those years when you weren't paid a salary. Then you helped to build up the business. You deserve a hefty slice of the selling price. Besides, you had a relationship, didn't you? That qualifies you for palimony payments. And you had a ghastly shock when the bitch quit. We'll sue for emotional trauma and psychological anguish."

"I couldn't afford it," gasped poor Ruth.

"No need to worry about that, darling. We operate on a no-win, no-pay basis. If Naomi lives in San Diego now, we'll clobber her under Californian law. I know they call us ambulance-chasers. But we do offer a genuine service to the community."

In the end, after a third Bourbon, Ruth had agreed. She still felt deep bitterness towards Naomi; and Amanda's personal assertiveness was just impossible to resist. While proceedings were set in motion, Amanda had suggested that she take this cruise. A little luxurious break would do her the world of good. Amanda would make the booking for her. With Naomi's money, she could afford an upper-deck stateroom with a verandah. What a chance of meeting new people!

But she hadn't met new people. Or, at least, not anyone she would ever wish to see again. At her table there were only that voluble English couple who were so against the Pentagon, that spooky Swedish widower who kept trying to rub his foot against hers, and the jovial young Greek doctor who seemed far too friendly with the curly haired chorus boy.

RICHARD PARSONS

The cruise had been rather a misery. Trying to read on the sun deck had given her sunburn and she wasn't any good at deck games. The girl in the beauty parlour had made a mess of her hair and she detested roulette. Nor had she much enjoyed the ports they visited so briefly. She found Jamaica too crowded, Trinidad too hot, and Barbados too British. She would be glad to come home to Massachusetts where they didn't shout so much.

Ruth had tried to be careful about money, but she knew the ship would be billing her for a few small items. There would be charges for the shore excursions, the bar drinks and the bottle of scent for Bessie the cleaner. It had been explained that accounts would be drawn up that evening, while the passengers slept, by an official picturesquely described as the Night Auditor. The final statement would be slipped under her door some time before dawn.

She must have been thinking about the Night Auditor as she dropped, at last, into a fitful slumber. That explained her dreadful nightmare. She was standing before the Night Auditor. He had made up her final account, a detailed analysis of her behaviour over a lifetime. It was the Great Judge himself, flanked by the hooded figure of the Angle of Death, her terrifying escort. Ruth's sins and omissions flashed before her eyes. The tea party where she had been so rude to Uncle Daniel, the almond croissant she had thoughtlessly pinched from a stall on Cape Cod, the private place in her body she had allowed that impudent boy to explore. Above all, she remembered that legal action she had begun against poor, misguided Naomi. The Night Auditor shook his head when he heard of that. It would weigh against her in the Final Judgement.

RODE HE ON BARBARY?

Ruth woke with a scream. The Belgian couple next door banged on the wall. A thin sliver of paper had been slipped under the door. She opened it, trembling. What was the verdict of the Night Auditor? Eternal damnation? No, just a few dollars to be paid by credit card. Of one thing, Ruth was quite clear. As soon as she got home, she would ring that pushy Amanda to cancel the whole of her claim against Naomi. Let the poor woman loll undisturbed on her Pacific beach. It was the only possible way to make her peace.

Later, as they were leaving the ship, Ruth noticed at the Reception Desk a youthful girl who looked very unsure of herself. Somebody's young sister perhaps. She asked the Danish Chief Purser who this might be.

"That, Madam," came the reply, "is the Night Auditor."

The Vladimirka Road

It's not really a road, more of a great wide dirt track made by the passage of thousands of horses and carts. It stretches across the dark green plains towards distant, ever-greener forests. Unalterably flat, ineffably tedious, this landscape. Above all, the scudding white clouds of our Russian skies.

Natasha is to follow me in a few weeks time, once we are settled, with some of the other wives. I begged her to stay in Saint Petersburg, to go to balls, to be happy, to forget me for ever. But I knew all along that she would never agree to that. Her company will be the one thing I have left to live for in the wilderness. It was her locket that I wore against my heart when I served with old Kutusov at Borodino, fighting for the country fourteen years ago. I was young then, more fitted than I am now for the physical ordeals ahead.

They are making us march all the way. I hope to God that my boots will last out. Also that they will allow Natasha and the other ladies to ride in a carriage, or at least a cart. She is, after all, still a Princess.

Ours was such a pathetic rebellion. More of a

demonstration really. We were badly mistaken in the Grand Duke Constantine. We thought he would lead us, but he failed us and opted for a quiet life. All we did was to parade on the Senate Square, though admittedly we refused to disperse. Then the new Tsar Nicholas brought up his artillery to break us up with gunfire. Can you imagine it? The Tsar himself ordering the Army to fire on the Pavlosky Guards! Those who tried to flee were drowned as the gunfire smashed the ice on the Neva. I felt so terrible for my poor, brave men who had trusted and followed me to this disaster.

In the Peter and Paul Fortress they said I was lucky not to be hanged. They even botched the hangings, you know. At the execution the ropes broke. Poor Russia, she cannot even hang decently. The Tsar himself questioned me, as he questioned many other Guards officers. I think he spared my life because I had served his brother and accompanied him to Paris and Vienna in happier days. Nicholas seemed genuinely interested in trying to find out what my motives had been. After all, I had great estates, an ancient name, a fine position in society. I was hardly a typical revolutionary. I did not belong to the Society of the South, or even to the less extreme Society of the North. I was mild by nature and I had much to lose.

I explained to the Tsar that my whole attitude had been changed by my friendship in Paris with English and French officers. They had made me believe in the rights of man; the equality of all human beings in the sight of God. I thought the serfs should be freed and each given a small plot of land. There should be a constitutional monarchy along the lines successfully established by the British. It was a mistake for the Tsar to go on trying to rule our huge country through a system of personal absolutism. We were no longer in the Middle Ages. Power must be shared with the respectable classes. We must change the system now while there was still time. If we dallied, it would be too late. The spirit of the French Revolution would submerge us all one day, and we should all be carried away.

"So you wish us to be ruled by our liberated serfs," snapped the Tsar.

I explained patiently that this was not our idea in the Pavlosky Guards where we ourselves were nobleman. The Tsar could be assisted by a real Parliament in which the nobility, the educated classes and the higher bourgeoisie would sit. I tried to show that I was not a rabid revolutionary, and that my political ideas would not seem outrageous in a London club for gentlemen.

The Tsar waved to me to be silent.

"You are not the worst of them, Prince," he said. "Only foolish and misguided. And you have done the State some service in your time. But I cannot have such pernicious prattle on the Nevsky Prospekt. You must join your comrades on the long march east. May God help you!"

"I am a loyal officer, Majesty. I was doing this for the sake of the Monarchy."

The Tsar made an impatient sign and rough hands dragged me away. Now we have already been on the road for some days. My feet are sore and bleeding. I am not sure that I shall make it to the end. And, if I do, what life can possibly lie ahead of us? Will we ever be allowed to return? If so, only perhaps when we are very old and are thought to present no danger.

RODE HE ON BARBARY?

But they themselves are the dangers, the unwise counsellors who have encouraged the Tsar to remain an autocrat. We offered a chance of reform, but it has been rejected. One day our Holy Russia will be engulfed in the flames of revolution, and that will end our entire way of life and perhaps our Religion too.

"Be cheerful, Prince," calls a brother officer, himself a gaunt scarecrow. He cannot eat the peasant food.

"Thank you," I reply gravely. "But in the wilderness, no man is a Prince." Or a woman a Princess, I think to myself, imagining Natasha with her delicate, white hands created by God to play Scarlatti.

At night we lie down beside the road on rough blankets under the stars. We would be frozen to death if it were still mid-winter. I dream of the Bronze Horseman and the Summer Garden.

I have a horror now of the Vladimirka Road. It leads to only one place: Siberia.

Dumping

Hate at first sight would be an accurate description of my relationship with my mother-in-law. Even in appearance we verge on the extreme. I am tall and well-built, if perhaps on the fleshy side, while she is a small mouse-like creature with a sharp tongue and venomous eyes.

We got off to a bad start from the first. Jessica, then my fiancée, had brought me home to be introduced after we got engaged. Our courtship had taken place among the café bars of Soho since we were both studying in Bloomsbury. What a sweet little thing she was! Megan, the ghastly mum, was safely ensconced in a village of slate houses under the Brecon Beacons. Here she reigned supreme over the pork butcher's shop established by Jessica's father, now dead, no doubt as a result of exhaustion. So we had not met before, though I had heard only too much about her.

After a short conversation, I left the sitting room to powder my nose, as Megan quaintly put it. I closed the door and put my ear to the key hole. You can learn quite a lot that way.

"What do you think of my Bobby?" asked Jessica nervously.

"You could do better, dear," replied the old harridan. "Much better."

I was incensed. It was so unfair. I know I do not actually have a job, but I am brilliant in bed, though you could not expect Megan to know that. To add to the injury, when I went back into the room, I could hardly fix the old bitch with one of my steely glares. That would have revealed my little ploy.

Jessica had been brought up under her mother's greasy thumb. During school holidays, she had even been made to work in the shop. No wonder she later became an enthusiastic vegetarian. She only escaped from that narrow Welsh atmosphere when she got to London University. There she had a chance to broaden her horizons and meet interesting people like myself. She was fascinated to hear that I had decided to become a great poet. And she certainly did not share her mother's silly idea that I ought to take on some routine work, just in order to make money to live on. I have explained to her that early rising to go out to work would stultify my creative processes, which often flourish best during the midnight hours. After all, Coleridge wrote his greatest poem in a haze of opium. And Browning never had a job.

We have been ensconced now for some years in married bliss in a cosy home in the north London commuter belt, an area known as a leafy suburb. It does not look at all like a poet's abode, but there is plenty of hot water and it is the inner thoughts that count. Fortunately, Jessica has got a good job at a local bank where she advises the indigent on debt re-phasing. She gets home in good time to prepare our supper, by which time I am usually dressed. I had hoped to take up haute cuisine myself since I am fond of food and need a good deal of it. But I have been diverted by the constant need to polish my poetic gems. I have not, so far, found an editor who wished to publish them, but that surely is only a matter of time.

My one fear is that Jessica might become pregnant and have to take time off work. In the last resort, I could do stacking again at the local supermarket, but I found that rather tiring, and not the right sort of job for a literary man.

Jessica has proved to be the ideal wife for me. Her loyal, obedient nature has transferred its natural reverence from her mother to myself. My clothes are always well pressed, and my shoes polished. Indeed, I must be one of the tidiest professional poets in the country. There is only one snag. You guessed it, that awful mother. I should have preferred Jessica to cut her links with Megan altogether, but I recognise that this would be asking too much. I am, after all, a perfectly reasonable man, and Jessica seems to retain a quite foolish degree of affection for that malevolent old busybody. Apparently Megan gets lonely in her off-duty hours when she is not cutting up the dead pigs and parcelling them into juicy packets.

Every so often Jessica goes off to Wales to pay short visits to her mother. I say short because that is what I insist upon. It is no joke to be deprived of one's hot dinner every evening, though my dear wife does leave cold plates in the fridge, each one carefully labelled with the appropriate date. She also rings me every night to say goodnight, sweet dreams. At her mother's expense, I am glad to say. I feel sure that Megan is doing her best to put Jessica against me. That is hardly likely to succeed since, as you will have deduced by now, I am a model husband. Megan's other great effort is to fatten Jessica up. For some reason, which I do not understand, my dear little wife seems to have lost a good deal of weight during the happy years she has been married to me.

The real trouble arises when my mother-in-law comes to visit us. I allow two invasions a year, each limited to three days. One is in the summer, which is not too intolerable since I can get out of the house most of the time. I take my little notebook with me and jot down poetic ideas. Sometimes I wander across the common, gazing at the skylarks like Shelly. More often, when I can get at Jessica's purse, I am to be found in one of our local pubs imbibing alcoholic refreshment like Dylan Thomas. It is satisfying to think that I have already outlived both these poets.

The far more intractable maternal visit occurs at Christmas every year. Jessica insists that her mother expects to come, and would feel intolerably lonely if expected to lie low among the scenic beauties of Wales. The woman arrives on Christmas Eve, cluttered with paper bags containing presents of negligible value. Then the annual grim farce begins. I am obliged to decorate the tree and to attend midnight mass in the proximity of the wheezing beldame, a horribly untuneful belter-out of hackneyed carols. Megan assists Jessica next morning with the cooking of the Christmas goose, and there is much cackling laughter from the kitchen. As a result, the goose arrives late and, quite often, burned. The silly ritual with crackers and paper hats follows. Megan forces me to take a large helping of Christmas pudding and brandy butter, which gives me acute indigestion. I attempt to listen to the Queen's Speech, stifling my burps, but am distracted by Megan's comments and Jessica's juvenile giggles. Women always seem sillier when they are allowed to get together.

One year, the impertinent crone attempted to confront me.

"Why are you always such a misery, Bobby?" she asked. "Especially at Christmas." I could see poor Jessica, in the background, desperately trying to silence her.

"I am not a misery," I retorted coldly. "I have a lot on my mind."

"You make the most awful faces."

"That is my normal face, Megan, the one I was born with. It is quite good enough for your daughter, if not for you."

"Is he always like this Jessica? Or only when I am here?"

"Only when you are here," I snapped.

After that, I was determined to punish her. The occasion arose on the day after Boxing Day when normal activities began again. Megan had insisted on remaining with us for one more day, and poor Jessica had to take a day off from the bank to look after the withered hag. I offered to take them both for an afternoon drive. They accepted with surprised pleasure.

"Where are we going?" asked Megan.

"Wait and see," I riposted. "It is a special treat."

I should explain that one area of our household activities has always been under my personal control. I am an almost obsessively clean and tidy man, so I did not feel able to leave this sector to Jessica who pretends to be constantly on the go. Anything to do with waste disposal is therefore in my personal domain. Each week I fill the wheelie-bin and push it to the roadside to be collected by the Garbage Collecting Team sent round by the council. In addition, from time to time, I parcel up recyclable items, such as paper, bottles and cans, and take them to be placed in the appropriate giant containers at our nearby recycling facility, known locally as the dump. Thither we were now bound.

"I wonder where we are going," mused my mother-in-law. "Rickmansworth perhaps for a nice tea? Or Whipsnade to see the new Siberian tigers?"

"We have to pay a call first," I announced, as I drove through the gates of the dump.

"It's not very pretty here," commented Megan.

"We won't be here long, Mother dear," said Jessica in her conciliatory way. "Then I am sure that Bobby has an interesting surprise in store for us."

"I do indeed," I thought grimly.

Both the women got out of the car with me and helped me to put the various bags of recyclable material into their appropriate repositories.

"You take this paper to the bin, Jessica," I said. "And you, Megan, please pop these bottles into their container."

"There's nothing else to get rid of," said my wife when the car boot had been emptied.

"Oh yes, there is," I announced triumphantly. With a sudden gesture, I seized the diminutive, if articulate, frame of my mother-in-law and dragged her across the yard. At first she was too shocked to utter a sound, but she soon made up for that with some blood-curdling shrieks. Pulling her up some iron steps, I pushed her to the top of a huge metal container marked 'General Waste. No bottles of plastics', and then let her fall down on the other side with a most satisfying plop. I gave a hearty laugh.

Jessica came running.

"What on earth are you playing at, Bobby?" she gasped.

"Revenge," I snapped with a manic glint of satisfaction. "She has joined the General Waste."

"Are you all right, Mother?" my wife called.

"No, of course I'm not all right. I can't get out. And I think I've injured my leg."

Other people rushed up. Somebody blew a whistle.

"I did warn you, Jessica," came a well known voice from the depths of the General Waste container. "I told you he was a few buttons short."

"It's his massive brain," moaned Jessica. "I think it has snapped at last."

"I've done nothing wrong," I shouted triumphantly. "The woman is neither plastic nor a bottle."

They took me away, but it was good while it lasted. It is quite comfortable here, and there is a television and spittoon beside every bed. There is talk of sending me to a nice place in the real country for a prolonged rest, which I certainly deserve. An eminent consultant from one of the big London hospitals is due to examine me tomorrow. I asked what his speciality is, but they didn't seem to want to say.

In due course I look forward to returning to domestic life. I have urged Jessica to use the time profitably by giving our house a thorough spring clean.

The Table by the Window

Roger and Sylvia were happily married. They were both sure of that, and so was everyone around them. Their circumstances were propitious. Roger had recently retired from his architectural practice, which had taken him abroad a good deal, mostly to places like the Persian Gulf where the clients had oil money to spend. Sylvia was good at occupying herself. She liked to think of herself as a writer. Not exactly of blockbuster novels, but of clever little articles and the occasional poem which she sometimes managed to get published. They depended on each other, but not too much.

After selling up advantageously in Saint John's Wood, they had retired to a large farmhouse near the coast in the north of Norfolk. Roger's skill and experience had enabled them to do the place up and make it comfortable. Apart from the capacious sitting rooms, each of them had their own working space, Roger's at one end of the house and Sylvia's at the other. They met cheerfully for meals. With two cars, neither was unduly dependent on the other. Their children had obligingly grown up and moved away, ringing up only when they needed money.

RICHARD PARSONS

It took Roger and Sylvia a little time to realise that living in Norfolk was not the same as residing in London. The village nearest them on the coast was fashionable, and indeed generally known as Chelsea-on-the-Sea. There were expensive restaurants, a couple of boutiques, a good second-hand bookshop and a semi-disused church where they organised classical music concerts which would not have disgraced the Wigmore Hall. But there was a lot of wind, and the sea was usually too cold for bathing. In the winter, the place shut up and the restaurant proprietors left for the Seychelles.

Roger and Sylvia were not fond of field sports. They liked to eat animals, but not to kill them. Roger played a bit of golf and enjoyed reading. Sylvia seemed to occupy herself happily enough with her mysterious scribbling but, especially in the short winter days, time dragged a little for Roger. You could hardly goggle all day at television. It was something of a boon, therefore, when he decided to take up the internet. Sitting alone in his cosy den surfing the net kept him content for hours until it was time for sherry. You met such a wide range of extraordinary characters in that way. And you never had to encounter them again, unless you wanted to.

Sometimes, however, you took to a correspondent and built up quite an internet friendship. He had joined a chat room which claimed to specialise in introducing attractive single people to others of the opposite sex. Just a little bit of fun, was how he thought of it. He had conversed with a number of girls in this way, thus pleasantly relieving the tedium of the winter evenings. There was no point in admitting his real age, in the late fifties, so he usually described himself as being thirty-five, athletic and good looking with a mane of dark hair. The girls all sounded very attractive too.

One day he made contact with Hermione. They got on like a house on fire. He could sense at once that she was just his type. She too was in her early thirties, she said, with a trim figure, blue eyes and long, fair hair. She enjoyed everything he did – travel, food, drink, having laughs and perhaps even a spot of ... fun. It was all so magically easy, clicking away at the laptop, well out of the reach of Sylvia, safely ensconced at the other end of the big, old house. Sometimes Roger felt a bit guilty, but he comforted himself with the thought that it was only innocent amusement and he wasn't doing Sylvia any harm.

Over some weeks he and Hermione got to know each other rather well, though they never exchanged addresses. That, apparently, was part of the etiquette of the chat room. She had to live a quiet life in the Lincolnshire Wolds, it seemed, looking after her elderly, disabled grandmother in an Old Rectory. Only occasionally could she escape to London to visit the Royal Academy and the National Theatre. Roger was too much a gentleman to ask directly, but he received the impression that Hermione was still a virgin, though not by choice. She sounded, he thought, perfectly delightful.

Hermione too seemed to like what she had gathered about Roger, who always called himself Tim. Early on in their acquaintance, he had incautiously admitted that he lived with a girlfriend called Claudia. He rather regretted that now, since it would have been more amusing to pose as a carefree bachelor. His internet partner at once wanted to know all about Claudia. Did he still love her? Had he ever thought of breaking away? Roger was basically an honest man, if a bit of a fantasist. He felt obliged to tell the truth. Yes, he still loved Claudia. Sex with her was not what it had once been. But that had been replaced by strong feelings of gratitude and deep affection. He would never leave her and he hoped to God that she would never leave him.

Roger had expected the young woman to be disconcerted by this frank admission. But she said it was good to hear it. She was glad that he was not some silly would-be seducer only out for selfish pleasure. He felt better after that. Their friendship deepened.

Soon it reached a point where Roger felt that he simply must meet this remarkably percipient and understanding young woman. By now she seemed to know him so well and to be such a marvellous partner for his deepest thoughts. He was delighted to find that Hermione was also anxious to see him. He told her that he lived in Suffolk. It was only a small lie. They agreed to meet for lunch in King's Lynn, a pleasant old town half way between their two houses. He had told her that he was a freelance public relations adviser, so it was understandable that he could take time off to meet her. She would find a kindly neighbour to sit with her grandmother.

Roger nominated a pleasant riverside restaurant as the venue for their tryst. He had booked the best table, the one by the window. The prospect filled him with a delightful thrill of excitement, reminiscent of younger days. In spite of the high-minded tone he had taken on the internet, he could not help hoping that Hermione would turn out to be a bit of a slut. There was a large, anonymous looking hotel on the main market square, just round the corner from the restaurant he had nominated. He wondered whether they hired out rooms by the hour.

On the evening before this exciting assignation, he had dinner as usual with Sylvia.

"Delicious, as always," he said appreciatively. "You're a wonderful wife, darling."

"I do my best," riposted Sylvia calmly. Was it just guilty conscience, or did he detect an element of cynicism in her tone? He was beginning to feel just a little bad about deceiving his wife. But then he thought of Hermione's delicious young boobs. How thrilling to instruct a complete beginner, keen to make up for lost time, in the art of love.

"I'll be out tomorrow," he said cautiously. "Going to Norwich for a committee meeting of the County Archaeological Society. They've roped me in, as you know. We're planning a series of lectures on the Saxon Churches."

"That's all right, dear," said Sylvia in her matter-of-fact way. "I'm off to Swaffham myself with the Womens' Institute."

He kissed her goodnight with special affection. A Judas kiss, perhaps. They no longer shared a double bed. Sylvia had complained of his snoring.

Next day, at the appointed hour, Roger sat at the table by the window, a glass of good sherry in front of him, gazing down at the River Ouse as it flowed swiftly northwards to the Wash. He was all psyched up for the encounter with Hermione. Was it, he wondered, the right month to order oysters? And was it true that these had a dramatic effect on the libido?

Suddenly he sensed movement. The waiter was coming towards him, leading a female customer. For one instant, he could not see her. A thrill of excitement ran through him. He was about to see Hermione's lovely laughing face and the frank invitation in her come-to-bed blue eyes.

Then he sprang with horror to his feet. What incredible bad luck!

"Sylvia! What on earth are you doing here?"

"I could just as well ask you the same question, Roger. But, as we are both here, I might as well join you."

It was all too ghastly, thought Roger. She had somehow got into his laptop and come here deliberately to shame him. What the hell would happen when Hermione arrived? He imagined the women brawling and him sneaking out alone.

"You came to meet Hermione, I understand," said Sylvia with infuriating calm.

"You've been spying on me," he shouted, growing red in the face. His doctor had warned him about blood pressure.

"I didn't need to, dear. You see, I *am* Hermione."

National Heroine

"Go away!" screamed the woman. "I'm not letting anyone in."

"I am Inspector Carlos Vitoria of the Serious Crimes Squad," shouted a voice outside. "I'll put my identification card through the letter box. It is essential that I see you immediately, Señora."

Isabel was a prosperous, well-groomed woman of middle age, who normally prided herself on her upper-class calm. Most of her girlfriends in Argentina went in for a good deal of shouting and even screaming, when the occasion demanded. But Isabel, with her French grandmother, liked to think of herself as possessing sophisticated European manners. She and Juan Francisco, her banker husband, lived in an elegant apartment in the Avenida Alvear. It was handy for the best shops and the Palermo Park, not to mention the Retiro Cemetery where they held the smartest funerals in Buenos Aires.

Isabel's pleasant daily routine had been rudely shattered. She usually rose late, like many wealthy Argentine matrons, spending the day drinking coffee, gossiping with friends and perhaps trying on a new dress. In the evening she would join her husband for cocktails and dinner, often at a foreign Embassy, or they would attend the Opera at the Teatro Colon. As one of the country's leading bankers, Juan Francisco and his wife were automatically considered to be pillars of high society. It is not easy to be an Argentine banker. As her husband often pointed out, the country's financial stability was often threatened by the absence of reliable political institutions. The constant strain could be detected on his worried, fleshy face with its double chin and untidy moustache. But then, thought Isabel, other countries like Britain, France and the United States, not to mention Italy and Greece, had some pretty rotten politicians too. Meanwhile, she tried hard to enjoy herself.

Now something quite terrifying had happened. Something that people like Juan Francisco dreaded all the time. It was the shadow that hovered over the daily life of the well-to-do. He had been kidnapped. Two days before, he had failed to return at his usual evening hour. Distraught, she had telephoned his office. Shortly afterwards his chauffeur and bodyguards had arrived at the flat to break the news to Isabel that their employer had simply disappeared. For reasons of security, he usually took the special directors' elevator straight down to the VIP car park underneath the bank. This evening there was no sign of him, though his secretary confirmed that he had left the office as usual. He was particularly keen not to be late. He and Isabel were due to have a quiet dinner at home and then go out to their box at the Colon where the great Venezuelan soprano Angelina de las Rosas was opening in Norma. Her coloratura trills were reputed to be simply too thrilling and Isabel was anxious not to miss a note.

RODE HE ON BARBARY?

What was Isabel to do? Should she go on to the Opera and trust to her husband to join her there? She had already dressed and Bellini was one of her favourite composers. At that point the full horror of the situation had not sunk in. Shortly afterwards, Rafael Figueras came round to see her. A slim, dapper man, considerably younger than her husband and unencumbered with a wife, he was one of her husband's principal colleagues, as chief legal adviser to the bank. There was nobody that the increasingly distraught Isabel was happier to see in an emergency. She invited him to sit down with her to eat the delicious crab supper prepared for herself and Juan Francisco.

"What has happened?" she gasped, motioning to Rafael to pour out the Mendoza Chardonnay. "Don't try to keep anything from me."

"I am afraid, dear Isabel, that you must prepare yourself for very bad news."

"Oh, do hurry up," she gasped. At this rate, they were going to miss the first act.

"Juan Francisco is in the hands of the Black Condors." Isabel knew exactly who they were, a ruthless and extreme left-wing group called after the savage vultures terrorising the high places of the Argentine Andes.

"The Black Condors!" she repeated in horror. "But that's terrible."

"I'm afraid so."

"How can you be so sure?"

"They have just telephoned me at the bank. They demand a huge ransom."

"We can't possibly afford it," shrieked Isabel. "We are poor people."

Rafael knew this to be spectacularly untrue. But his experience of the rich had taught him that the affluent usually pretended to be totally indigent. That was how they managed to remain rich.

"The bank should pay," said Rafael. "I will talk to Don Antonio." He referred to their chairman.

"Thank God!"

"We must keep it a strict secret. The bank's declared policy is not to pay ransoms. Otherwise we should be at the mercy of any criminal gang that cared to kidnap our staff."

"Will the Black Condors preserve the secret?"

"They will have good reason to do so. They present themselves to the public as political idealists, not extortioners."

"Please get him back as soon as possible, Rafael. This very evening." There were long intervals at the Opera. They might still be able to make it for the last Act.

"That will not be possible, Isabel. I must first obtain the Chairman's authority, as I told you. I cannot reach him until the small hours. They say he is somewhere down in the Boca judging a tango competition. I could only leave a guarded message at his mansion. Even then, I am not in a position to liberate our dear Juan Francisco. For reasons of security, the Black Condors have given me no way of communicating with them. They have promised to ring me sometime tomorrow to hear our answer over the ransom. Until then, we can do absolutely nothing."

"But Juan Francisco will be suffering. He is used to his evening cocoa. And he likes a clean shirt every morning."

"We can only pray," replied Rafael unctuously. "Meanwhile, it is absolutely essential that nobody else knows. I have told your husband's secretary that he has had to make an emergency visit to a dying and wealthy aunt in up-country Tucuman. That's the kind of consideration they understand in financial circles. On no account must we speak to the police. With their oafish blundering, they might well provoke the Black Condors to kill poor Juan Francisco. They have a reputation for doing that … rather unpleasantly."

Isabel shuddered. There was no guarantee that her husband would be back by the following evening. She could hardly attend the Opera without him. People would notice, their box being naturally one of the most prominent and luxurious. The opera next day was to be Aida, a nice noisy piece, one of her favourites.

"Can I talk to no one?" she asked piteously, in the small, pathetic voice which had frequently subdued strong men. "Not even to Pilar, my dearest girlfriend?"

"Certainly not," snapped Rafael. He knew how women gossiped.

"Then you must stay with me," said Isabel. "I cannot bear to be alone at such a terrible time. It will drive me mad."

Rafael took this threat seriously. Her family had never been conspicuously sane. Her brother Salvador, an unemployable playboy, was only too well known on the nude bathing beach at Punta del Este. He agreed to move into the apartment. His mobile phone was wired into his office number known to the kidnappers. So there was no danger of missing their call.

Around midnight he might hope to speak to Don Antonio. Meanwhile, there were a few hours to kill. Who better to spend them with than the buxom, highly tactile Isabel?

Reached at last, the Chairman agreed to the ransom, though with a marked lack of enthusiasm. Rafael had to spend the whole of the next day with Isabel. They got on rather well. In the evening the Black Condors rang. They made the call very short, fearing to be traced. To Rafael's astonishment, they no longer seemed content with the ransom. They had decided to make a political demand as well. They would be in touch again later.

"How is my poor husband?" shrieked Isabel.

"They claim that he is still alive. Though complaining vociferously about the cuisine and the quality of the wine."

"That has the ring of truth. Poor darling Juan Francisco, he is used only to the best."

On the following afternoon, Rafael was obliged to leave Isabel alone in the apartment. He had other duties which could not wait. Surely, she thought, her husband would be home by the weekend. In the next week, they would be starting the Ring Cycle at the Opera. Hermann Gloggnitz, the great Heldentenor, was coming especially from Berlin with his wife, personal trainer and masseur. Isabel adored Wagner. It was nice and long and loud, and right through it you could enjoy pleasant little chats and even a refreshing nap.

It was on the evening of the second day, with Rafael still absent, that Inspector Vitoria made his unexpected appearance. Isabel was astonished to hear that he knew all about the kidnapping.

"Don Antonio contacted us," explained the Inspector. "Very sensible. Dealing with the Black Condors is not for amateurs like Rafael Figueras. They are brutal and ruthless in the extreme."

"When are they letting my husband out?" gasped Isabel.

"That depends," replied Carlos Vitoria enigmatically. Isabel liked his cute little ears. "We have at last received their political demand. They insist on the release of five of their group, now in the high security prison at Mar Del Plata awaiting trial for murder. They want that as well as the ransom."

"All for my poor little Juan Francisco?"

"They regard him as a big fish, Señora."

"What are we to do?"

"That is partly for you to decide. Or, at least, recommend."

"I don't understand," said the bewildered Isabel.

"I have just been with the President of the Republic at the Casa Rosada," announced Carlos portentously. "It was necessary to consult him personally, and in great confidence. The release of these five known murderers, in response to a terrorist demand, would be an appalling blow to the prestige of the government and indeed the nation. On the other hand, it would be a pity to lose your distinguished husband. The President has thus been presented with a ghastly dilemma. He has consulted his Personal Confessor and also his Public Relations Adviser and he has reached a decision."

"What is that?"

"He has decided … not to take a decision. He is leaving it to you."

"Me!"

"Yes, dear Señora. If you ask him to do so, he will cave in to the terrorists and release the criminals. The nation will suffer, but your husband will be safe. If, however, you choose to support the dignity and prestige of our beloved Argentina, then the terrorist demand will be rejected."

"And my poor husband could die a painful death."

"That could be. One does not really know."

"A hard choice, Inspector."

"Indeed, Señora. So the president passed it on to you. That is how one becomes a Head of State in this part of the world."

"I must have fifteen minutes to think," countered Isabel. "I shall take a nice hot bath. Please sit down and read La Moda En España. It has the latest fashions."

On her return, swathed in an elegant dressing gown and smelling of a deliciously fragrant perfume, Isabel announced her decision.

"I cannot ask the nation to give in to terrorists," she said simply.

"Magnificent, Señora," said the Inspector, bowing deeply. "Spoken like a Roman matron. The president will make public the part you have played in this decision. You will earn the admiration of your countrymen for your noble contribution to the honour of this great nation at immense personal sacrifice. May I have the honour and joy of embracing you as a national heroine?"

"Let me ask you again. What will happen to my husband?"

"I can only repeat that I don't know, Señora. From now on, it is nothing to do with us."

"Perhaps he will give them one of his lectures on fiscal policy," said Isabel hopefully. "He might bore them so much that they will send him home."

Rafael called in later. He too seemed to think it

appropriate to embrace the heroine.

"Between the two of us," he murmured discreetly. "Don Antonio is delighted. There will be no ransom to pay."

At the beautiful Retiro cemetery, a week later, Isabel was the star worshipper at her husband's funeral Mass. The Cardinal Archbishop attended, and so did the President of the Republic. Isabel looked quite ravishing with her neatly tailored black dress and bunch of white lilies. People commented on her extreme pallor and the traces of suffering in her huge dark eyes. She wanted to lean on Rafael's arm, but she felt instinctively that this would not look quite right. For music, she had chosen the Verdi Requiem with its pleasant suggestion of nights at the Opera.

Her husband left her well provided for. And she would never have to play bezique with him again.

A few weeks later, Rafael moved from his bachelor pad into Isabel's much more spacious apartment. For reasons of respect to the dead, their wedding was quiet and unfashionable in a little church on the Tigre delta.

Rafael's career at the bank has gone from strength to strength. He has been promoted to take over Juan Francisco's job. At the theatre and other public places, Isabel quite often receives an ovation. They are out at some function nearly every night.

Rafael does not greatly care for opera and he detests Wagner. He has converted Isabel to the joys of operetta. That's where they go now. Their favourite is *The Merry Widow*.

Senior Citizens

It was peaceful in the little sitting room overlooking the rose garden at Warminster. Just the two of them, Emily and Tom Pargiter, a middle-aged couple of respectable appearance. Emily was listening to her six CD boxed set of *The World's Great Lullabies*. It was remarkably inexpensive, having been recorded in Bratislava. Tom had brought it especially to keep her quiet and prevent her turning on noisy TV chat shows while he got on with his own literary work. He had found the laptop computer somewhat beyond his powers, and was content to bash out his opus with two fingers on an antiquated typewriter which had trouble with capitals. Tonight, as usual, he was tapping contentedly like a domesticated woodpecker, while his wife leaned back on her reclining armchair and happily imagined rough male fingers fondling her breasts. It was one of her main hobbies, and never failed to afford an innocent pleasure.

Retirement had presented a problem for Tom. After a career in the Army, he was used to constant activity. Time at first had hung heavily on his hands. It had been a mistake, Emily had suspected, to go and live in Wiltshire. There were too many other Army people around. Against this background, the Pargiters could hardly be regarded as big fish. Tom had retired with the comparatively modest rank of Major. Emily, a beauty in her day and considered something of a catch in Aldershot circles, was a little disappointed by this since she had expected him to rise to levels where he would command huge armies like her own eminent father. She could never quite understand why he had not. He dressed nicely and had a pleasant manner. But the truth was that God had not actually given Tom a very big brain. It was really Emily who had kept him going all the time with her vivacious smile and large doe-like eyes which seemed to appeal to senior officers. That was just as well. They had occasionally needed support from his tolerant superiors.

His career had been punctuated by a series of small but unfortunate episodes. There had, for example, been his failure to remember to notify HQ of his impromptu night exercise, culminating in the capture and compulsory disrobing of the Brigadier, a dignified officer of the old school.

It had been exhausting, thought Emily, traipsing round the world with the regiment to places like Germany, Northern Ireland and Hong Kong. It was a blessing to settle down, not too far from the children. Emily, as usual, found little things to do around the house. She was no great reader, but she kept her eyes and ears open and had a capacity for enjoyment. Tom, however, was soon bored. You could not shoot all the time, and he didn't have the brains, or the memory, for bridge. He had hoped to secure further paid employment in order to supplement his modest pension. But somehow nobody seemed to need his services. He was not up-to-date in technology, and he didn't have the financial background for the jobs available to his contemporaries, like secretary to a Golf Club or Bursar at a minor public school. Nor was he keen to offer himself for voluntary work. He didn't care for the clacking of old biddies who priced the battered jerseys at the Oxfam shop. His pacing round their small abode like a caged panther was beginning to get on Emily's nerves. It was sad to see what time had made of a man she had once regarded as a bright young hope. He had lost his youthful sense of fun, while she had retained, and even developed, hers.

"I've got the very thing for you, dear," she burst out at last. "You must write your memoirs."

"My memoirs?" he echoed in astonishment. "You know I'm not a literary gent."

"It doesn't have to be literary, darling. Just the story of your life, written in that concise, straightforward prose they taught you at Sandhurst."

"Nobody will want to read it. I'm not interesting."

"Everyone is interesting, dear. We are all reflections of god. At least that's what Canon Bartlett says. And you have been to some awfully odd places. Like when you were seconded to train those mountain warfare troops in Bhutan. And guarding the Princess of Kensington on her Antarctic tour."

"No publisher would take it. They only want books about celebrities. Unless, of course," he added, brightening, "I could become notorious. Like poor old Pogo who exposed himself in that public lavatory at Waterloo."

"I don't think that would be a good idea," said Emily hastily. "Don't forget that I'm on the Parish Council.

People round here are quite conventional. No, I've got a better plan. There is a nice man near Sherborne who publishes books from his Old Rectory. He specialises in authors who want to record the story of their lives. You order five hundred copies, or whatever you want, and then you can give them out to your children and friends. He produced my uncle's book *With Rod And Gun In Pategonia* and everyone loved it."

"There must be some snag," retorted Tom. He had become slightly bitter, with the boredom and the pain in his back.

"Well, *he* doesn't pay. You have to."

"They call that vanity publishing."

"Never mind. No harm in a little vanity."

"It will cost thousands. We can't possibly afford it."

"I could. With my legacy from Aunt Grace."

"You should keep that for emergencies."

"This is an emergency," said Emily, but only to herself.

And so it was agreed. On the assumption that the book could be published from the Old Rectory, Tom would work on it every evening between tea and the Happy Hour. It gave Emily great satisfaction to see the new contentment on her husband's usually peevish old face as he bent over his masterpiece. Now that he was safely taken care of, she herself could relax and indulge in her pleasant dreams and private activities.

Tom showed no disposition to discuss his efforts, even with Emily. She could read it all when it was finished, he snapped. After each working session, he pointedly locked up the manuscript in a rather fine old lacquered box and took away the key. Emily was not all that interested in the book itself. She found it impossible to believe that Tom's literary efforts would be exactly sparkling. She had only suggested the enterprise to keep him happy. But the precautions so obviously taken each day to prevent anyone, even her, from seeing the book did rather intrigue her. What on earth could her poor husband have to hide? She decided to treat herself to a little snoop. But she would have to bide her time.

As the months went by, Tom became increasingly immersed in his work. His hours of labour now extended to much of the day, rather to his wife's secret satisfaction. She was able to go out on her own for long spells without provoking any objections on his part. Her social life became … enjoyable. To watch her husband at his writing was amusing too. He worked very slowly and with great deliberation, savouring every word. What on earth could he find to fill all those pages? The contentment had faded from his face, and it had a curious expression as he wrote; quizzical, cynical, perhaps even bitter. Was he recording the occasions when he had been passed over for promotion? Emily became intrigued.

Her opportunity came suddenly one morning when Tom was summoned by a neighbour to rush out and help him remonstrate with the council who were about to cut down a shared hedge. In his frenzied haste, Tom failed to lock away his manuscript. He must have forgotten the omission since, soon afterwards, Emily saw him walking down the lane with his friend for a session at the local pub. He would not be back for a couple of hours. Now or never, thought Emily, seizing the typed pages.

She was appalled by what she read. The book wasn't

about Tom at all. It was about her and her adulteries. She had assumed that Tom neither knew, nor cared. But he *had* known and he *had* cared. This was to be his revenge. It was all down in black and white – from her first timid infidelities with charming little Ben Wakefield in Catterick, right through to that last passionate affair with the Air Chief Marshal in Cyprus. He was even writing up her current entanglement with gentle Valentine Montrose, now Dean of Trowbridge, who had been their Brigade Chaplain. He was spoken of as a future Bishop. Exposure would ruin his career.

Fortunately, he did not live far away. Emily picked up her mobile phone and dialled feverishly. Mrs Montrose answered.

"May I speak to Doctor Montrose please?" she asked.

"Who wants him?" asked the wife suspiciously.

"I am the Archbishop's secretary," replied Emily resourcefully. That was the fun of adultery. You got to use your wits.

Her lover came on the line.

"I must see you tomorrow," she hissed, "same time, same place."

"Very well, Your Grace," replied the Dean, who was quick on the uptake.

Next day, in the cosy teashop in Bath, the Dean tried to calm her.

"One is not unused to these little contretemps," he intoned in his beautiful light baritone which made Emily feel quite faint. "I have a plan. As you may remember, I was once Chaplain to a refuge for … difficult young people. The locals used, jokingly, to call it the 'home for Backward

Boys and Forward Girls'. I still retain contacts with some of my old … alumni. It is wonderful what they will do for auld lang syne."

On the following night the Pargiters' house was broken into. A few items of some value were stolen, including the old lacquered box containing the manuscript of the Major's memoirs.

"A very odd business," commented Tom gravely.

"Yes, dear," replied his wife calmly. She was an experienced liar by now.

"I don't think I shall have the heart to go on with it. All that effort thrown away.

"Never mind, dear. We'll think of something else."

At her prompting, they have taken up croquet. They rather enjoy it and have become quite good. Better, in fact, than most of their neighbours. Hitting away your opponent's ball, just when it was about to be driven through a hoop, is such an effective way of ventilating one's feelings.

The Beast Inside

I'm twenty-one and I've only worked in the bank for three months. But already something very peculiar has happened. Mum says I should write it down, in case I ever forget it. Not very likely!

I had passed my school exams and trained in both shorthand and IT. I didn't want to go to university, and I did want to get a job. It would be nice to have my own money coming in regularly. Dad suggested I should apply to the bank. Banks, he said, were solid. You met a reliable class of person. Perhaps he was thinking of my elder sister, Chloe, who has gone to live under a railway bridge in Hackney with a rock guitarist. As mum pointed out, I am now their only hope. Dad and mum like to see life in simple, straightforward terms. As this story will show, you can't always do that.

Banks have changed in recent years and some of the older customers don't quite seem to realise that. You don't get many employees actually working there any more. Most of the transactions are processed through the internet, or by a machine. Some of the branches don't even have a real manager. But ours does. We have still a lot of small businesses in our town, and our boss has to decide whether or not give them loans. Again, many managers now rely on their laptops and the telephone operator, but our manager, Mr Harold Cogswell, insists on having a real flesh-and-blood girl to act as his Personal Assistant. When he sets his mind to something, he usually gets his own way. So that's the job they gave me.

I have enjoyed working for Mr Cogswell. He is quite a character. He is not all that old for his important job, perhaps early forties. He is a good-looking man, not too fat, with a nice little moustache. They say he exercises regularly before coming to work and that would explain his trim, muscular figure. He is very good at his job, snappy and decisive. He can examine a loan request and turn it down, all within five minutes. Sometimes I think he rather enjoys that side of our activities. I have to soothe the rejected applicants, and Mr Cogswell kindly says I am good at that.

"We make a splendid team, Sophie," he said recently. "I am the hard man, and you are the soft woman."

I found myself blushing with pleasure. I never can help that. The girls used to tease me at school.

Mr Cogswell never once mentioned his family. I had to assume that he was a bachelor. But was that likely? The forward sort of girl would be all over him. More likely a divorced man, or perhaps a widower. I liked to think of him as a lonely widower needing tender, loving care. It was difficult to find out. Mr Cogswell had a rather intense manner, at least at the bank, and I did not think he would relish a direct question. He never received private telephone calls at the office and made it clear that he did not approve of them. Indeed, under Mr Cogwell's regime, our branch has become a rather serious place altogether, but we are renowned for our professional competence. Dad says I can learn a lot from Mr Cogswell.

I have at least discovered one thing about his private life. He is mad about football. Every weekend he goes off to watch some match or other. I know about that because I have observed him booking tickets on the internet. I did say, quite casually, that I should be interested to see a game, but he did not take the hint. He is quite nice to me in the office, but that's about the end of it. I wonder what he wears at the football. Surely not one of his nice, dark suits with crisp, white shirt and blue tie. I think he wants to keep all that separate from his life at the bank.

There is just one small negative side to Mr Cogswell. Usually he is very polite to everyone, including me, but occasionally he does suddenly fly in to a dreadful rage. I still remember the awful day he went for me after I had made a small mistake. It is so easy to confuse hundreds with thousands, and you are not supposed to do that in a bank.

"You are a fool, Sophie," he shrieked in a voice loud enough for all to hear. "A fucking great idiot. You deserve a bloody good spanking, silly little wench."

He went on for some time, using other rude words familiar to me only from the television after the watershed. I knew the others would all be listening, and I had gone brick red with embarrassment. Miss Barnstaple, our Deputy Manager, who is a keen feminist, said afterwards that the word 'wench' could be regarded as a breach of my human rights and I could get damages. But I didn't have the heart to follow this up, because Mr Cogswell apologised very nicely the next day, giving me both a dozen red roses and a huge box of mint chocolates, to which I am partial.

It was a bit of an eye opener, all the same. I began to think of our Mr Cogswell as a smouldering volcano. Perhaps he was under some kind of stress.

One Friday morning he arrived at the bank with a small, smart suitcase.

"Going away for the weekend, Mr Cogswell?" I asked, in my usual chirpy way. Sometimes at the secretarial college I used to be described as a 'little ray of sunshine'.

"I am indeed, Sophie," replied my boss with an unusually friendly smile. He was obviously in a very good humour. "I am flying to Barcelona tonight. For the big game tomorrow, of course I shall be back on Sunday night, ready for the bank on Monday."

"I hope you have a lovely time, Mr Cogswell," I said.

"I live for these trips, Sophie," he explained. "They bring out ... the other side of me."

I wondered what that other side could be. But I thought it better not to ask.

On the Monday morning I was looking forward to seeing Mr Cogswell again. At the least, he might tell me a bit about Barcelona which I have never visited. I did also slightly hope that he might have brought me back a little present. Wasn't Catalonia well known for its pottery? It would have been nice to have something to show Mum and Dad, and perhaps put on the mantelpiece in our lounge.

But Mr Cogswell never appeared. I assumed that his plane had been delayed and spent some time ringing round to postpone his appointments for the day. Then Miss

RODE HE ON BARBARY?

Barnstaple summoned me to her cubby hole.

"I think you should know, Sophie," she said, "that Mr Cogswell has been delayed in Spain. That's all you need to tell people."

"Oh dear," I said. "When is he coming back?"

"I haven't the slightest idea," snapped Miss Barnstaple. She and Mr Cogswell have never got on. They are both the world ruler type.

"Has there been an accident?"

"Not exactly."

"Can't you tell me more?"

"No, I can't, Sophie, or rather, I don't intend to. We don't encourage prattling in this office." She can look awfully severe, with those big spectacles.

I went home feeling rather bewildered. Mr Cogswell hadn't always been nice to me, but I had grown fond of him, in the way that you do with a big, old dog.

Dad was the first to spot it next morning. There was a big splash in the local paper under the headline 'Local Bank Manager Arrested in Spain for Football Hooliganism'. It turned out that the British fans had rioted after the game and gone on to attack shops and the local police. Some had thrown bricks and used truncheons brought for the purpose. Among these were Mr Cogswell. He was in prison in Barcelona awaiting trial. Stiff sentences were expected.

I was utterly astonished, but Mum, as usual, liked to pretend that she had suspected something like this all along.

"I know you were a bit sweet on him, Sophie," she said, "but your dad and I always thought he had strange, staring eyes."

"He was a bank manager," I gasped. "So tremendously

respectable."

"That's the trouble with that type of man," said Dad. "They have to maintain the façade. And underneath there's a boiling cauldron. It's a ghastly strain and, in the end, something has to give. We had a sports master like that."

It wasn't so interesting at the bank after Mr Cogswell left. Miss Barnstaple took over and cut down on the lunch hours.

I followed Mr Cogswell's case in the papers. After his sentence, he served a short term in a Spanish prison and was then transferred to an English one, not far from our town.

I went to visit him one Saturday. He looked rather deflated in his prison outfit. It was hardly surprising.

"Oh, it's you, Sophie," he said. "I was told that a young lady was here to see me." A look of disappointment crossed his face, when he realised that it was only me.

"I'm awfully sorry, Mr Cogswell. About what has happened to you, I mean."

"No need for that, my dear. One has to let off steam from time to time. It was a calculated risk. I did enjoy whacking that pompous Civil Guard Captain. There's something quite fascinating, you know, about leading a double life. Financial adviser combined with football hooligan."

He gave me a grin which I found rather disconcerting. I think I shall change my mind about waiting for him outside the prison on the morning they let him out. As Mum says, there is a bit of a beast inside Mr Cogswell and that would not make for a calm relationship.

Alma Mater

"Oxford is going to the dogs," said Marcus Phillips, Fellow of Holy Redeemer College and University lecturer in Ancient Assyrian.

"It always has been," retorted his friend Lewis Haliburton, also a don at Holy Redeemer, tutor in Modern History and a world authority on scutage in 14th century Yorkshire. "Duns Scotus complained about it in the thirteenth century."

The two bachelor academics, both in late middle age, were sunning themselves on the grass at the nude bathing pool for men on the Cherwell, commonly known as Parsons Pleasure. This was their usual practice on warm afternoons during the summer terms. Public opinion was not their concern. It did not worry them that they made an unlovely sight.

"The university will soon be bankrupt," moaned Marcus. "We have to take in too many of these ghastly foreign undergraduates because they pay more. And our best people are being pinched by the damned Yanks. Potterton has just left for Harvard. No doubt he will treat them to his unsound views on the exact location of ancient

Nineveh."

"The university may have run out of funds," admitted Lewis, "but Holy Redeemer, thank God, is not exactly broke. In the senior common room, as you well know, we have the best claret in Oxford." Fifty years before, an astute Bursar had sold off college livings in rural Lancashire and invested the proceeds in blue chip companies. Special prayers for the repose of his soul were said every year in chapel on the eve of Budget Day.

"What worries me most," continued Marcus, scratching his hairy stomach in a not very attractive way, "is this modern emphasis on useful subjects. I have always taken pride in the fact that my work is of no possible use to anyone. Utility is not the purpose of a great university. All I have done is to push out, just a little, the frontiers of human knowledge. We shine torches into the darkness."

"And we train their young brains too," said Lewis. "My undergraduates emerge with a tremendous capacity for public life. They are versed in the twin arts of picking up a little knowledge with the minimum of effort and then displaying that knowledge with the maximum of effect. Don't forget, the Prime Minister was once one of my flock."

"I can well believe it," said Marcus rather nastily.

"Don't worry, Marcus," continued Lewis. "Holy Redeemer will last out our time. And a good deal longer than that."

"I do hope so. I should like to be associated with the college, even after my death which cannot be far away."

"A monument in the chapel, you mean," said Lewis. "You would have to leave money for that in your will."

"A monument be damned," snapped Marcus. He could

be more decisive in manner than Lewis, who was really rather gentle. "I plan to be there in person."

"What on earth do you mean?"

"I have decided to believe in reincarnation. Millions do in Asia, as you know. Some of us do seem to be able to carry talent and knowledge on to a future life. It is the only possible explanation for the phenomenon of the infant genius. They have brought it with them into the world. Look at Mozart. I myself was composing quite passable Greek iambics at the Dragon School at the age of eight."

Marcus was a vain, and somewhat malicious, old bachelor. As college rowing coach, he had earned the reputation of hanging round the changing room at the Boat House and being rather keen on his young men.

"In what shape do you plan to return?" asked Lewis.

"That will be for the Gods to say. But, in some form, I shall be around in the Old Quad for some time, enjoying the dappled light in the lime trees and the muffled roar from the High."

"I am very devoted to the College, too," said Lewis. "I should like to stay there indefinitely, though the prospect of metamorphosis does rather alarm me. There are people there of whom I am rather fond."

"You refer to the Domestic Bursar, I suppose," chortled Marcus. "The nubile Miss Molly Orchard."

Lewis Haliburton's little foible was well known too. Although he had never actually been able to find anyone willing to marry him, it was understood that he tended to entertain hopeless sentimental passions for the more spirited type of young woman. He blushed, thinking how absurd it was to do so at his mature age.

"Miss Orchard is certainly charming," he agreed cautiously. "But the dear old college has other attractions. Professor Gillespie, for example, with his Nobel Prize and his magnificent beard."

"It is agreed then," said Marcus. "We stay on and we stay at Holy Redeemer."

"Look out," shrieked Lewis. "There's a boat load of women coming this way." That did happen occasionally in spite of the warning notices. A feminist don at Lady Margaret Hall was trying to get the whole system changed, and would no doubt succeed some day.

Lewis snatched up a towel and carefully wound it round his middle. Marcus, however, took hold of his white panama hat and placed it over his face as he reclined.

"Why on earth did you do that, Marcus?" asked Lewis when the badly rattled girls had beaten a hasty retreat.

"I don't know about you, my dear Lewis. But in Oxford I am known by the face."

They set off to travel back to College in Marcus's battered Peugeot, which he drove extremely badly. Outside Wadham they had a head-on collision with a taxi and both men were killed outright. The Master of Holy Redeemer paid a graceful tribute at their joint funeral, emphasising how greatly both eminent scholars would be missed. Lewis had left everything he had to the college while the assets bequeathed by Marcus were to go, somewhat curiously, to a young Moroccan gentlemen resident in Soho and currently involved in the leisure activity business.

Soon afterwards an irascible looking ginger tom cat appeared in the Old Quad. Nobody quite knew how he had got there, but nobody liked to kick him out. Ginger had a rather bossy, magisterial manner as if he owned the place. He liked to stretch out and sun himself on the lawn underneath the founder's statue. Any attempt to remove him against his will tended to be countered by an offensively shrill miaow and the threat of a scratch from a claw. So people left him alone. Ginger seemed to be rather clever at finding his way around Oxford, sometimes he was spotted in the changing rooms at the college boat house where he seemed to bring good luck. Holy Redeemer became Head of the River, and stayed there for some terms.

Molly Orchard is planning to get married soon. Her fiancé is a promising young cardiologist at the Radcliffe. She has enjoyed her job at Holy Redeemer but, unfashionably, would rather bring up babies, at least for the next few years. She was pestered for a time by a large, and very ugly, black beetle which just seemed to be sitting wherever she went.

"Almost as if the horrid creature were following me around on purpose," she remarked one day to the Master. English grammar was one of her strengths.

One day Molly stamped impulsively on the black beetle. It lay very squashy and still. It has not been seen again. Molly was seized with a regret for which she could not account. She tried to make friends with Ginger, but the lordly creature did not seem at all interested.

On the Beach

"Could this be the right place?" asked Moses Oduwole doubtfully as they arrived at the line of modest bungalows overlooking the beach. He and Patience had dressed up specially for the occasion in their robes as a Yoruba Chief and his wife. The fine costumes looked rather conspicuous in England, but Moses felt, rightly, that the traditional outfits gave them a certain dignity. They did not come much to England these days. Like other successful Nigerian business men, Moses had concentrated recently on contacts in the United States, and even in Canada and Australia. But they had both studied in London years ago; Moses as an accountant and Patience as a nurse. Indeed they had met at the student hostel in Brunswick Square. That had been in the old colonial days, long since gone. Young Africans had been treated then as an interesting rarity in Britain before the influx of black people on a larger scale. Both Moses and Patience had liked what they saw of the English, colonialists though they might be, and had developed an affection for the country. They belonged to the ageing group of Nigerians now sometimes regarded by their younger successors as black people with a white heart.

RODE HE ON BARBARY?

After independence, Moses's export-import business had taken off, once Nigerians were free to trade more widely than with British firms. He had become rich and successful. Five of their children were working in his enterprises, which comprised everything from oil to bananas. Patience, now a distinguished matron, was chairman of the Motherless Babies' Home in Lagos, for which she organised glittering social events. They were, of course, frequent guests at the British Deputy High Commission in Lagos, the High Commission itself having moved up-country to the new capital at Abuja. In that way they had kept in touch with the news about Sir Edward.

He had been the great panjandrum of their youth, the British Governor of the Western Region, an area larger and more populous than many a European country. Sir Edward Pemberton and his wife Virginia had, in theory, not been popular among the many Nigerians who wanted to see an early end to colonial rule. But those who actually met the distinguished Gubernatorial duo found them to be surprisingly unstuffy and open hearted. Among these were the young, newly married Oduwoles. Patience had been called in to look after a guest at Government House who had slipped on a highly polished floor. She had been rewarded with an invitation to one of the Pembertons' grand receptions, to which she had been allowed to bring Moses. They had been kindly received by the gracious Governor and his elegant Lady. They had not forgotten.

Moses was not without faults. His fairly numerous enemies and failed rivals alleged that his considerable fortune had been built up through a good deal of financial sharp practice. But he did have one great virtue. He was always grateful to those who had been kind to him in his early years. He had heard that Lady Pemberton had died, but Sir Edward, now a very old man, was still alive and living on the south coast. It was not difficult to discover his address in Sussex, near Hastings. Moses had written to ask if they could pay him a visit and had received a card in reply, in a shaky hand, saying they would be very welcome. A time was assigned. Moses and Patience came down from their pied-a-terre in Chester Square in their hired Mercedes. The glaucoma was beginning to affect Moses's eyes now, so Patience did the driving.

They found Hastings disappointingly run down. They had happy memories of a youthful visit to Brighton, but the English seaside had changed for the worse. The cheerful families who once frequented the little guesthouses now went further afield to warmer climes for their holidays. They had expected Sir Edward to live in an elegant mansion and were shocked to discover that he resided in a modest area where a seedy esplanade overlooked the sands. The English Channel seemed flat and cold, so unlike the foaming Tarkwa Beach near Lagos where the Atlantic breakers rolled in, warm, long and lethal.

They had assumed that they would be received by a servant, but Sir Edward himself answered the door. He looked fragile and somehow smaller. He was dressed in an elderly pullover, casual trousers and a pair of ancient carpet slippers. It seemed a far cry from his white uniform, sword and plumed hat, which had seemed so impressive in Nigeria.

"We are Moses and Patience Oduwole, Your Excellency," said Moses. "Do you remember us?"

"Of course I remember you both," replied the old man.

"You do look smart. How very kind of you to visit me. I don't see many people these days. Come in and sit down. I was just making a cup of tea."

"We were so sorry to hear about Lady Pemberton," said Patience.

"Thank you. Yes, it was a great blow. We just didn't make our golden wedding anniversary. Poor Virginia, she was crippled with arthritis in her last years. I had to give up my voluntary work to look after her. Then I hadn't got the heart to take it up again."

Mark and Patience exchanged glances. Surely people like the Pembertons would be able to afford servants, or a resident nurse?

Sir Edward was glad of the company and become quite chatty. In the course of the next two hours, they learned a good deal about him and his circumstance. They had retired from Nigeria with only modest savings and had lived since then on his Colonial Service pension. Lady Pemberton had inherited from her parents a pleasant house, with a garden, near Haywards Heath. But they had been obliged to sell it, in order to pay the debts accumulated by their son Harry, who had been something in the city. Moses received the distinct impression that, but for this relief, Harry would have found himself in prison for fraud. He was now residing abroad, somewhere unspecified. Their only daughter lived alone in the not particularly affluent suburb of Crouch End, where she supported herself by teaching the oboe. Sir Edward was sustained only by carers provided by the council who came in twice a day to get him up and put him to bed.

"I know what you're thinking," he said cheerfully. "It must be a lonely, dull life for me. But there are always books and music, and walks along the sands. I still have my mind. And my memories."

"I felt so sorry for him," said Moses as they drove home.

"So did I," agreed Patience. "Once so big, and now so small. All that grandeur in Government House, peacocks on the lawn, guards at the gate."

"I don't think that matters," said Moses, "but it seems a shame that he hasn't got any money. He hasn't done very well by his family either. In Nigeria, he must have had ample opportunity to make a fortune. He had all those government contracts to give out. People would have been willing to pay him a lot, to make sure of obtaining the right decision. He was a silly fool not to make the best of it."

"That's what you think, Moses dear. But you know the British weren't like that, at least not in the Colonial Service. They would have called it corruption."

"It's a question where you think your loyalties lie. With us, as you well know, one's first duty is to the family and then to one's village and own people. I have done well for them. I built them a hospital and a school and a road. I am proud of that, and I know they are grateful."

"You had the money for it, Moses."

"Of course I did. And I made it myself, even if I had to cut a few corners. I've spent a lot too, Patience, on giving you a good, comfortable home and setting up our children in life. That's nothing to be ashamed of. It's Sir Edward who ought to be ashamed, living in that mean way without any help. And he has never provided properly for his wife and family, in spite of all those chances to get rich. I shall never really be able to understand the British."

"They are different from us, Moses. Or, at least, some

of them used to be. Government servants of the old school like Sir Edward. He is proud of being poor but honest."

"It's a funny thing to be proud of," grunted Moses, as his wife swung the big, comfortable car into the Purley Way.

A Dish to Die For

"I gather," said Sir Emrys Aberdovey with a certain complacency, "that we are in for rather a treat."

'He looks like a greedy old satyr,' thought Ben Callaway, with that slightly red nose and the jutting jowls. They had already consumed a good deal of sake, the Japanese rice wine which tasted innocuous but actually had a kick like a mule. The restaurant in Tokyo was luxurious in the extreme. Sir Emrys, being a visiting celebrity, had been placed with his younger guest at a special table with red upholstered bench seats in a discreet alcove beside a window. The head waiter had served them in person, a magisterial figure who could have doubled as Malvolio. The Japanese, decided Ben, certainly knew how to push the boat out, when the occasion demanded. He had never been anywhere so grand in his life. It was a far cry from his modest bachelor pad in the wrong part of Battersea.

Ben, in his early thirties, had been a professional actor for ten years. He had not exactly been a success so far, but he was still mad about the stage. It was the only thing he had ever wanted to do. He had appeared for tiny sums in several fringe productions in the remoter areas of London.

RODE HE ON BARBARY?

He had ventured, more than once, to the Edinburgh Festival where the average audience for a daytime fringe production numbered eight people. But the lusher pastures of the West End and television had eluded him almost completely. Most of the time, he lived on the benefit and ate one meal a day. His mother reproached him for not taking up that nice job in the estate agents in Godalming. Ben liked to think of himself as the victim of bad luck, but the truth was that he was not really a very good actor. He had an efficient and quick memory, but all he could do was to regurgitate his lines in a somewhat mechanical manner. He lacked the born performer's gift of getting into the skin of a character as if it had been his all along. At best, he might have made a stuffy straight man for a gifted comedian to make jokes at.

One day, he read in *The Stage* that the eminent old Thespian, Sir Emrys Aberdovey, veteran of the Royal Shakespeare Company and National Theatre, had formed his own company to tour cities in the Far East with *Macbeth* and *The Tempest*, he himself playing the leads, of course. Ben auditioned, as usual. He spent a great deal of time offering his services at auditions, mainly without success. But this time he had a spot of luck. He was accepted to join the company, much to his surprise and delight. For reasons of economy, many of the actors were to take several of the smaller parts each, Shakespeare being so tiresomely prodigal of these. In the Scottish play, as the actors insisted on calling it for reasons of superstition, he was to appear as The Witch, the Drunken Porter in Act 2, and the Cream Faced Loon in Act 5. It would make quite a lively evening. In *The Tempest* he would come on as the shipwrecked boatswain, a Strange Shape at Prospero's nightmare banquet and a Reaper in the Graceful Dance in the fourth Act. Ben had hoped for something better, but the Director, Adrian de Coverley, a ruthless young Cambridge graduate with big spectacles, curtly informed him that he was too plump for Ariel and not quite ugly enough for Caliban.

Ben was glad to get anything at all. There would be exotic places to visit – Singapore, Hong Kong, Tokyo, and finally Los Angeles and New York. Sir Emrys, though somewhat over–the–hill, was still a big star, world famous not for his distinguished stage work, but for his film appearances as Grandpa Reuben in the Oscar-winning sci-fi drama *Tommy Tucker*, in which he was reputed to have a share in the gross. He clearly saw himself now as one of the old actor managers, venerable monsters who controlled every aspect of the life of their companies, including the clothes to be worn by actors at off-stage parties. This was not at all to the liking of Adrian de Coverley, but Sir Emrys, having underwritten most of the tour, was in a position to get his own way.

It was he who decided that he would like Ben Callaway to act as his understudy and personal assistant, in addition to playing small parts. Both the director and Ben himself, were mystified by this. Ben looked a good deal younger than his real age, with his saucy smile and pert, turned-up nose. Surely there were several more mature actors in the company who could have made a better stab, in emergency, of the huge parts of Macbeth and Prospero. But Sir Emrys had brushed such objections aside, pointing out that anyone could be made to look old, with a stuck-on beard and some false facial hair. The reverse was more difficult. He himself had recently been, regretfully, obliged to give up his Romeo and incomparable Hamlet – not before time, according to one bitchy critic who had been blackballed by Sir Emrys for the Garrick Club.

In choosing Ben, Sir Emrys had two motives, both known only to himself. First, he had no intention of allowing his understudy ever to take over his roles. He was never ill and, if he were, he would still totter onto the stage. Besides, he did not want too capable an understudy. If Ben ever did perform these demanding parts, he could be relied upon to seem a mere simulacrum of the star. That would suit Sir Emrys, even on his death bed. He was rather a jealous old man, and he was not in the habit of encouraging competition.

The star's second motive was more arcane. He and Lady Aberdovey were the 'great married couple' of the British stage. Everyone knew about their wonderful partnership, both in stage and film and their famously happy married life. The truth was somewhat different. Since Tatiana had taken to the bottle, she had become decidedly difficult to work with. Sir Emrys had hoped to tour with *Antony and Cleopatra* and *School for Scandal*, but Adrian de Coverley had ridiculed the idea of Tatiana as Cleopatra and Lady Teazle, pointing out that the poor old lady would forget her lines and bump into the scenery as she had in the disastrous national production of *Hedda Gabler*. She had accordingly been left behind in Highgate, bemoaning her fate.

This had secretly suited Sir Emrys quite well. He liked women, but he was even keener on young men, a fact not usually known even in the tolerant world of show business. Tatiana Aberdovey, a famous Medea in her time, would be a frightening sight in a rage. She tended to throw glass ornaments. Sir Emrys was anxious to avoid that. So discretion was his watch-word. On first seeing Ben Callaway, with his amusingly retroussé nose, he had privately decided that he liked boys who were not too skinny, and he rather fancied this one. That was, in fact, the reason for the younger man's appointment. Sir Emrys knew nothing about Ben's sexual tastes but, in his experience, aspiring actors did not usually resist an invitation to the casting couch from a big star like himself. He decided to bide his time and wait for an opportunity. At least Ben would be unable to avoid him and they would have to spend hours in each other's company.

On their last night in Hong Kong, with Sir Emrys bringing the house down as Prospero, as usual, he had managed, in the atmosphere of euphoria, to persuade his understudy to spend the night with him. That had not been an entire success. The great actor was too tired for anything more athletic than sentimental groping. Ben had not enjoyed himself at all. Indeed, he had concluded that nothing would cure a man more decisively of homosexual leanings than an evening of passion with the great Thespian. Next day, they had both felt some embarrassment. Sir Emrys knew it had all been a mistake and must not be repeated. Now, he feared that young Ben might betray him. The press were following the tour with interest, and there was tabloid money to be made from an exclusive scoop.

Ben also felt anxious. He was a sensitive man and he knew that Sir Emrys was disappointed. Perhaps the boss would take it out on him by sending him home, on some other excuse. If so, he would never get the chance to do even in his Cream Faced Loon on Broadway. He simply could not afford to alienate his star employer. So he felt relieved when Sir Emrys, presumably to ease the tension, invited him to join him for supper, after their first night in Japan, at this grand restaurant in Tokyo.

"I hope you like fish," said Sir Emrys.

"Oh yes, Sir Emrys," replied Ben.

"You may call me Emrys, when we're alone." The great actor gave one of his toothsome smiles. "I have accepted the Maitre D's recommendation. He speaks quite decent English. I took the opportunity of ordering while you were in the cloakroom. We are going to have fugu, a kind of blowfish native to the Pacific. Apparently, it is absolutely delicious. The speciality of the house, he says. And a great rarity."

Ben scrutinised the menu. "It looks awfully expensive," he said.

"Never mind about that, my boy," said the great actor expansively. "This is on me, of course."

Ben tried to smile appreciatively. In fact, he felt tired and longed to go to bed. The thought of Sir Emrys as a lover filled him with disgust. The man was a hideous old gargoyle, with his creased actor's face.

The fish arrived. It came on large, circular dishes covered with paper-thin slices of flesh, delicately arranged. The two diners toasted each other in Japanese wine and then bit deeply into the tasty looking food.

"As I thought," proclaimed Sir Emrys triumphantly, "So delicate, even ethereal."

"Yes, it's gorgeous," agreed Ben with feigned enthusiasm. They both took a couple more mouthfuls and smiled appreciatively.

At this point they were approached by Kazuo Yamagata, the Japanese impresario who had organised the Tokyo leg of their tour. Unusually large and powerfully built for a Japanese, he was followed by a small posse of hangers-on.

"Congratulations once again, Sir Emrys," he said. "A wonderful Prospero! The audience were enchanted, and the critics will be too. I was sorry about those empty seats at the back but, with good word of mouth, we must hope for full houses for the rest of your fortnight."

Sir Emrys bowed his head in silent appreciation. He was not unused to full houses.

"I had hoped you might join us for supper," continued Kazuo, "but I see you have already made your ... arrangements."

Ben felt decidedly uneasy. The role of star's boyfriend did not come easily to him. Sir Emrys also felt awkward. He wondered whether he should have taken Ben to a more discreet location. Would Kazuo blab? These promoters would do anything for a juicy story to get bums on seats. But then the young man was his personal assistant. It would be natural enough to offer him the occasional meal.

"This is a very famous restaurant," said the impresario. "I am so glad you were directed to it. It is especially popular among theatre people, like the Ivy in London and Sardis in New York. Over there is one of our most famous Kabuki actors. I would introduce him, but he only speaks Japanese. He is noted for playing old ladies."

Sir Emrys was hungry. He took another two large mouthfuls of the delicious fish and motioned to his guest to do the same. He hoped that Kazuo would take the hint and move on to his own table.

"That looks tasty," commented the Japanese implacably. "What are you eating?"

"Fugu," replied Ben. He thought it was about time to show that he, too, possessed a tongue.

"Fugu!" exclaimed Kazuo. "Did you say fugu?"

"Yes."

"But that's terribly foolish."

"What on earth do you mean?" Sir Emrys almost shouted.

"Don't you know what fugu is?" said the Japanese. "It is the most dangerous fish on earth. A dish to die for. The gut, the ovary, the skin, and particularly the liver, contain a lethal nerve agent called tetrodotoxin. It is some one thousand, two hundred and fifty times as strong as potassium cyanide. Fugu poisoning results in a rapid and violent death."

"Good God!" yelled the great Thespian. "We have both eaten this ghastly dish. Get the stomach pumps quickly. It is our only hope."

"Keep calm, Sir Emrys," said Kazuo. "You may well be all right. Fugu is not dangerous when prepared by an expert chef, as it will have been in a restaurant of this calibre. There are strict safeguards, and last year there were only three fatalities."

"I still want to be pumped out," shouted the eminent actor. "My death would be a terrible loss to the world."

"It is too late for that, my friend," said Kazuo with annoying sang-froid. "Nothing can be done now. The poison is either in your system, or it is not. If it is, the symptoms are nausea, convulsions and paralysis, followed by total respiratory failure."

"Like being strangled?"

"Something like that."

"Why on earth do restaurants serve the damned stuff at all?" moaned Ben. He was still young, he remembered, and had a life to live.

"It's the excitement," explained Kazuo. "The thrill. Like Russian roulette, dancing with death."

"I should have been warned," moaned Sir Emrys.

"The restaurant will have thought you already knew. This place is so well known. It is their great specialty."

"How long before we know, one way or the other?" gasped Sir Emrys.

"About five minutes from now, I should say."

"This is terrible for us,"

"And for me, too," replied the Japanese impresario. "I had to borrow on the strength of my wife's jewellery to finance your show. I could lose much money. And now I suggest a period of total silence. Even perhaps a prayer."

"Just one question," interposed Ben Callaway. "Could one of us be poisoned and the other not?"

"Quite possibly. It is a question of who happened to get the poisonous portion."

The two men lowered their heads and thought quietly. Dear God, spare me, thought Sir Emrys, recalling early days in the Chapel at Trefeglwys before his talent had been recognised. He had beseeched the Good Lord to get him accepted for the chorus of that amateur production of *Lilac Time*. Now, I am too valuable for the world to lose, he told himself. They expect me in Hollywood in the spring for the sequel to *Tommy Tucker*. And then we start rehearsals in London for *Cymbeline* at the Haymarket. Besides, Tatiana needs me to keep her from going completely bonkers.

If anyone has to succumb to a lethal nerve agent, continued the great actor's thought, let it be that wretched boy sitting opposite me. He hadn't been very enthusiastic about their night of passion in Hong Kong. He might easily be a closet straight. He could be tempted to blab to the press for a fee. Then the fat would be in the fire. Tatiana would blow a fuse. She could start chucking his precious Herend porcelain around as, last time, she had demolished his Aunt's Spode. Ben Callaway was no good as an actor either. He would be better out of the way.

Then he himself could move on to another target, thought Sir Emrys. He already had his eye on that charming young man, Charlie, who made such a spritely Ariel in his skimpy costume. He looked as gay as a bird and would, almost certainly, respond warmly to advances from his eminent leader. A Prospero-Ariel partnership, wasn't that what *The Tempest* was all about? But he wouldn't want to scupper Ben's chances. Charlie wasn't that kind of boy. So Ben must go. Was it just imagination, thought Sir Emrys hopefully, or was Ben already looking a bit green around the gills?

The other diner was also lost in thought. Dear God, thought Ben Callaway, please spare me. There were so many things he had never done. He had never been to Petra or Angkor or New England in the fall. If you need anyone, please take that horrid old Sir Emrys. A glittering future would then fall into Ben's lap. He would have to take over his roles for the rest of the tour. He knew the lines already, and had rehearsed well. Just think of it, Prospero in Tokyo and Macbeth on Broadway. It would be the making of a brilliant career. He thought with pity of his contemporaries at drama school who were now mostly staffing theatre box-offices, or cleaning offices to scrape a living. He would be kind and generous to them all. One could afford compassion when one was a huge success. Besides, Mummy would be delighted. The famous star, he noticed, was already looking rather queasy. Could that be nausea coming on?

Both men smiled feebly at each other, concealing their dark thoughts.

"The five minutes are up," announced Kazuo Yamagata. "You should both be safe now."

"Of course they are safe, Mr Yamagata," said the head waiter, bustling up. "We have first-class chef, who cleans away all the poisonous parts."

Ben got up and, with a theatrical gesture, gave the great actor an enormous hug.

"Thank God you are safe, dear Emrys," he shouted. "What a loss to mankind you would have been." Relief and joy were written all over his face.

"I am so happy for you too, dearest Ben," rejoined Sir Emrys, returning the hug with tremendous panache.

"The tour can continue then as planned," said Kazuo, mopping his brow. "This episode will bring us a lot of valuable publicity."

"You know, my dear Ben," remarked Sir Emrys with a certain irony, "I always knew that I myself had acting talent. But now I'm starting to think that you may have it too. From your performance just now, a casual observer might well imagine that you adored me."

Ben tried to grin.

Kazuo moved away to have a little chat in Japanese

with the head waiter.

"Well done," he said. "Here's the little present I promised you."

"Thank you, Mr Yamagata. I hope we didn't frighten your two friends too badly. They were never in the remotest danger, of course. We served them mackerel and charged them for fugu, just as you instructed."

"No harm done then. It will be a splendid story for the world media. The object of the exercise."

"Curious people aren't they, these foreigners," opined the head waiter.

"The English don't consider themselves to be foreigners anywhere," remarked the impresario. "Other people are the foreigners. It is one of their national oddities."

"Everyone is a foreigner somewhere, sir."

About the Author

Born in 1928, the son of a doctor in Saint John's Wood, London. Educated at Arnold House School in London and Bembridge School, a progressive independent school evacuated to the Lake District during the war. From there he won an Open Scholarship to Brasenose College, Oxford. There he took part in amateur shows with people like Sandy Wilson, Donald Swann, John Schlesinger and Ken Tynan who achieved fame in the theatre. He left Oxford in 1949 with an Honours Degree in Modern History.

The next two years were spent in the Army on military service. Having begun in the Rifle Brigade, he ended up as a commissioned officer in the Royal Army Educational Corps and then as an Intelligence Officer at a Brigade Headquarters on Salisbury Plain. He also directed a production of *Arsenic and Old Lace* which toured widely, being especially successful at the Porton Down Germ Warfare Centre!

RODE HE ON BARBARY?

In 1951 he passed the exam for the Senior Branch of the Foreign Service where he worked until retiring at the age of sixty in 1988. He served in a variety of posts throughout the world; such as Washington, Laos in Indo-China, Argentina, Turkey and Nigeria. In the Foreign Office itself he also had a number of interesting positions such as Private Secretary to the Secretary of State (the temperamental George Brown) and later Head of the Personnel Department sending people round the world, which gave him a further opportunity to explore from Chile to south Africa and then Japan.

He married in 1960 Jenifer Mathews, the daughter of a Hatton Garden expert in precious stones. She tragically died in 1981. They had three sons and two grandchildren. He is now happy again with a civil partnership.

In 1976 he was promoted to the rank of Ambassador. From then until retirement he served as Ambassador to Hungary, Spain and Sweden, passing the Foreign Office language exams in Hungarian and Turkish. He was awarded the honour of Knight Commander of St Michael and St George in 1982. He also served as Leader of the UK Delegation to the European Security Conference in Belgrade in 1978, which involved publicly debating with the Russians and their Allies on the subject of human rights. Never a dull moment.

On retirement he has served in several honorary positions such as Governor of the Sadler's Wells Trust and later the Hospital Trust in King's Lynn, and also the Chairmanship of the Ruskin Foundation and now of the West Norfolk Musical Society. He has also travelled widely as a lecturer on Swan Hellenic and other cruise ships including four visits to Australia where he was nearly eaten by a crocodile.

In addition he has pursued a literary career. Apart from his first story, published in *The Nursery World* when he was seven years old, his second career really began in 1967 when his first novel *None of Us Cared For Kate* was published by Cassell (and Dutton in New York) under the pseudonym of John Haythorne to avoid giving his superiors the impression of frivolity! Four more novels have since been published and so the new venture by the Melrose Press will be his sixth novel. During this time he received support from his agents in both Curtis Brown and Peters, Fraser and Dunlop until they sadly retired and died respectively.

He has also written for the stage, his plays having been produced professionally at the King's Head Theatre in Islington and a dozen other fringe theatres in London, Brighton and Edinburgh. His plays have been published by Samuel French, earning royalties from some unlikely spots. He is particularly big in Bangalore! Finally, the periodical *Poetry Today* has published several of his poems. So it has been a full life and still goes on!